Also by Lucinda Rosenfeld
What She Saw . . .

Why She Went Home

a novel

Lucinda Rosenfeld

Ballantine Books / New York

Ballantine Books Trade Paperback Edition

Copyright © 2004 by Lucinda Rosenfeld
Reader's guide copyright © 2005 by Lucinda Rosenfeld and Random House, Inc.

Published in the United States by Ballantine Books, an imprint of The Random House Publishing Group, a division of Random House, Inc., New York.

BALLANTINE and colophon are registered trademarks of Random House, Inc.
Ballantine Reader's Circle and colophon are trademarks of Random House, Inc.

Originally published in hardcover by Random House, an imprint of The Random House Publishing Group, a division of Random House, Inc., in 2004.

Library of Congress Control Number: 2004096693

ISBN 0-8129-7171-X

Printed in the United States of America

Ballantine Books website address: www.ballantinebooks.com

9 8 7 6 5 4 3 2 1

Text design by Mercedes Everett

For my mother and father,
Lucy Davidson Rosenfeld and Peter J. Rosenfeld

Home is the place where,
When you have to go there,
They have to take you in.

—Robert Frost,
"The Death of the Hired Man" (1915)

Why
She Went
Home

At sixty-five, despite waning lung power, Leonard Milton Fine was still lead oboist of the Newark Symphony Orchestra. He was also one of few musicians in the troupe whom Newark's car thieves hadn't scared off from driving to work; he figured his 1986 Yugo hatchback wasn't tempting even for spare parts. On the evening of the NSO's season opener, he set off down the New Jersey Turnpike with a full car. Next to him in the front, a lugubrious cellist wearing loafers that looked like bedroom slippers stared blankly at the toxic plumage of two dozen industrial smokestacks, which was bleeding into a violet and gold sunset. In the back, Leonard's younger daughter, Phoebe, barely visible beneath a battered cello case covered with stickers from obscure music festivals, attempted to make conversation with the cellist's flute-playing wife, a dark-browed blonde who seemed to have memorized the seating chart of every musical ensemble in the tristate area. Phoebe's left ear was pinned against the neck of the case. As uncomfortable as she was, she considered herself lucky not to be sitting up front, in the death seat. Her father had the alarming habit of turning around while driving to talk to the passengers behind him. Earlier in the trip, while regaling them with tales of his many superlative buys on rain-gear at Burlington Coat Factory, he had narrowly avoided scaling the turnpike divide and then swerved into the middle lane, where he nearly got swiped by an eighteen-wheeler.

"Jesus, Dad!" Phoebe had cried, even though they were both secular Jews.

"Sorry there, folks." Leonard had sounded incongruously cheerful after veering out of danger.

"Trying to give us a scare there, Lenny?" the flutist had asked. "Anyway, as I was saying, apparently Trudie Fisher is now playing *third chair* at the Pops, if you can believe it. I really can't. The woman is *always* out of tune."

"It's amazing there's any air left to breathe in this state," the cellist had muttered to himself.

Leonard's driving didn't improve much after they got off the highway and made their way through downtown Newark. After almost shearing the door off a parked police car, he just missed mowing down a group of teenage boys playing stick-ball in the street. Eventually, to everyone's relief, they arrived at the auditorium. Leonard found a parking place just around the corner, in front of a boarded-up house, and the four of them dispersed—the musicians through the stage door and Phoebe through the main entrance into the lobby. There, she spent the fifty minutes until showtime skimming a work of "women's fiction" from the 1970s she'd grabbed off her parents' bookshelf before leaving—to her surprise and chagrin, she was unable to locate a single sex scene—and perusing the arriving crowd, who were mainly old and feeble and white-haired (if they had any hair at all) and were yelling "Whaaat?" at each other as they futilely adjusted their hearing aids. There weren't too many of them, either.

Indeed, as she settled herself into the first row of the mostly empty balcony, Phoebe was distressed to discover that, with the orchestra and the full chorus, there were twice as many people onstage as there were in the audience. Even more depressingly, a high percentage of those in attendance were probably nonpaying friends and relations of the musicians, such as herself. She hadn't always empathized with her father's setbacks. During her college years a decade earlier at Hoover University, when she saw the world primarily through the lens of race, class, gender, and sexual orientation (mostly her own, but still), she had even reveled in the NSO's consistently paltry turnout, since the orchestra bore the name of a predominantly Hispanic, Arab, and African-American city, despite being an almost exclusively Asian and Caucasian organization. Never mind the fact that the music they played had all been composed by dead European males. Or that the structure of the orchestra was, by design, inegalitarian. Or that the house auditorium was, in fact, a converted mosque.

More recently, however, Phoebe had decided to try and bolster her father in the twilight of his musical career—a career that was already, by nature of the kind of music he played, obscure. In addition to having trouble blowing into his oboe, Leonard was finding it difficult keeping time and, by extension, track of where he was in the score. While he'd never been a virtuoso—never been *that* good—it physically pained Phoebe to imagine him lost in a sea of notes. She found his incompetence a little pathetic, just as she had always found everything about her father simultaneously endearing and exasperating. At the same time, after a lifetime spent dreading his classical music concerts, she had begun to look forward to them, if only for the opportunity they provided to sit in a chair doing absolutely nothing for two hours and not feel guilty about it. (Domestic plane travel, she'd found, offered similar comforts.)

One glance at the evening's program changed her feelings on the subject. First up was Gustav Mahler's "Resurrection" Symphony in D minor. If Phoebe remembered correctly from her teenage days playing second violin for the All County Orchestra, it was a bombastic monstrosity. Back then, of course, classical music had only been a burden, a built-in inadequacy, a zombie motion she went through to please her parents. It had never entirely lost that quality, though it had gained others as well. In Brahms, she had come to hear the tragedy of it all; in Chopin, the excruciating tremolo of lust in the spring. But there was something so inescapably pompous and irritating about the whole penguin-suited business. It was only in the dark, or when she closed her eyes, that she could even hear the music—the mystery and beauty that had outlived its own century.

Still, she was curious to lay eyes on the NSO's new conductor, a certain Roget Mankuvsky. According to the program notes, he was not only the youngest conductor ever to perform with the NSO, he had studied with the great Uli Rindfleisch in Vienna, followed by the lesser-known Heinz Zimmerfenster in Berlin. Barely two years later, Mankuvsky became the assistant conductor of a small early instruments consortium in Lausanne, Switzerland. Then, at just thirty, he had been appointed the musical director of the Cherry Hill Community Orchestra. To Phoebe, who at twenty-nine had not yet decided whether she was a breakfast person or a lunch person, Mankuvsky seemed like a prodigy. (The verdict: neither and, at the same time, both.)

At two minutes past eight, a flock of late-arriving concert-goers having failed to materialize, the NSO's slinky Japanese-American concertmistress, Nanette Yamaguchi, appeared onstage in a wraparound dress that gave full play to her protruding clavicles. The way she swung her hair around while bowing the tuning A showed that she lorded her power over the other orchestra members. *That could have been me,* Phoebe thought to herself, while also realizing how glad she was that it wasn't. Mankuvsky came out shortly afterward. He was short, dark, stocky, and not particularly handsome, with bulging eyeballs and a mashed-in nose. He bounded onto the podium in brown shoes, his ruffled shirt only half tucked into his concert tails, his spiky hair sticking out of his head. From the back, he looked like a sea anemone.

His conducting style, as it soon emerged, had more in common with the bat-trapped-in-the-attic type of flailing made famous by Leonard Bernstein than it did with, say, Fritz Reiner, the old conductor of the Chicago Symphony, whose hand movements were so miniaturized that it was once said, "When he reaches the third button, it's a downbeat." (For her twenty-ninth birthday, Phoebe's parents had presented her with a gossipy book about the great conductors.) But Mankuvsky's gestures were so overwrought as to make even Bernstein seem repressed. While the cymbals clashed and the triangles dinged, he manipulated his body into strange pretzel shapes. His need to express himself wasn't limited to body language, either. While the guest soprano strained for an F sharp, Phoebe could have sworn she heard the words "fucking migraine" wafting off the podium.

The audience sat politely and with limited squirming for the entire symphony, causing Phoebe to wonder if they weren't just deaf but dead. On the other hand, they performed the usual number of holus-bolus coughing fits between the symphony's five movements, thereby demonstrating that they were still breathing. Phoebe also wondered why it was that the sound of one person exorcising phlegm incited others to do the same. (Of the many things that baffled her about this world, that one ranked in the top ten, along with how all those plastic bags wound up dangling from trees. Seriously, who put them there?)

It seemed to take a lifetime to get to intermission, and the second half of the concert seemed just as long. It was an arduous journey through late-nineteenth- and early-twentieth-century Czechoslovakia, beginning with the cloying strains of Dvořák's "Slavonic Dances" and ending with an orchestral suite from Janáček's infrequently performed (for a good reason) opera, *The Cunning Little Vixen.*

At the end of the evening, the applause was tepid, except from a community college music appreciation class seated downstairs in the orchestra section. They howled with approval—probably out of relief that the show was over, Phoebe thought. Still, she was thankful that her father had made it through the program without incident, taking his entrance cues when necessary from his far-younger deputy, Benson Smith. With a shudder, she remembered the time, a year before, when Leonard had lost his place playing Prokofiev's *Peter and the Wolf*—the stun-gunned look that had overcome his face and hands, his eyes buggy, his mouth frozen around his mouthpiece. Phoebe hadn't been sure if the conductor had noticed or not, but Benson surely had. He could have removed a finger from his keys long enough to point Leonard to the right bar, but he hadn't bothered.

The curtains having lurched to a tremulous close, Phoebe ventured backstage in search of her father. It was an uninviting space, dark and rank and windowless; both the walls and the floor had been painted black. She found him huddled in the corner with the NSO's octogenarian timpanist with the Merlin beard. Leonard was peeling twenties from his wallet with the slow hand of a magician procuring scarves from a supposedly empty hat. Not wanting to intrude on what was clearly a private interaction, Phoebe stationed herself ten feet away, behind a steel column plastered with program announcements and FOR SALE ads—beechwood music-stand lamps were among the articles of limited usefulness being sold—and strained to overhear their conversation.

From the words and phrases she was able to make out ("odds," "field goal," "payout," "sign over your check"), she could only assume that her father had participated in some kind of sports betting pool that had cost him the bulk of his playing fee for that evening's performance. How long had this gone on? Was this why, during her childhood, her family never seemed to have enough money to go around? Or had Leonard's penchant for gambling arisen in the intervening years? Whatever the case, the revelation of his involvement in the world of vice, however peripheral, left Phoebe strangely jubilant, as she considered the possibility that her father wasn't half the emasculated "new man" she'd always imagined him to be.

Their eyes met as he was tucking his wallet back into his tuxedo pants—no small feat, since they appeared to have been shrunk by the dry cleaner. That, or he'd experienced a late-life growth spurt, which seemed unlikely. "Well, hello there, Phoebe!" he said with uncharacteristic theatricality, as if not yet resigned to the idea that he was no longer onstage. Or maybe he was just embarrassed to have been caught settling his debts. "Enjoy the concert?" He came over to where she stood and hooked a spindly arm over her shoulder.

"Oh, yeah, it was great," she lied. "Especially the Janáček. The guy can really riff on a theme."

"Yes, I've always thought Janáček's opera music was underrated," Leonard muttered dreamily, as he looked around him. Then, taking her by the elbow, he began to steer her across the room. "I want you to meet Roget, our new conductor," he announced, at some point along the way. "You know, he's exactly your age." He leaned closer into her ear. "And a handsome young man to boot! Or maybe I should say, 'to baton.' " He chuckled merrily; he was the only one. Phoebe had never met anyone who made worse puns than her father.

Or who found his own so amusing.

Before she had the chance to feign a bathroom emergency, however, Leonard had tapped his conductor on the upper arm. "Pardon me, Maestro," he began, "but there's someone here I'd like to introduce to you." At which point the maestro turned around to face the two of them, his ferret eyes shifting from one to the other. "Along with being my daughter, Phoebe is quite a violinist in her own right," Leonard went on. "Though I'm afraid we've lost her to the other side of the musical spectrum."

"Wazzup?" said Mankuvsky with an up-and-backward jerk of his jutting chin.

"Hey," said Phoebe, eking out a pained smile as she contemplated the idea—really, the horror—that she had arrived at such a point of desperation in her personal life as to be reduced to having her own father pimp for her.

Still, whether for reasons of ego or interest, she felt compelled to clarify her father's introduction, and she cut in with, "What he means is that I play the electric violin."

"Electric violin—that's cool," he replied, in a monotone that suggested he'd heard cooler.

"Well, I'll leave you two young people to get to know each other better!" a now-giddy Leonard declared, clearly under the impression that he'd negotiated some kind of history-altering alliance along the lines of the Molotov-Ribbentrop pact struck by Nazi Germany and Communist Russia before World War II. Then he walked away.

The maestro didn't look particularly fazed. He stood there, scowling and silent.

From Phoebe's perspective, it really couldn't have been more embarrassing; her father might as well have handed them a room key to the Tollgate Motel on the Fort Lee side of the George Washington Bridge. "I really enjoyed the concert," she offered finally, if only to replace the sound of Leonard's last words.

"Well, you must not have been listening," said Mankuvsky, "since it sucked shit."

Not inclined to argue, and taken back by his response, she laughed queasily and said nothing.

"So, you live around here?" he asked next, with another chain pull of his chin.

Insofar as it forced her to acknowledge the reality of what had happened in her life thus far—or, really, failed to happen—the question put Phoebe in a minor panic. She found herself maniacally curling a baby hair around her index finger and gazing at the crumpled curtain fabric overhead, before she told him, "It's sort of complicated, actually. I mean, I was living in the city until recently, at which point I really wasn't anymore." She shrugged with entirely performed insouciance. "There was some stuff going on, and it just seemed like the right thing to do, under the circumstances, which there were a lot of."

"I guess you don't want to answer my question," he shot back.

"Well, I only met you ten seconds ago!" she cried out, in her own defense, even as she recalled the many men before him who had tarred her with similar allegations of insincerity. Kevin McFeeley, for instance. She thought back to the ten-page, single-spaced, chicken-scrawled sheaf of translucent parchment with which her singer-songwriter ex-boyfriend of many years before had left her after she left him: *I'm sure your slick, empty existence will lead you to that special some-*

one, he'd written. Only Kevin had been wrong. Here she was, as alone as she'd ever been.

Of course, *alone* was a relative term. "And in case you hadn't noticed, my father is standing five feet away from us, listening to every word of our conversation," she added.

Both she and the maestro turned in time to watch Leonard take a frantic step backward into a half-collapsed music stand, whereupon the two of them (man and stand) came crashing to the floor. Pretending for his sake not to notice—even while the sight of his crumpled limbs made her cringe—Phoebe let her father's timpanist-bookie friend prop him back up; considering he'd extorted Leonard out of his paycheck, it seemed like the least he could do.

When it became clear that Leonard was okay—he could now be heard laughing good-naturedly about the whole thing—Mankuvsky turned back to her and said, "Your father's one weird dude."

"Tell me about it," she murmured in agreement, as she wondered if she'd ever love another man as much as she did Leonard Fine.

Then again, there was an intensity to the conductor's black-eyed gaze that drew her closer. And at the same time, there was a sweetness to his face—in particular, his rosy cheeks—that implied the makings of a potentially sympathetic husband and father himself. (Oh, the hell of being a woman! To be driven to look at every new man in this hideously pedestrian way!) Or maybe it was the fact of his being a musician—like her father, only a more commanding version; maybe it was music that had been missing from her past relationships—the understanding that it could speak what she couldn't. Or maybe it was Mankuvsky's directness.

So many of Phoebe's past loves seemed to have been actors of one sort or another, albeit mainly out-of-work ones.

"Anyway, as I was about to say," she began again, on a coy note, "it's possible that I'd be willing to explain my situation in greater detail at some later date."

"When?" said the maestro.

"When what?" said Phoebe, as flattered by his interest as she was suddenly panicked by her own forwardness. In truth, she had been tagged "needy, aggressive, and demanding" just as often as "emotionally paralyzed and duplicitous." Then again, she had been called pretty much every negative word in the English language.

But he came right back at her. "When would you be willing to explain your situation in greater detail?"

Again, Phoebe's eyes traveled up to the curtain rolls before she told him, "Well, I'd have to look at my book."

"Gimme a break," he scoffed. "Your schedule's wide open."

"That's so insulting! How do you know?" she protested, as offended by his presumption as she was impressed by his perceptiveness.

"I just do," he replied with a shrug. "Besides, people always find time if they want to find time."

"That's probably true," she had to agree. "Well, where do you live?"

"Off Route Forty-six, in Little Ferry," he told her.

"Little Ferry—wow," said Phoebe, reflecting how, in her homophobic youth, the town's name had been a source of great hilarity to her.

"You like pasta?" he asked.

"I guess," she answered.

"There's a place in my neighborhood that serves a mean egg parm." The chin was jerking backward again—this time to the right, presumably in the direction of the egg parm. "I'll see you there on Wednesday at seven."

"Okay, but where am I going?" she said, suddenly dubious and wondering what she'd gotten herself into.

"Main Street, corner of Grand."

"By any chance does the place have a name?"

Now the maestro folded down his lips and lifted up his shoulders, as if it were a bizarre and ultimately superfluous question to be asking. "As far as I know, it's just a pizza ristorante."

"Oh." Phoebe nodded, dread consuming her. In her experience of the world so far, people were disappointing when you got to know them any better than you already did.

"Speaking of names, what did you say yours was?" he wanted to know.

"Phoebe," she told him.

"You look more like a Hope. Or a Dawn. By the way, you can call me Roget. Now, if you'll excuse me, I have to go puncture the balloon of a local composer in pursuit of a commission. See you Wednesday." He charged off.

"Right—bye." Phoebe raised her left hand in a phlegmatic wave as she mulled over the implications of Mankuvsky's earlier comment. Was he trying to imply that she seemed like a good bet for the future?

Or maybe just an early riser?

Just then, Leonard reappeared at her side. "Ready to go, Crumpet?" he asked. There was a small tear on the knee of his pant leg. Neither of them mentioned it.

"Whenever you're ready, Daddy Dukes," said Phoebe,

herself resorting to childhood nicknames, having given up trying to get either one of her parents to acknowledge her evolution from ten-year-old "gifted and talented" student and not-quite-prodigy violinist to almost-thirty-year-old— well, something else.

Then again, it must have been confusing for them having her back at home again, moping around the house in her favorite Camp Beverly Hills T-shirt, making muffins out of breakfast cereal, playing with her stamp collection, and complaining about how there was always someone in the bathroom when she needed to go.

2

What, precisely, was Phoebe doing there, in the leafy back-water Podunk of Whitehead, New Jersey (current population 7,968), six miles southeast of Paramus? That was the question she asked herself as she sat alone most nights on her junior-sized trundle bed in her childhood bedroom, frantically scribbling in her notebook.

So far, she had come up with ten reasons for her recent move back home:

1. She hated her job
2. Her apartment depressed her
3. Yet another relationship had failed to live up to its promise of everlasting love
4. Therapy had become a prison from which she saw no escape
5. Where once they'd been vaguely irritating *I*'s, all her old friends had lately turned into extremely wearying *we*'s

6. She was tired of trying (and failing) to be someone
7. She was drinking heavily
8. She actually missed New Jersey
9. Images of sneaker-sized water bugs haunted her dreams and waking thoughts alike
10. Her mother was ill

   To be fair, though, Phoebe hadn't hated her last job any more than she'd hated the one before it. Or the one before that. Indeed, for the past however many years, she had been bouncing from one peripherally creative but ultimately clerical administrative position to another, all of them at mid- to large-sized media and marketing conglomerates. She never stayed long enough at any one of them to climb to any position of authority, earn a premium salary, or accumulate any marketable skills—even as she managed to antagonize whatever boss she reported to with her sullen demeanor and defensive posturing. That said, she had always responded poorly to authority figures, who tended to inspire guilt and resentment well before she had made her first non-work-related, long-lasting, long-distance phone call on the company bill. Though it was also true that, over the past several years, her tolerance level for working in general had decreased precipitously. Her chief gripe, aside from having to wake up at a reasonable hour in the morning? The admonitory Post-it notes her colleagues felt compelled to fasten to the soy-based beverages they stored in the personal-use refrigerator—e.g., *Drink this under threat of execution.* Also, she felt she had better things to do with her time, such as write and record a solo album for electric violin and voice that she planned to call *Bored and Lonely* but was currently too busy and too lazy to contemplate undertaking. It was Phoebe's keen hope, however, that the company of her classical music–obsessed parents would inspire not only her return to creative endeavor but her actual musical compositions. She feared they were likely to err too much on the side of ennui and not enough on the side of the eternal human struggle—should she ever get around to writing them, never mind recording them.

And not that she had ever made any attempt to fix her apartment up—or even, for that matter, to finish unpacking. It had never seemed worthwhile. With its paltry ceiling height and eminently forgettable location in a white-brick building in the Murray Hill section of Manhattan—combined with her own lack of a discretionary income with which to purchase contemporary Italian design innovations—the place could only fail to live up to her expectations. Which is to say, the standard of living she had once achieved with another of her ex-boyfriends, budding cable-TV executive Neil Schmertz. In Phoebe's early- to mid-twenties, the two had rented a charmingly antiquated Brooklyn brownstone floor-through made au courant with Danish modern furniture in the living room and, in the bathroom, tinted glass and stainless steel canisters for the dignified corralling of cotton balls and swabs. (If only Neil hadn't also lived there, Phoebe might have stayed forever. But he did.)

And at first, therapy had seemed like a bargain. While two years Phoebe's junior and dowdily dressed—how, Phoebe worried, could a woman who wore nude panty hose understand the cloud she operated under?—the so-named Jackie Yee had agreed to see Phoebe for free as a part of her doctoral thesis on overachieving children who end up angry and disappointed in their adult lives. Phoebe should have heeded her own fashion alert. By week two, she had become convinced that Jackie ought to have been writing *her* checks. Why? A crimson flush and hangdog smile crept across her student therapist's doughy face at the mere mention of the word *sex*. Was it any wonder that Phoebe became suspicious of the young woman's frequent attempts to get her to lie down on the cheap distressed-leather Door Store couch that took up half the floor space of her windowless office on University Place? But by then it was too late; Phoebe was hooked, not only on the receipt of Jackie's relentlessly ingratiating responses ("What's important is how *you* feel, Phoebe," Jackie would timorously cheerlead Phoebe's admissions of moral depravity), but on not hurting Jackie's feelings. Three years later, Phoebe was still her only patient. It was a bad situation made that much worse when Jackie asked Phoebe if she'd be interested in going out for drinks sometime. And did she know any attractive single men? There weren't any in her Ph.D. program, and she was feeling "very alone." Having an unstable and unprofessional therapist was only the half of it, however. Phoebe had grown tired of her own problems. She already knew she was a hopeless case: insecure, underhanded, overcompensating, sexually impulsive, paranoid if not delusional, all messed up about her mother and sister. Talking about it only seemed to make it worse. But when she tried to tell Jackie that she wanted to quit, Jackie simply called attention to Phoebe's "need to sabotage what she couldn't control."

And she wasn't the only one who couldn't get along with

Alex Kahn. A civil liberties lawyer for the ACLU, his nickname around the office was "Genghis." Later, it struck
Phoebe as incredible that you could spend nearly three years
of your life with someone, albeit breaking up and getting
back together every few weeks, only to find at the end of it
that the other person had literally made no impression on
you. And yet this was precisely the case with Alex. While she
vaguely recalled having once noted to herself that it shared
certain features in common with a neighbor's pit bull, she
could finally, scarcely, even remember the man's face. And
when she thought that he had once presented himself as the
solution to her problems! Or, at least, she had hoped for as
much—hoped that Alex's combative personality and general
disregard for other people's feelings (in traffic jams, he rode
the shoulder) might deter her from dismissing him as yet another feckless dullard along the lines of Neil. Having convinced herself that make-up sex was almost always preferable
to making love, she had even taken pains to instigate quarrels
with Alex when none appeared of their own accord. She'd tell
him how much she admired Tipper Gore for getting warning
labels about explicit lyrics pasted to the front of all those
misogynistic rap albums. He'd accuse her of condescending to
the masses—a charge she'd counter with an elevated middle
finger, which he'd naturally try to topple, leading to further
power struggles and eventually to the floor. There, they'd assume one of several favored positions, all of which eliminated
the possibility of eye contact while indulging Alex's appetite
for lurid fantasy role-play involving teen runaways plucked
from the sulfurous stairwells of the Port Authority Bus Termi-
nal. In truth, Phoebe found the scenario sexy, sometimes, sort

of. But mostly, she couldn't wait until it was over so she could go to sleep or, even better, back to her apartment in Murray Hill, which, even though it was depressing, still had a door she could lock on Alex Kahn. In short, far from constituting an aphrodisiac, the constant bickering became as predictable as talking baby talk and playing house had been with Neil.

To be sure, there were notes of harmony and mellifluence. Together, Phoebe and Alex renamed the streets of New York City to suit the sophomorically off-color sense of humor they shared (perhaps the one thing). Rector became Rectum. Bond became Bondage. (They left 69th Street well enough alone.) But even comic genius has a shelf life. And one day, their alternative map lost its ability to charm or titillate. They would still refer to it in passing, as in "Let's meet at the little Italian place on Dingleberry—what's it called?—you know, the one with the really good meatballs right above Birth Canal." Then they stopped referencing it altogether. A half dozen more breakups ensued; for the stress involved, each paid the other back with half that many extracurricular flirtations and, in one or two cases, actual infidelities, which led to more screaming fights and only slightly fewer tearful reunions, during which time, with decreasing conviction, they professed undying love for each other. Eventually, after the hang-ups wore out their efficacy, the phone stopped ringing. (Eventually, Phoebe wished for nothing more than to bowdlerize Alex Kahn from the text of her life.) But it wasn't just Alex; it was all of them, the short ones and the fat ones, the tall ones and the small ones, the pink ones and the tan ones and the blue ones, too. It had become clear to Phoebe there were only so many more men she could afford to take on, take in, before she'd be all filled up, the victim of her own false hope and fake orgasms, a living motel with a permanent NO VACANCY sign. And at the same time, who was to say how much longer they'd want *her*? Even if she was still pretty, she could no longer be described as a pretty *young* anything. In recent years, her skin had grown a little dull, her hair a little thin. Just the other day, she'd spotted her first varicose vein. It reminded her of an alternate route on an old map of nowhere.

And the irony was that, before meeting and marrying a venture capitalist named Chad, Phoebe's on-again, off-again, but mostly off-again best friend and former bandmate Holly Flake had never been in a relationship for longer than six weeks (she claimed six months). Now Holly left messages on Phoebe's machine to the effect of "Hey, Phee. We just got in. We're going out for a bite to eat. We'll be back in an hour if you want to call us." Without fail, Phoebe didn't, the one exception to her anti-couples bias being Leonard and Roberta Fine, not only on account of their being her own parents but because, to Phoebe's mind, their union had an inevitable quality about it. It was as if two overlapping and finally undifferentiable clouds had merged into one cumulus, poised between the stratosphere and outer space. The secret to her parents' marriage? From what Phoebe could tell, it came down to a failure to engage fully with planet Earth.

And she wasn't just tired of trying to be famous and rich and important and beautiful; she was tired of feeling as if she had to be at the right party in possession of the right bag and shoes, the right straight hair, the right straight date, the right gay platonic "going out" friend who pronounced her the modern incarnation of Audrey Hepburn or Dorothy

Parker or Coco Chanel, the right cocktail of ebullience and ennui so that she might appear wildly successful without appearing to care that she was. Where did these social pressures originate? Always happy to blame others for her problems, Phoebe—with Jackie Yee's encouragement, of course—had long assumed the culprits to be her "withholding mother," "distant father," and "domineering older sister." More recently, however, Phoebe had begun to see her plight in sociohistorical context. She believed that, as the stock market had soared in the late 1990s, an unapologetic strain of Social Darwinism had taken root in the city's unconscious, with the disparity not just visible but flaunted on every street in the city, with its packs of crisply suited winners, upright and strutting, while the losers lay prostrate beneath them like felled forest game. Where did Phoebe fit in? With her college degree, pale skin, culture literacy, and access to establishmentarian institutions, she clearly ranked among the privileged elite. But in her own peer group, she felt perpetually inadequate.

Is it any wonder that on her New York nightlife sojourns she was stowing away cheap champagne (and, occasionally, high-end bourbon) with greater and greater enthusiasm? The result was that, at least one morning per week, Phoebe awoke to the sensation of having been hit over the head with a baseball bat. At least she knew she was alive. On the other hand, it hurt like hell. She was therefore able to see the advantages to living in a dry town, far from the limelight, as Whitehead was. How had it gotten that way? According to town historian Mildred Finch, the ban had its origins in the Colonial period, during which time the native Lenni-Lenape Indians got a little too interested in the Europeans' firewater, leading them to dance and carouse with the settlers' wives in ways the settler husbands didn't necessarily appreciate.

And Phoebe had had her fill of the Barneys New York sales staff, who always made faces and acted inconvenienced when she asked to try things on. And maybe, also, she found she could relate to her hometown state's reputation as a literal and figurative swamp. Whatever the case, having spent the previous twenty years running away from the place—and even denying that she had been born and raised there—she found herself increasingly drawn to a life of quiet anonymous pleasures of the type found in New Jersey's malls and plazas, her hair pulled back in a plastic butterfly clip, her aspirations reduced to buying a new antiperspirant at a competitive price and hoping there was something good on TV that night.

And the sneaker-size water bugs.

And the exhaustion and the headaches and the car alarms and the bus soot and the bullshit.

Thankfully, the doctors to whom Phoebe's mother, Roberta, had begrudgingly surrendered—her relationship to the medical establishment being cautious at best—were insisting that the prognosis was good. But hers was still a sufficiently advanced case of cancer—or the "c-word," as she preferred to call it—that, following "a few little tests" the previous summer, she had been ordered a preventive six months of treatment. Which turned out to be another euphemism, this one for a prolonged course of poison. And while Phoebe's motives for sticking close by her formerly voluptuous mother in her time of vanquishment had as much to do with showing up her older sister, Emily, as with anything else, it was also true that she had started to care about other people in ways she never had before.

At a cost of fifty bucks a month, Phoebe had rented a storage locker in the neighboring town of Pringle, New Jersey. In it she deposited her bed, desk, the still-unopened packing boxes that had lain dormant in her Murray Hill hovel for the past two-plus years, and her velvet painting of two ships passing in the night. She took her violin, amplifier, two suitcases of clothes, a box of books and sheet music, and another of shoes and accessories home to Whitehead with her. At first glance, the place was exactly as she remembered it. As she settled in, she was reminded of a picture puzzle that used to appear in her favorite magazine when she was growing up, *Highlights for Children,* in which the reader was asked to identify the historical inconsistencies. For example, Ben Franklin would be shown tooling away in his study, inventing electricity and whatnot, but a modern telephone would lurk amid the kites and jars and fountain pens—ripe for circling.

By virtue of both its small population and its not being off a direct exit of any main interstate, Whitehead had staved off the onslaught of chain stores that had turned so many neighboring hamlets into nondescript "every towns." The exception that proved the rule was the Whitehead CVS, which had taken over from Klein's Drugs after Stew Klein was caught writing prescriptions for anyone who wanted one. But all the signage on the mom-and-pop stores was in English *and* Korean now. Some of the English names had changed, as well. The old twenty-four-hour convenience store had become Happy Market. Sportino's Fine Jewelry was now Pretty Nice Necklace. And Sal's, the old pizza joint that Phoebe had frequented during free periods at Whitehead Middle School (before she developed a fear of grease, born of the excessive reading of dieting columns in women's magazines) had mutated into a sushi bar called Sushi Bar. What's more, where Vinny's Karate had once monopolized the town's martial arts industry, there were now four jujitsu studios within a two-block radius—none of them operated by Sicilians.

The Canadians had moved in too—or at least the Canadian geese had; you could find them waddling on every last triangle of undeveloped land around town, shamelessly expelling a trail of murky gray turds.

In the Fines' dilapidated Depression-era bungalow at 281 Douglass Street, on the other hand, mass migrations appeared to have been kept at bay. So had the passage of time, with desuetude more or less the normal state of things. The 1970s hi-fi was still blasting Mozart and Berlioz. The antique clocks that had never worked continued not to do so. Where so many of Phoebe's friends' mothers, in an attempt to ameliorate their grief over their suddenly empty nests, had converted their children's bedrooms into retirement offices, TV dens, and guest bedrooms within days of their leaving for college, Roberta had left the scenes of her daughters' maturations untouched for more than ten years. Revolutionary hero Che Guevara still gazed commandingly out from over Emily's school desk, with its purple plastic clock radio and 1980s NO NUKES mug filled with broken pastel crayons and electric-green-haired Smurf-top pens. Phoebe's fantastically buxom runner-up tennis trophies from high school, a quarter-inch-thick blanket of dust settled between them, continued to crown her childhood bookcase. What's more, the same poly-cotton leggings, Orlon socks, mismatched pom-pom Peds, and souvenir T-shirts continued to impede the movement of her dresser drawers—while the same Swedish clogs, Fayva pumps, and no-name sneakers lined the floor of her closet. (Hanging above them were rayon dresses and blazers with giant shoulder pads whose Frankenstein aesthetic was now impossible to comprehend.)

To be fair, there were practical reasons for the Fines' fail-ure to renovate their home. Roberta and Leonard had never had much money. Nor had they ever been good at saving it. In recent years, the situation had only grown worse. Roberta's medical care had already cost the family a small fortune, and Leonard wasn't getting hired for as many free-lance oboe gigs as he once had. Since he had never had a regu-lar job, there had been no company pension or 401(K) account waiting for him on his sixty-fifth birthday, either—only a modest social security check to cover groceries and in-cidentals. And now Phoebe had reason to believe that he was gambling away even that small sum. To aggravate matters, the Fines had taken out so many home equity loans that, after thirty years of living there, the bank still owned their house. Little wonder that an air of weariness permeated the place now—weariness that bordered on resignation. Even the ivy seemed to have won out. Or at least it had grown unruly enough to give little indication of the stucco siding under-neath, the purple color of which had caused Phoebe so much embarrassment growing up. (Who lived in a purple house?)

Inside was pretty much the same story. The stairs creaked

like bad ankles. The cobwebs had commandeered entire portions of the ceiling. The lettuce in the refrigerator (aka the icebox) was spewing brown juice, while the carrots and onions had sprouted green stalks and bulbous second heads, like a science project gone berserk. There were never enough windows open, either, and a gamy fug had permeated not only the kitchen area but the upstairs bedrooms as well. (Sometimes, it was enough to make Phoebe want to jump out of one.) And while she would still occasionally spot one of Roberta's favorite coffee cakes heating up in the toaster oven, its squiggly white glaze shimmying beneath the burners, its body sagging and drooping over the sides of the tin, the chamber-music parties at which such confections had once been staples were no longer in evidence. The extra music stands had been folded up and sent out to the garage.

And Leonard—it seemed to Phoebe—was even daffier than he used to be. The reasons? It was said in the music world that oboists, if they kept at it long enough, eventually blew out their brains. And while Phoebe had long dismissed the saying as wishful thinking on the part of other wind players, she had begun to wonder if there might be some truth to it. Her father would make toast, then forget to eat it. Or else he'd turn on the shower, then disappear in the Yugo to buy caulk, even though it wasn't time to put up the storm windows, or grout, even though there were no tiles in need of relaying. (Both substances now figured prominently on Phoebe's list of Ugliest Words in the English Language.) Certainly, the oboe was a challenging instrument to play. Not only was the space between the reeds as slender as a keyhole, the ventricle that ran down the center of the instrument was so narrow that an oboist who let out too much of his air all at once could find himself choking on his own breath as it backed into his mouth. But while there was little reason to believe that anyone had ever died this way (though one or two had surely gotten woozy), it raised questions as to the long-term effects of spending your days with your cheeks extended like a chipmunk's, pumping out oxygen with the fervor of a balloon sculptor, as Leonard did.

Owing to the "c-word," the signs of age and illness in Roberta, though six years Leonard's junior, were far less ambiguous. Her facial skin had taken on the translucent quality of the flaky white integument of a garlic clove. Where once they'd resembled a semicolon, her rosebud mouth and pointed chin now mimicked the lower portion of a right-hand bracket. Like pebbles on the shoreline after a crashing wave had retreated, her once-bright eyes appeared to have sunk into her skull; and now there were dark crescent moons underneath them. And who could get past the awful auburn wig with the short bangs to which she'd been reduced in recent months? (Phoebe couldn't.) The irony was that Phoebe had spent most of her adolescence being mortified by her mother's hippie hair, which Roberta had worn long and wild and practically to her waist, occasionally restraining its argent mass in two Heidi-esque braids. By contrast, most of Phoebe's classmates' mothers had sported frosted flat tops or sensible earlength bobs. And now, what she would have given to see her mother's rat's nest returned!

Now—was this so awful to say?—there was a part of Phoebe that, as much as she wanted to be helpful, wished to flee the entire anti-spectacle of her aging parents.

It wasn't the prospect of the "d-word" (as Roberta naturally chose to call the end awaiting us all) that Phoebe couldn't face, it was the shifting of the generations that Leonard and Roberta's deterioration implied. Phoebe didn't feel she'd accomplished enough to play the adult one, with all its concomitant responsibilities and prerogatives. And her unhappiness over being rushed into a role she imagined to be beyond her only exacerbated the resentment she already harbored toward her mother on account of the moratorium Roberta had placed on all discussion of negative subjects—at least insofar as they affected her own family. The list of forbidden topics included depression, illness, anger, envy, hurt, poverty, and even casual sex. How Phoebe had envied those few friends of hers while she was growing up whose toenail-painted and terrycloth-romper-wearing 1970s-styled moms had, on the occasion of their daughters' sixteenth birthdays, presented them with contraceptive show-and-tells featuring not just the sponge but the contraceptive jelly that invigorated it!

That said, Phoebe and Roberta had long maintained a relationship that, while ultimately distant, was always cordial. Conversation revolved around the latest books and movies and sometimes the neighbors' dysfunctional kids. Rarely did a phone call conclude without a filiation-confirming *I love you*. Phoebe began to feel a strain only after she moved home and Roberta became her chief talking mate in life. At the same time, Phoebe couldn't necessarily deal with the "d-word" either and found herself trying to distract Roberta from the grim reality she had once longed for her mother to intrude upon. So the two filled their days playing gin rummy and

Scrabble and watching old Fred Astaire movies on the family's black-and-white TV set. And when Roberta was up to driving, or Leonard wasn't playing or teaching, they went outlet shopping in Secaucus, to garage sales in and around Whitehead, to the consignment store in Fort Lee (Tahari blouses for $36 this month, only $18 after October 1!), or to the art-house cinema in Paramus. Phoebe found herself admiring her mother's will to deny and dissemble insofar as it prevented Roberta from succumbing to the self-pity and dramatization in which so many people, Phoebe included, seemed to become mired.

She was further impressed by the fact that, no matter how poorly her mother felt, Roberta insisted on sitting down to dinner each night—with cloth napkins no less!—even if she wasn't hungry, and Leonard had gotten take-out sushi (his new obsession) from what all the old-timers in town continued to call Sal's, even though Sal had long since moved to Menlo Park to be closer to his grandchildren, his wife, Helen, having d-worded. And now Phoebe sat between them, except on those intermittent evenings when she took the bus into Manhattan to hang out with a crowd of perpetually single, deeply neurotic, and possibly insane female friends she had made in the past several years. Since they were all in therapy three to four times a week, they never stopped berating her for having sacrificed her own needs in the interests of her parents'. Still, to the extent that they made her feel functional—if only by comparison—Phoebe found their presence comforting.

In the end, however, she preferred the company of her parents. In fact, she found she was happy living in Whitehead. The terrain felt safe and familiar. There was no pressure to be someone she wasn't. As anxiety-inducing as it was to wake up and have nowhere to go, it was an equal pleasure not to have to report to the same dreary office morning after morning. Yes, there were times when she felt lonely—for love, for sex, sometimes just for drama. There were also times when she felt as if she were wading through knee-high sand, so oppressive was the silence, so arduous did every step forward seem to her.

Mostly, though, she was just relieved not to be fighting with men and composing furious e-mails:

I think it was a perfectly sensible suggestion on my part that we go somewhere cheaper to eat than Nobu. But no— suddenly, I'm not contributing my equal share to this relationship, since I seem to you to have "plenty of money to buy boots, just not anything that has to do with us." (Not true; and, for the record, those boots were on a huge sale.) And then, having finally gotten to the restaurant, you have to freak out because you think I look annoyed that you're ordering the steak frites, even though you've gained fifteen pounds since we met and your cholesterol is dangerously high for your age. (Hey, your business if you want to die young! Just don't expect me to sit around watching it.) Next, I make a completely innocuous comment about how bad my skin has been lately. Your response: "Phoebe, I'm trying to enjoy my dinner—do we have to talk about this right now?" and you have to say it in this really snide tone of voice designed to make me feel even uglier than I already feel. So I say, "Actually, Alex, this isn't about you right now!" Since it actually isn't. After which point you start complaining about how you're the "sick one here" (sorry, I forgot you had a cold), and I'm stealing your limelight by daring to talk about my career for all of two seconds. (So much for that topic.) And then, after dinner, you decide to get furious at me, because why? Because I want to have a cigarette, and you don't want to come to the bar with me—as if I've even asked you to come to the bar with me! (Honestly, I don't know why you couldn't just have sat at the table for three minutes while I had my smoke. Is it that hard for you to be alone?) And then later, at your apartment, I happen to mention that crazy girl in the spangled outfit who was sitting next to us at dinner and how ridiculous she looked, and you have to make your little point by asking, "How would you like it if she called you a flat-chested acne-scarred bitch?" (Really charming, not least because you were the one making fun of her at dinner!) Okay, you apologized for that comment. How long does the apology last? Right before we go to sleep, I offer to read to you from my book, since you've made this huge production all night about how you're literally on your deathbed. Also, I thought you'd enjoy it since it's called The Trial, *and you're a lawyer. Your response? "You're acting really neurotic, Phoebe. No, I do not want you to read to me, play the violin for me, or do anything else to entertain me. I just want to go to sleep. Okay?" I think that was an unbelievably hostile thing to say, not least because I was just trying to be sympathetic about your cold. The final straw? In the middle of the night, I ask if we can open the window since it's about a million degrees in there and I can't sleep, and you completely go off on me for waking you up! (As if that's some kind of crime against humanity—I mean, sor-ry!) Alex,*

I know people get cranky when they're not feeling well, but this is getting to be too much. Maybe your personality is just too abrasive for me. Maybe you're acting out because you feel hurt that I never tell you I love you and I still haven't decided whether I want to be with you or not. Well, is it any wonder? I mean, right now, you're making me want to run far and away from you. And you telling me you love me every five minutes isn't helping. Seriously, I'd rather you told me you loved me less often, and we got along better. The problem is, I'm not sure we can. Alex, I'm starting to have serious doubts about our long-term compatibility. . . .

Of course, Phoebe's parents ticked her off regularly, too.

"Bebe, it makes me feel bad that you're cooped up in here with your old mother, when you could be out socializing with the young and restless. . . ." Roberta started on a familiar gambit a few nights after the season opener of the NSO, as she lay resting up following a "few more tests." Phoebe sat nearby, reading aloud from a lesser Dickens novel with too many coincidences to be believed. "You know I don't need you here."

"I *like* being here, Mom. How many times do I have to tell you?" Phoebe told her, sighing with frustration that her mother was so busy pretending nothing was wrong all the time that she never stopped to think about how comments such as "I don't need you" might be hurtful to hear. Moreover, it seemed to Phoebe that Roberta actually *did* need someone at her side just then, as evidenced by the catch pot currently positioned to the left of her bed. "And *The Young and the Restless* was a stupid soap opera from the eighties that no one watched!"

"Yes, but you could be out meeting a new beau or—who knows?—your future husband," she told Phoebe, lowering her tortoise-shell glasses down her aquiline nose—her best feature, everyone always said. "You *do* want to get married someday, don't you?"

"Well, sure, someday." Phoebe recoiled into her rocker, her discomfort at talking to her mother about personal things outweighing even her conviction that her mother was in some way neglectful.

"Well, I won't tell you marriage solves all of life's problems," Roberta went on, in a wizened tone. "Frankly, your father has been a lot of work over the years; I nearly have to pick out the man's socks in the morning! Do you remember the time he wore two different-color ones to play the oboe for all-school assembly at WMS?" Staccato-like chuckles exited from her throat.

"Believe me, I remember," said Phoebe, laughing too, if mostly out of relief to be onto a new subject. In fact, she could still recall how the sight of Leonard's lone green sock peeking out beneath his pant leg had summoned that most excruciating if universal of childhood emotions—namely, the sensation of being unable to prevent your parents from making complete and total imbeciles of themselves.

"But at the end of the day," said Roberta, returning to the dreaded subject, "it's a lovely thing to have a man around the house to install blinds when you need them."

"Why would anyone install blinds at the *end* of the day when the sun has already gone down?" asked Phoebe, just to be difficult. (It was easier than being defensive.)

"Don't be silly," her mother scoffed. "*At the end of the day* is an expression!"

Phoebe didn't answer, and her eyes went to the window. Outside, the rain fell thickly and relentlessly, and she thought with pity and irritation of the new grass that Leonard planted so diligently in the backyard each spring—only to watch dirt and weeds prevail the following autumn. He always blamed sea-level issues, combined with too many tall trees blocking the sunlight—without ever mentioning his own complicity vis-à-vis the desiccated oak he refused to tear down, on the grounds that, come spring, the robins and cardinals used it to build nests. Leonard was supposed to be the green thumb of the family; like so many family reputations, his seemed entirely undeserved.

"Fine, if you don't want to think about these things, then I won't, either." Roberta's lovely nose reached into the air.

"If I get desperate I can always find that deaf guy Emily went out with in college," Phoebe finally offered. "He'd probably marry me. What was his name, Jack something? We'd probably get along really well, since I don't know sign language." Roberta had always had a unique talent for bringing out Phoebe's surly side. Just as Phoebe had always made her mother shake her head and wonder how she ever begot this splenetic, dark-witted child.

And yet, these days Phoebe found herself longing to regain her mother's affections as quickly as she had rejected them. "Actually, you'll be relieved to hear that I have a date tomorrow night with the new conductor of the NSO," she went on to inform her.

Almost instantaneously, Roberta's grimace turned into a

grin. "Did you think I didn't know?" she trilled. "Why, I've been literally counting the hours!"

"Oh, Mom!" cried Phoebe, shielding her eyes from what was beginning to look like a family-wide conspiracy, and a humiliating one at that, since the implication was that she couldn't possibly procure a mate on her own. "Please tell me you're lying."

But her mother showed no signs of compunction. "I have little enough to entertain my imagination these days," she told Phoebe. "And what could be more fun than following the progress of my glamorous younger daughter's sexual conquests?"

"*Mooooom!*" Phoebe couldn't believe her ears. For as long as she could remember, Roberta had avoided words like *sexual* in favor of moonier, more graceful adjectives like *passionate* and *amorous*.

Then again, it was nice to know (at least) that her mother entertained no illusions about her younger daughter still being a virgin. It seemed like a lot to ask of an almost-thirty-year-old.

3

Little Ferry had the quality of a town created as much by de-fault as by will, trapped as it was between Teterboro Airport (to the west), the Hackensack River (to the east), and Route 46, which sliced through its northern quadrant with a desul-tory procession of carpet emporiums, hubcap depots, bunting-rich used car dealerships (¡CARROS BONITOS, BARATOS, Y BUENOS!), MSG palaces with lion statuary (Ming This and Ming That), hourly rate motels (Turnpike, Jade East, Airport, Stage Coach, Capri, and Congress—aka Sexual Congress), and hot-dog huts, most prominently Bubba's, at the Little Ferry traffic circle, not to be confused with Hank's Franks ("Buy eight get one free") in Little Ferry proper. Only the town's southwestern border was unencumbered by nature or infrastructure; it flowed directly into the mainly treeless mu-nicipality of Moonachie, which was home to the Wonder Hostess Bakery Thrift Shop, which sold "expired" Twinkies at discount prices (the Arnold equivalent was just up the road, in North Bergen).

Little Ferry itself resembled a slightly more downtrodden version of Whitehead—just without the Koreans or the Jews. Over by the river, on one of many dead-end blocks, there was a nightclub with black glass windows that you could rent for weddings and other special events; it was adjacent to the pumping station and across the street from a family-owned construction company and another marble and tiling one. A block down from Muffler World, on Main Street, was a Veterans of Foreign Wars hall swathed in purple flags and advertising champagne breakfasts on select Sundays. The old brick public library was still up and running, but the bank building had been vacated. It was unclear if the misspelling at the center of the Monna Lisa pastry shop was intentional or not. On the northwest edge of town was a Lithuanian, Latvian, and Estonian social club with anticommunist iconography on its front door—a hammer and sickle with a red slash through it, and another slash nixing a Soviet tank.

On the other side of the Route 46 traffic circle, there was an upscale Asian supermarket called Han Ah Reum; it was attached to a discount department store that, with its half-lit neon Gothic signage, in-house popcorn vendor, abandoned drive-in movie screen, and uneven parking lot with mysterious tar clumps, seemed to belong to an earlier era of retail. The town also claimed an industrial park, which was located across the street from Teterboro Airport and was home to Bridge Casket Co., the Bunn-o-matic corporation, and Iberia Foods. Diagonally to the south of the airport was a tiny, cramped trailer park. Finally, on its southern tip, Little Ferry touched on a slip of land—really, no more than an old clay pit—that, for reasons no longer recalled, the town of South

Hackensack claimed as its own despite the fact that the actual municipality of South Hackensack was located several miles north of Little Ferry, mimicking the situation of West Berlin during the Cold War divided-Germany years, albeit with somewhat less controversy.

There seemed to be a pizza ristorante on every corner.

On the night of her date with Roget Mankuvsky, Phoebe had Leonard drop her off half a block away from the one Roget had selected for their date. Her fears of detection proved unfounded, however, as she was the first one to arrive. She was also the only customer, and one of two human beings in the place. The other was a morose-looking giant with a unibrow who was slumped behind the counter. Taking a seat at the table closest to the door—and on a metal fold-up chair of the variety stored in church basements for addiction meetings—she looked around her. The place appeared more pizza than ristorante. The floors were linoleum. The lighting was strictly halogen tube. The extent of the wall décor was a framed mirror advertising a notoriously watery beer and featuring a mostly naked lady with a protruding tongue. The menu selections were spelled out in letter magnets, which were attached to a white board over Unibrow's head. Someone had left a copy of the previous week's *Record* on the seat next to her. Opening the paper, Phoebe found an article about a sewage treatment project gone awry in Secaucus and another one about the pending retirement of a beloved fourth-grade teacher in Leonia.

It was another ten minutes before the maestro arrived—in belted, stone-washed jeans, bright white sneakers, a leather bomber jacket, and a two-sizes-too-large turquoise T-shirt.

Though clearly well built beneath his tent, he was also (off the podium) shorter than Phoebe remembered and greener in complexion, though it may simply have been a reflection from his chest. "Luigi, my man," he said, lifting his chin in the direction of Unibrow, who grunted in reply and went back to his Nintendo game. Then Roget turned to Phoebe. "Yo," he said, pulling out the chair opposite hers.

"Hey," she smiled fakely, fighting the impulse to dismiss her date on his outfit alone. Had she not fled New York precisely to get away from the kind of people who judged others on such superficial attributes? Besides, if and when she knew the man better, she might begin to make subtle suggestions as to how he might tweak his wardrobe to reflect a more updated look. Not that, in three years, she had ever gotten anywhere persuading Neil Schmertz to rid their Brooklyn home of his hideous pleated balloon pants with the tapered legs and sewed-down cuffs.

To be fair, though, she was hardly dressed in high style herself that evening: brown corduroys and a plaid blazer with a nipped waist discovered in a box in the attic marked ROBERTA—WINTER—DRESSY.

"So, you ready to order?" began Roget, shaking off his bomber jacket. "I'm frigging starving." Had he never heard of small talk?

"To be honest, I hadn't really thought about it yet," Phoebe told him.

"Well, I'm having the egg parm." Slapping his palms down on the wood-look tabletop, he gazed up and around him and began to whistle, apparently waiting for her to finish deciding.

Though tempted to launch into a tirade about the need for manners in a civil society, Phoebe instead decided to give him the benefit of her doubt and turned obligingly around in her seat to survey the offerings. (Maybe he really was starving.) "I guess I'll have the spaghetti and tomato sauce," she announced after a short interval, thinking it sounded like the safest bet.

"You want a Coke or anything?" he asked, standing back up.

"Do they serve wine here?"

"Does it look like the kind of place that serves wine?"

Phoebe made a face and said nothing, irked to have been called on her own stupidity.

"Hey, if you really can't deal, there's a liquor store around the corner," Roget offered.

"That's okay," she said, bristling at the insinuation. "I'll just have water."

"Up to you." Roget approached the counter, where he engaged in a complex handshake and upper-arm slap session with Unibrow before putting in his and Phoebe's dinner orders. "So listen, we're gonna have one egg parm. That's for me. And the lady would like your spag with pomo." Luigi grunted and hit him again. Then Roget hit Luigi back. Then, to Phoebe's horror, they banged heads.

Returning to their table, Roget propped his elbows upon its surface and said, "I should start by telling you that, generally speaking, I find the violin an extremely shrill instrument. And this is coming from someone who actually digs the piccolo. However, I'm prepared to make an effort not to hold it against you."

"Hold *what* against me?" asked Phoebe, her eyes narrowing with derision and confusion.

"The violin," he replied.

Her eyes grew even narrower, as she tried to comprehend how she'd ever agreed to go on a date with this moron.

"Hey, lighten up, it was a joke!" he exclaimed.

"Hilarious," she muttered.

"Thank you." The maestro smiled cordially. "One of the reasons I became a conductor is that you get to be a total schmuck. I'm serious. It's practically part of the job description. It's like that joke—*what's the difference between a bull and an orchestra?*" He didn't wait for Phoebe to guess. "*The bull has the horns in front and the bunghole in back.* God, that's a good one." Laughing raucously, he slapped the table again, while the evening stretched out before Phoebe like a nonstop from New York to Sydney, confirming her suspicion that the world was a bad place, best survived from inside your own home, with the shades drawn and the lights off.

No more than three minutes later, Luigi appeared with their meals. The speed of the transaction suggested to her that their food had been reheated, as opposed to cooked. Phoebe found it a disturbing concept to entertain, especially since it involved pasta, a food group that, from what little she knew about cooking, having resisted self-reliance for as many years as she could, suffered from reheating. What's more, she could have sworn that her "pomo sauce" was a close friend of ketchup, but no matter. She figured it was only one night of her life—only one more failure. With any luck, it would be over soon. And she would be back in bed with her notebook making lists of palindromes, prime numbers, Roberta's fa-

vorite euphemisms, her own favorite baby names and orchestral works, her worst dates ever. (This would qualify.)
"Grandma de Luca really appreciated the visit last week,"
Unibrow was now telling Roget. "Also, she loved the record
you got her. The Three Tenors, right?"

"There'll be two tenors soon if Pavarotti doesn't lose
some weight," replied Roget, tucking his napkin into the
neck of his T-shirt as if it were a lobster bib. (Phoebe averted
her eyes.) "But glad she liked it. Nice lady. Too bad she can't
see anything. That must suck."

"Well, she already saw some stuff." Luigi shrugged helplessly and disappeared.

Then Roget turned back to Phoebe. "This is service,
huh?"

"And it looks so fresh," she mumbled sarcastically, her
fork twirling at half speed through her spaghetti pile.

In truth, her dinner wasn't as bad as she'd feared. Or
maybe it was just that her stronger impulse was to avoid talking, and eating accomplished precisely this. Roget, on the
other hand, seemed to feel that chewing and chatting were
mutually compatible activities. His makeshift bib bobbing as
he bent over his plate, he began to recount his life story so far,
beginning with, "So, let me tell you a little about myself—I
have no sisters or brothers and I was orphaned as a small
child."

"I'm sorry," said Phoebe, her sympathies momentarily
going out to him; it was hard for her even to imagine her life
without her family making it difficult.

But he asked her, "Why are you apologizing? You weren't
there. Oh, hey, you got some sauce on your chin. . . . No, to

the left. . . . A little higher. . . . Yeah, that's it, you got it. Anyway, back to me. . . ." He went on to recount a difficult adolescence spent bouncing between distant relatives' houses and foster homes provided by the states of first New York and then Ohio. It was in Columbus, apparently, that Roget got involved in the school music program and learned to play classical guitar. Later, he won a full scholarship to the University of Florida at Gainesville, where he met his mentor, Guillermo Something de Something, who introduced him to conducting and arranged for him to study in Europe. He was over there for nearly a decade and had moved back to the U.S. only two years before. He could have commuted to the NSO job from New York or Philadelphia—never mind Newark—but he preferred small-town life. He found the people less stuck-up, the distractions fewer. And while he wasn't religious per se, he had certain issues with evolutionary theory ("I mean, take the giraffe. Have you seen one lately? I'm sorry, those things are too fucking freaky-looking. Don't tell me they're the product of any naturally occurring, evolutionary—").

"Do you want to get the check?" Phoebe interrupted his soliloquy at twenty-six minutes past seven, as she pushed away her half-eaten plate. (Roget had already wiped his clean.) With any luck, she figured, the whole date would come in under a half hour. But was it Roget she sought escape from or everyone and everything?

"Whatever," he answered with a shrug, seeming (understandably) a little put out. "I didn't get to hear much about you."

"I'll tell you next time." Phoebe smiled unconvincingly.

"Sure." Roget turned around in his seat and called out to

his friend: "Yo, Lu, the lady would like to know what the damage is."

But at the sight of the check, Phoebe felt suddenly ashamed of her own behavior. The maestro was a semi-grotesque figure, to be sure. And yet, here she was, abandoning him before it was time, just as his own parents had done. "Here, let me split the bill," she said, eager to make amends for her negligence, as she drew her wallet from her purse.

Secretly, she was expecting him to protest. Far from it. "Oh, thanks," he said. And then, after reviewing the figures, he asked her, "Hey, since your spaghetti cost seven and mine cost more like six, do you think you could throw in an extra dollar or two? The NSO isn't exactly making a killing these days."

"Did anyone ever tell you that you're really cheap?" she grumbled under her breath, incensed all over again, as she yanked two extra bucks from the fold.

"I don't get the feeling you like me very much," said Roget. He'd heard her.

"I like you fine," Phoebe lied. "I just want to point out that I don't have *any* job right now. So whatever you're making, I guarantee it's a lot more than me!"

"We're looking for ushers," he offered.

"I'd rather prostitute myself." The words filtered through her clenched jaw. (Her careerist nerves were too raw to find the idea of handing out programs and showing old ladies to their seats at her father's concerts even vaguely comical.)

"Really?" Roget's eyes twinkled.

"I meant that metaphorically."

"Well, I also have to pay for the gas," he added, grabbing

his bomber jacket off the back of his chair and standing back up. "That is, assuming I drive you home."

"I'll give you two dollars," Phoebe told him. Above all, she was eager *not* to have to call Leonard and ask him to pick her up. (He probably wasn't even home yet from dropping her off.)

"One would probably be fine," Roget told her, as he started toward the door.

"You're really amazing," she said, shaking her head.

"So I'm told. Oh, hey, car's back at my house." The chin was on the move again. "Don't worry—I'm not trying to get you to go home with me, *that's for sure*." He laughed caustically.

"Believe me, I'm not worried," Phoebe assured him, as she followed him out.

But the comment had gotten to her. Never mind the fact that she didn't particularly want to sleep with Roget. Did he not want to sleep with her either? She could recall a time when, to her fury and excitement, it had seemed that every man wanted a piece of her.

And now, it seemed, they didn't anymore.

A muted, mauve sun was holding on, just enough to light the way down a block of modest frame homes constructed of clapboard and brick and set close enough together to imply row houses that had changed their mind at the last minute. Their screen doors were scalloped, their wrought-iron hand rails had been painted white. On the far corner, there was a newly constructed Mafia palace with an over-landscaped garden. Roget lived in an aluminum-sided dollhouse on a shady lane off Redneck Avenue, which traced the eastern edge of Teterboro Airport before meeting up with Liberty, which was also known as Moonachie Road and had once been home to a slave burial ground—or so Roget claimed in a sidewalk tutorial on the history of Little Ferry. Then he shifted his attention to a vintage white Corvette parked out front. "Meet Arturo," he said.

"Nice car," said Phoebe, wishing she were about to pull out her *own* ignition key.

How, in almost thirty years, had she managed to avoid that suburban rite of passage, the driving test? In truth, until moving back home, there had never been a compelling reason to take it. In high school, her mean, insecure, doggedly loyal best friend, Rachel Plotz, had driven Phoebe everywhere in Rachel's stepmother's Mercedes coupé. And on those rare occasions when Rachel had plans of her own, such as accompanying her real mother to the Concord resort hotel in the Catskill Mountains for one of their singles weekends, Leonard had done the honors in one of a half-dozen Electra station wagons he had driven while Phoebe was growing up. (While he had been a terrifying driver even then, the Electra's gargantuan hood had at least created the illusion of safety through distance.)

And Hoover University was located in the Allegheny Mountain region of Pennsylvania, where there was nowhere to go, so no one had a car, with the exception of a few restless frat boys with a special feeling for the town of Altoona. And after college, Phoebe had moved directly to New York City, where everyone took the subway or a cab, or walked.

Meanwhile, upon her graduation from Tufts University, Rachel Plotz had moved to San Jose, California, to work in the technology sector. There, she met and subsequently married a software titan named Bill, with whom she went on to conceive identical twin boys named Connor and Tucker. Phoebe had recently learned this in her prep school alumni bulletin, the *Pringle Post,* the class note section of which she pored over twice a year as if in possession of a religious text, divining evidence wherever she could find it that she had failed in some spectacular and irrevocable way.

"*Entrez, madame,*" said Roget, holding open the passenger door for her.

"Thank you," said Phoebe, ducking into the car.

The seat was so low she felt as if she were sledding. Even so, she felt far safer on the ride home than she had on the ride over, with Leonard. Even more propitiously, Roget played Beethoven's *Third Symphony* at full volume the entire way back, rendering further conversation impossible. (For its *Funeral March* section alone, the symphony was also number six on Phoebe's list of favorite orchestral works ever.) That evening, its plangent tones reminded her of all the people she knew who were now in the ground—to be honest, not that many yet. But how soon before that changed? Or what if there never was a *yet*? What if she were the first to go? And in a way might that not be preferable? The worst part of being close to someone, it had occurred to Phoebe more than once, was the utter devastation that his or her death promised to deliver.

If his violently nodding head was any indication, Roget seemed to be enjoying the music too.

"Thanks for the lift. I owe you another twenty-five cents," were the next (and last) two sentences out of her mouth as she handed him three quarters.

"You can give it to me later," he offered.

Whenever that is, Phoebe mouthed to herself as she made her way up the crooked slate path to her family's house, relieved to be home but also just a little bit sad.

She found Roberta stretched out on her favorite old divan with the silver duct-taped arms, watching a documentary about the Indian railroad system. ("It took eleven thousand men eight years to lay all thirty-two thousand sixty-three kilometers of steel tracks between Jodhpur and Bhubaneswar.") "Back so soon?" she said. Phoebe could tell that her mother was sorry to see her back so early. But was it disappointment that her daughter's date hadn't gone better, or that Phoebe hadn't left her alone for a few more hours?

And what if the truth were that, far from being unable to manage a moment without her, Leonard and Roberta actually couldn't wait for Phoebe to leave? She was suddenly furious at them all, furious because she felt unwanted, unneeded. "Yeah, well, he was a total freak and I had a terrible time," she told her mother, not in the mood to spare her the "negative news" she so despised. "I mean, I feel sorry for Dad for having to play for him every week."

"Are you sure you gave him a chance?" asked Roberta, her eyes still on the Indian steam engines.

"A chance?" cried Phoebe, even more on the defensive. Her mother had a way of always seeming to blame the victim.

"I was ready to call Dad and ask him to pick me up before we even started eating! Literally the *first* thing out of his mouth was how shrill he finds the violin." Phoebe realized as soon as she said it that she could hardly expect much sympathy from Roberta on that front. As with so many other violists who had begun on the violin but found the competition too stiff, her mother probably couldn't help but take pleasure in hearing the ever more popular fiddle derided. In fact, a nanosecond-long giggle—really, a snort—escaped her nose, propelling her shoulders and torso forward.

What bothered Phoebe far more was her mother's need to change the subject—her answer, it seemed, to all strife. "Oh, did I tell you that I ran into Mrs. Rosenbloom at the Happy Market this afternoon?" she began anew. Just like Roget, she didn't wait for an answer. "She told me the most shocking thing about the Axelrods!"

"Who are the Axelrods?" asked Phoebe, even though she could name all three kids.

"You don't remember the Axelrods?" Roberta cocked her head in surprise. "Mr. Axelrod is a mathematician at Fordham, and Erica Axelrod was a year below Emily—a very unfortunate-looking girl, poor thing. Anyway, the oldest one, Carl, who I believe was a year above Emily, apparently got himself in some terrible trouble with drugs down in Florida. And now, Carl's second wife—well, to be honest, I don't know if they ever married, I believe she was a drug addict, as well. In any case, she's disappeared with both children, both of them under the age of five. It's really very sad. Such nice parents, too."

"Definitely sounds like a major setback," said Phoebe,

who was now holding back tears, not on the Axelrods' behalf but rather on the Fines'. For it seemed to Phoebe that there was a threat lodged at the core of Roberta's encomiums for her neighbors' lost innocence, a *don't forget that terrible things happen to other families, not ours.*

Except it wasn't true. Devastating things had already happened to the Fines and, in all probability, would continue to do so. For that matter, at least the Axelrod wastrel had fulfilled his biological duty and produced some grandchildren for his own parents to fawn over in their declining years. It was a shame that his spouse equivalent had to kidnap them, but at least he'd tried.

It was more than anyone could say for Phoebe or Emily Fine.

4

For as long as Phoebe could remember, Roberta and Leonard had been saving both the twist-ties and the clear plastic bread bags they once cinched. They reused aluminum foil and paper towels too, draping the latter on a string over the sink, as if laundry left out in the sun to dry. The town of Whitehead, on the other hand, had come late to recycling. When it finally caught up, it implemented an elaborate every-other-week policy for the collection of reuseable types of trash. Leaf and Lawn Waste was carted away on alternate Thursdays. Commingled Paper (junk mail, old newspapers, unfinished novels, unread *National Geographic*s) went on Wednesdays. Mixed Containers (plastics, tin, and glass) were picked up on the first and third Friday of every month, and Household Junk (old board games, bookshelves, typewriters, and toilet seats) on the second and fourth Friday. What's more, whereas the town's ten full-time garbagemen once ventured down driveways and into cans, now residents were asked to take their collections out to the curb themselves.

Early in September, a famous penny-pincher in town named Mrs. Rossner came across an unchipped Limoges china tea set in front of the McCluskys' house. The McCluskys were an elderly couple with no children who lived on Lower Oak. Phoebe learned about the discovery from Roberta, who had run into Mrs. Rosenbloom once again, this time in the crackers and cookies aisle of the Fairlawn ShopRite. Just how much valuable stuff was being mindlessly tossed out twice a month, Phoebe wondered. Was Mrs. Rossner's finding a fluke? Had Mr. McClusky been dying to throw out that tea set for as long as he'd been married to Mrs. McClusky? Had he mostly objected to the floral pattern, which conjured up for him a certain hothouse feeling reminiscent of his unhappy childhood in Bayonne? And wasn't each marriage a kind of detective story with its own set of clues, its own red herrings, all of them destined to be buried with the central protagonists and added to the list of unsolved crimes?

And might there be an easy way to get rich, after all?

Phoebe wasn't paying rent anymore, of course, which relieved a certain level of financial stress. But she needed spending money, and there wasn't any coming in. As a result, her credit cards had already achieved "peak performance," her checking account currently hovered in the three-hundred-dollar range, and her savings consisted of a single twenty-five-dollar CD—presumably worth slightly more than that now—that had been awarded to her at the age of ten by the Whitehead Fire Department, for her second-prize-winning submission to its antilittering poster contest. Using watercolors, fabric snippets, and newsprint, she had rendered the image of an overflowing garbage can, accompanied by the following stenciled imperative: DON'T U B A LITTERBUG! Needless to say, Roberta had compared it favorably to Rauschenberg.

But there was a larger motive for Phoebe's money lust, as well. She had a distinct fear of ending up like her parents, counting change and clipping coupons and buying generic-brand products when she bought anything at all. Yet she seemed to be headed in precisely that direction. Given her dislike of reporting for work, it seemed unlikely that she would ever make a decent living. As for marrying someone who did, if her relationships with Neil Schmertz and Alex Kahn were any indication, there was just as poor a chance of that. (She seemed to have the highest success rate, at least in the short term, with anarchists, bartenders, and starving artists.) And to purposefully seek out a rich man for matrimony struck her as eerily akin to prostitution. Finally, unseemly as it was to contemplate, as far as Phoebe could tell, she and Emily stood to inherit little of value: a few divans in need of reupholstering—split by two?

But then, Phoebe's interest in Trash Night wasn't purely a matter of economics; it also had something to do with the thrill of the chase. In fact, her fascination with treasure hunting dated back to early childhood—for a while, *Treasure Island* was among her favorite books, second only to *From the Mixed-up Files of Mrs. Basil E. Frankweiler*—and formed a partial explanation for the frequency with which she once walked into walls. (Lest a gold necklace or ten-dollar bill had lost its owner, she kept her eyes earthbound at most times.) In a similarly speculative vein, she spent hours flipping through the Scott's catalog in search of the list price of each stamp in her collection, as she counted perforations, checked for exotic watermarks, and dreamed of happening upon a backward-printed Queen Victoria bust amid the Renoir reproductions from Togo. Her love of all things aristocratic informed her dollhouse as well, which she decorated in the style of Versailles, and her arts and crafts projects, almost all of which she spray-painted gold.

Back then, however, attaining great wealth was just one of countless fantasies Phoebe harbored. Others included winning a gold medal on the uneven bars and, as she got older, writing the next Bret Easton Ellis novel and marrying a Kennedy. It wasn't until adolescence that she became enchanted with money's practical applications. It was the Reagan eighties. Conspicuous consumption and civic duty had become fully enmeshed in the public imagination. And the Fines alone, or so it seemed to Phoebe, found fault with the needless half bathrooms and remote-controlled garage doors that were the mark of status in their suburban milieu. To make matters worse, Roberta made Phoebe and Emily shop for their back-to-school outfits at designer-seconds outlets and Midnight Madness sales. As such, their blue jeans had French labels no one could pronounce—not *Bon Jour* but *Au Revoir* and *Voulez-Vous*.

The irony was that, while her family occupied the bottom third of the economic spectrum represented by her mainly middle-class classmates, Phoebe was one of only a few students at Whitehead Middle School to have crossed the Atlantic. How did the Fines afford their European vacation? At four o'clock on the morning of their intended departure, Leonard had dutifully captained the Electra to Newark Airport, where he'd waited in a standby line at the People's Express counter until well past breakfast. Successful in his efforts, he had returned to the airport that evening with the whole family in tow. In this manner—and, wherever possible, by camping on expatriate musician friends with untraditional lifestyles—the Fines had traveled to Belgium, Luxembourg, France, and Switzerland. Roberta thought it was important for the girls to see Wagner's summer retreat on Lake Lucerne, but she didn't believe in spending sixty bucks on Nike or Adidas "tennis shoes"—as she called them—when you could get them for five at Caldor. (Sick of having her classmates call her sneakers "skips," Phoebe would have preferred the Nikes.)

Later, as a financial-aid student at tony Pringle Prep high school, she found herself on the receiving end of certainly subtler but arguably more invidious forms of snobbery. Her inability to load a pair of borrowed Rossignols onto the ski rack of Rachel Plotz's father's weekend Jeep, for instance, produced in Phoebe's best friend at the time a semblance of disbelief, followed by paroxysms of hysterical laughter. Depressed, overweight, and never kissed, Rachel herself could hardly have been characterized as a glamorous figure. Even so, Phoebe had come to see the world as divided between "the Excitings" and "the Borings," with the rich on one side of the equation, the Plotzes included, and the Fines clearly falling on the other. So she deduced by watching both the popular girls at school having important conversations with their boyfriends in the front seats of their silver Audis, and the characters on the popular evening soap operas, *Dynasty, Dallas, Knots Landing,* and *Falcon Crest* making delicious messes out of their debauched lives. (With Emily already away at Yale, Roberta had by then relaxed her one-hour-of-public-television-only-per-night rule.)

At the same time, despite the zeal with which she attempted to ape and longed to embody her moneyed classmates' style and mannerisms, Phoebe had inherited from her parents a certain reflexive snobbery toward those whose capital was primarily material, not cultural. If she never stopped lamenting her family's single bathroom with its grubby bowls and peeling contact-papered surfaces, for example, it was also possible for her to imagine that the Fines, with their Hans Hofmann calendars hanging over the Maalox, were of a more elevated species than most. Such feelings of superiority were especially ascendant in the company of her Jewish friends, the majority of whom hailed from families with more fresh fruit in their refrigerators than Franz Liszt in their record collections, the Plotzes again included. So that Leonard and Roberta, despite their fondness for canned peaches, sometimes struck Phoebe as a healthy corrective to an unflattering stereotype. Not all Jews, it seemed, were good with money after all.

And yet, the older Phoebe got, the more favorably she began to look upon that unflattering stereotype, and the more it seemed to her that being rich and scorned was still preferable to being poor and ignored. It had taken her by surprise as an adult to discover how much money mattered to her—how it could start to seem even more important than love. It wasn't just the things it could buy you, either; it was the things money could *prevent* you from having to do, such as picking through your neighbors' trash. Which is precisely what Phoebe set out to accomplish on the evening after her dinner date with Roget Mankuvsky, since the fourth Friday of the month was the next day.

As per custom Leonard was happy to lend his driving services to the expedition. More surprising to Phoebe, given his avowed anti-materialism, was that his interest seemed to surpass the desire to play the part of dutiful father. "What a curious idea," he said, a glint in his eye as he stroked the Vandyke he had worn since his beard had begun to look straggly. "And who knows? I might find something myself—something to buy or sell. You know, my students sometimes see things around the music room that they ask about—music-related trinkets and whatnot. And I'm not too proud to say that, at some point, I might be inclined to match their wishes, especially if it means making your mother more comfortable."

"Sure, why not?" said Phoebe, wincing at the idea of her college- and conservatory-educated father resorting to the practices of his peddler grandfather, Phoebe's great-grandfather, Isaac Feingold, late of Scranton (by way of Bavaria).

"I've actually been looking for a few things myself," said Roberta, appearing on the staircase moments later.

She and Leonard were ready to leave pretty much that second.

Phoebe had other ideas. Less than keen to be outed in the throes of an all-family Trash Night expedition, she insisted that they wait until dark to leave. So at quarter past seven that moonlit night, after a light snack of sardines and imitation Triscuits, the three of them piled into Leonard's Yugo and set off in the direction of Lower Oak, which, given Mrs. Rossner's findings a fortnight earlier, seemed like the natural starting point. Roberta sat up front with Leonard, blathering on about which of their neighbors, being spendthrift types, were most likely to be throwing away perfectly good household items. Phoebe sat in back with her head leaning out the side window, the better to inspect their neighbors' garbage and also to block out the sound of her mother talking. She felt sure that her current location constituted final proof that her standing in the world had fallen in immeasurable ways. Moreover, she had crossed over to some other side from which she could no longer expect to be rehabilitated. But since she was already here . . .

Leonard pulled up next to the McCluskys', and Phoebe got out. There were clearly still renovations going on somewhere in the couple's lemon-yellow Cape Cod. But while impressive in size, the pileup out front contained little of value, namely:

1. The mud-stained remains of a rope hammock
2. A metal footstool featuring more rust patches than white paint
3. An old plastic juicer, circa 1979
4. The hose portion of a vacuum cleaner
5. A garden rake with three teeth left to its bite
6. A wicker dog bed that appeared to have been crushed by a meteor
7. An electric-blue area rug rolled up like a log, its backside covered with mulch
8. An apple-green acrylic-knit sofa with its springs sprawled on the grass
9. The fake wooden shell of an ancient TV set
10. A rusted tricycle
11. A dented wastepaper basket
12. Two orphaned bureau drawers
13. A garden chair whose green-and-white webbed seat appeared to have been devoured by a wild boar

14. A plastic high chair decorated with caked red sauce
15. A bent snow shovel with a broken handle
16. A flaccid blue pool raft in the shape of a donut
17. A toilet seat whose brown spots either could or could not be attributed to chipped paint (sometimes, it's better not to know)
18. A short stack of *American Heritage* hardback magazines dating from the 1960s, with a color reproduction of Wild Bill Cody facing out (and in direct violation of Whitehead's garbage rules, since those magazines rightfully belonged to Commingled Paper Night)
19. A disassembled refrigerator, its hulking door and produce drawers propped up against a curbside catalpa (again, in flagrant breach of Whitehead's waste disposal laws, since, with regard to so-called white goods, residents were required to call in advance and arrange a special pickup)

Within minutes, Phoebe was back in the car and grousing, "All they forgot were the lead paint cans." (Hazardous Waste Collection Day was held quarterly at a local community college; following a license check, residents were directed to one of a half dozen check-in tables that had been set up in the parking lot, each of them devoted to a different type of ecological nightmare.)

There wasn't much of anything on the rest of the block, either.

"Well, that was an inauspicious beginning," declared Roberta, sounding none the less cheerful for it. (She considered *feeling discouraged* the eighth deadly sin.)

"We could always try Millcrest," suggested Leonard.

"Maybe the Wigglehams are throwing out an extra copy of the Declaration of Independence," muttered Phoebe. In addition to featuring the most expensive real estate, the block was home to Whitehead's only *Mayflower* descendants.

"Oh, Phoebe!" said Roberta, chuckling at the idea. While she rarely had anything good to say about the nouveau riche, Phoebe's mother hated their old-money predecessors, perhaps even more. "Did you hear that one, Lenny?"

"I did indeed," said Leonard, turning around in his seat to shoot his younger daughter a sly wink. "In fact, I like to think she got her keen sense of wit from me."

"Dad, watch the bike!" shrieked Phoebe.

"Sorry about that, folks." Leonard rounded the corner on what felt like two wheels.

Moments later, they pulled up across the street from a mini–White House in the shadow of a massive weeping willow tree. Without too much trouble, Phoebe could imagine that behind its fire-engine-red door and brass knocker lay an oppressively cheerful chintz-heavy living room with overstuffed floral sofas and a golden retriever farting beatifically by the fire.

Their trash, on the other hand, as Phoebe soon discovered, was somewhat less impressive in scope: a few board games and an unidentified engine, perhaps having once belonged to a leaf blower. Since she was already there, however—and on the off chance that a real bill or two had found its way into the scrip— she lifted the top off a battered Monopoly box.

She wasn't expecting the words "Excuse me, aren't you one of the Fine girls?" to greet her ears. Naturally, her first instinct was to flee.

But because (a) the voice sounded friendly enough, (b) running away might be interpreted as an admission of wrongdoing, (c) she had already been identified by family name, and (d) she was still, just maybe, more concerned about offending the male gender than she was in defending herself against their unwanted advances, she made the split-second decision to face her accuser. "Helloooo?" she trilled in as lighthearted a voice as she could muster, her body frozen like an ice sculpture, her flashlight pinned behind her back.

"Thomas Wiggleham here." A gangly man wearing a bright orange suit jacket emerged from behind the hedgerow. Owing to the angle of the streetlamp, he appeared to have only half a face, and a thin one at that, with a chin that seemed to stretch all the way down to his knees. "I believe you went to school with my younger brother, Ben." He extended a witchy-looking hand.

Phoebe met it with her own, her thoughts turning briefly if traumatically to the British banker's party she'd attended in a Tribeca loft a year earlier. Emerging from the bathroom with her hands still wet—the apartment's minimalist aesthetic apparently precluded hand towels—she had been introduced to a certain pink shirt named Henry. Or maybe it was Harry. Or Hiram. Or Hamish. In any case, the words "Don't worry, it's not urine" somehow found their way to her lips, prompting stunned silence on Pink Shirt's part. *Well, that's all in the past,* she tried to reassure herself, as she told Thomas Wiggleham, "Oh, right, hi, I'm Phoebe—Fine. What a nice surprise!"

"Where's that light coming from?" he asked, lifting his long chin and peering over her hunched shoulder.

Her face blanched as she yanked her hand up and away from his, flung it around her waist, and flicked the power switch on her flashlight to OFF with a nervous laugh and, "Oh, thanks!"

Whereupon the shadows on Thomas Wiggleham's face assumed an even more nefarious cast. "If you don't mind me asking," he continued, "what are you hoping to find in our trash?"

The sensation of burning acid now seized Phoebe's abdominal cavity. For the first time since moving home, she recalled her media and marketing jobs with nostalgia and longing. Maybe the work had been mind-numbing, the pace exhausting; at least she'd been able to show her face during daylight hours. "I'm on a scavenger hunt," she told Thomas. "It's for a good cause."

"And what cause is that?" he wanted to know.

"Poor children."

"I see."

"And also sick ones."

"Right."

"Oh, Phoeeeebeeeee." Turning around with a start, she was faced with the further unwelcome sight of her mother hanging out the passenger window of the Yugo in her bizarre wig. "Is everything okay out there?" Roberta called to her. Leonard was flashing his emergency lights for no evident reason. Then, even more inexplicably, and despite pellucid skies over northern New Jersey that evening, his windshield wipers went into overdrive with the resulting screech, as the wipers scraped against dry glass, calling to Phoebe's mind the rat she had once watched attempting to claw its way out of a sink full of soapy dishwater, the metal portion of a mouse-trap strapped to its back like an oxygen tank on an *Apollo 9* astronaut—a long story involving Alex Kahn and a country house-sit.

"I'll be there in one second!" Phoebe called back to her—to her still, after all these years, mortifying mother—before she turned back around to face her tormentor. Except she didn't face him at all. "That was my mother," she informed a wet leaf amalgam positioned next to her right foot.

"Well, I'll let you guys get on with your—well, whatever it is you're doing!" declared Thomas.

"Going to the—" On the cusp of saying "movies," she suddenly recalled her previous explanation and substituted "the scavenger hunt."

"Oh. Right. Well, it was a pleasure running into you! Our curb is your curb." Looking somewhere between amused and perplexed, he turned his back.

"Yeah, nice running into you," Phoebe mumbled back at him, her glee at the prospect of reentering her family's car unlike anything she had known before.

But quiet fury came over her just as escape became feasible. *No,* she thought to herself. It wasn't right for a guy in an orange sports coat to get away with mocking her family! The owner of the offending garment was already halfway up the stone path that led to his manse when she called out his name, whereupon his pea head swiveled around his long body like a carnival game target. "I just want to point out one thing before I go," she yelled, her heart at full gallop. "You can laugh at me all you want for going garbage collecting with my parents on a Thursday night. However, please note—you're here too!"

"Well, for one thing, my elderly parents, whom I try and visit twice a year, live here," Thomas replied, in a disconcertingly rational voice. "For another, my wife and I and our two children are on our way back to Jakarta, where we spend the other fifty weeks of the year, since I manage a developing markets fund for Morgan Stanley. In fact, we're leaving for the airport as soon as our car arrives. Our car is late, however, which is why I came outside—to look for it. Well, good night now."

The logic was inarguable.

Just then, the front door opened, revealing a tiny blond woman holding an even tinier blond person in her arms. "Baldy Nut, should I call the limo service?" she squawked shrilly across the lawn. (The embarrassing nicknames couples have for each other!)

Facilitator of sweatshop labor, Phoebe mouthed under her breath, as she skulked back to the Yugo in defeat. There could be no doubt that this ranked among the lowest points in her life. Nor did she have any particular desire to expatiate upon its origins and implications.

But Roberta was asking, "Who in the *world* was that?" before Phoebe had even slammed her door shut.

"I'll tell you in a second," Phoebe barked back at her. "First, it's imperative that we get out of here *now*."

"Sure thing, Crumps," said Leonard, pumping the accelerator.

The three of them flew backward in their seats like crash-test dummies. For once, Phoebe didn't object.

Roberta seemed to feel otherwise. "Lenny, *please*!" she squealed.

"Sorry about that, Bert," he said, laying a conciliatory hand on her knee.

"Do you *have* to call Mom that? Bert is a guy's name." Phoebe had been lobbing this charge at her father since before high school.

Her father's reply was always, "Don't worry. Everyone thinks I'm saying Gert."

"But why would you be calling Mom Gert if her name is Roberta?" asked Phoebe, as exasperated as ever.

"It's a nickname for Gertrude," Leonard explained.

"But Mom's not named Gertrude! Also, Gertrude gets shortened to Gertie, not Gert!"

Silence. (It was always the same story.)

"So, who was that anyway?" Roberta tried again. It seemed to Phoebe that her mother never let go of the subjects that begged for release, while the important ones always got shunted.

"One of the Wiggleham sons," Phoebe finally told her— why postpone the agony?—as they rounded the corner, past Whitehead's single historic landmark, a Civil War–era drill hall.

"The youngest, middle, or eldest?" asked Roberta.

"The shithead one," said Phoebe.

"Your language, Be!"

"Sorry, the dunghead one."

"Well, I don't know the sons, but I've never liked that mother," Roberta went on. "I know her from Whitehead Works. She isn't a bad fund-raiser, but she never gives a dime away of her own family fortune! And don't think it goes unnoticed by the other board members."

"Preppy murderers."

" 'Preppy murderer'? Isn't that what they called that

Robert Chamber fellow who murdered that poor girl in Central Park some years ago?"

"It's Cham*bers,* with an *s,*" Phoebe told her.

"That's what I said!"

"No, you said Cham*ber,* as in *chamber music.*"

"So what do you say we try Frost Lane next?" said Roberta.

"Doesn't matter," said Phoebe, her mood continuing its descent into abject nihilism. She was suddenly disgusted even by the air she was breathing: Why did the backseat of the Yugo always smell like old bananas?

The evening would have ranked as a complete and utter fiasco if they hadn't driven by the Marcianos' three-bedroom Tudor Revival on their way back to Douglass Street. A short, rotund man with salt-and-pepper eyebrows shaped like circumflexes, Vincente Marciano was the guy at the opera who sat in the little black box on the edge of the stage and fed the singers their lines, most of which were in Italian, which was no big deal for Mr. Marciano, since he'd been born in Palermo. How he got from there to Whitehead, New Jersey, was a matter of some speculation around town. (There were unsubstantiated rumors of petty Mafioso connections.) In any case, he had been in the employ of City Opera for at least the past twenty-five years, which was also the amount of time that Marciano had been waiting for the now-geriatric prompter over at the more prestigious Metropolitan Opera, a mere two hundred yards away in the Lincoln Center complex, to croak already, so he could take the old woman's job. Except the old woman kept mouthing "Mimi!" and "Carmen!" at the right moments (in *La Bohème* and *Carmen,* respectively). So Marciano kept waiting and praying. At least, so said Leonard's orchestral musician friends, most of whom had harbored dreams beyond the pit and therefore reveled in tales of others' equally thwarted ambitions.

It was Roberta who spotted the flame mahogany music cabinet with the flower detailing on the curb out front. Vincente had apparently found another place to store his libretti. Phoebe went to take a look. The piece was missing a hinge and in need of refinishing but was well proportioned, a pretty color wood, and sturdily built. And while it was unlikely to be a Chippendale original, it was bound to have some resale value, she mused to herself, her mood improving dramatically as her thoughts turned from her exposure by Thomas Wiggleham to practical matters such as how to transport the thing back to the garage. Since it was no longer in length than a cello, there was reason to believe that, standing on end and angled just so, it might fit in the backseat of Leonard's car. But upon further examination, Phoebe determined that the cabinet's legs posed too serious a decapitation threat to risk such a setup.

Luckily, Leonard found some elastic snakes beneath the driver's seat, and after a good deal of huffing and puffing he and Phoebe were able to hoist the piece onto the roof of the car and fasten it down. For a block or two, it seemed like an excellent solution. No sooner had they braked for a stop sign, however, than the thing began to slip-slide overhead, and they had to pull over and refasten the snakes—three separate times, as it turned out. It was enough to convince Phoebe that, should there be a next Trash Night expedition, alternative transportation arrangements would have to be made.

5

"Lenny, stop, there's a light on in the house!" cried Roberta, as they pulled into the lip of the mostly but not entirely gravel driveway. (Bottle caps, loose change, and bits of tinfoil had all been known to turn up in the farrago.) To amplify her point, she had extended her left arm across her husband's lithe frame.

"For heaven's sake, there *is*," said Leonard, as he pounced on the brakes, an action that failed to instantaneously curtail the car's forward momentum. (The Yugo had a few known structural flaws, this being one of them; Leonard had always felt confident that he could work around the problem.)

The skid was followed by an ominous-sounding *thud* overhead, prompting Phoebe to howl, "Dad, can you *please* not drive like a frigging maniac!" Then she unrolled the window and extended her head and torso through the opening.

She found the Marcianos' music cabinet still up there but—having slipped its moorings yet again—this time, halfway off the roof.

"For God's sake, Phoebe, will you get your head back in the car?" Roberta reprimanded her as she sat back down. "It could be an intruder out there!"

"You guys probably just left the light on," suggested Phoebe.

"Why would we have left a light on?" asked Roberta.

"It's a terrible waste of money," added Leonard.

"Whatever," said Phoebe, rolling her eyes at her parents' shamelessly penny-pinching ways—ways that never seemed to make a dent in their insolvency.

"I suppose we ought to call the police," Leonard continued, though in a tone of voice that suggested he wasn't in any particular hurry to do so. "Maybe I'll run over to the death house and use the Nathans' phone." Husband-and-wife bassoonists, the Nathans were the new owners of the windowless monstrosity next door, which had been built by a lesser-known nuclear physicist affiliated with the Manhattan Project at Columbia University, across the Hudson—hence its nickname in the Fine family.

"What, and leave us in the car? He could be armed!" Roberta clutched her macramé purse to her infirm bosom.

"How do you know it's a *he*?" asked Phoebe.

"Now isn't the time for your gender politics, Phoebe!"

"Fine, but could we all *calm down* for a minute?"

Just then, the back door was seen to flex on its hinges. Even Phoebe felt her chest constrict around her heart, while her mother shrieked, *"LENNY! DO SOMETHING!"*

"We're vacating the premises," he announced, in a deep granulated voice so much more evocative of fighter pilots and firsts-in-command than of the man Phoebe knew her father to be that she might well have burst out laughing had she not at that moment been so frightened—not nearly as much of the intruder in question as by the possibility of being left in a neck brace for years to come. (Leonard driving in reverse was no laughing matter.)

Thankfully (or not), before he had a chance to assault the accelerator, she happened to notice her older sister standing by the back steps, ashing on a cigarette. "Wait, it's Emily!" she cried, just in time.

"My goodness, it *is* Emily," said Leonard, squinting through the windshield as he maneuvered the gearshift back into neutral.

"Well, I'll be darned," said Roberta, pushing open her door.

"Hey, you guys!" Having pitched her cigarette butt in Leonard's doomed grass experiment, Emily began to wave with two hands.

"What a lovely surprise," Phoebe grumbled to herself. In fact, she found it anything but lovely. Simply by being in White-head, Emily threatened to usurp her role as their mother's chief caretaker. That is, in times of adversity, Roberta and Leonard had always deferred to their elder daughter, and there was little reason to believe that things would be any different this time.

Moreover, as surprised as Phoebe was to see her sister standing there—to her knowledge, Emily had no prior plans to come east from San Francisco, where she lived—she was even more shocked to find her wearing what appeared to be a short coat made of rabbit fur. Not only was it barely sweater season, but, for as long as Phoebe could remember, her sister's sympathies had lain with the humane-society crowd. A few years back, Emily had even landed a mention in a tabloid gossip column in New York for having participated in an anti-fur fashion-show stage-in, with (of course) a leading role—first fake-blood hurler. What's more, just the previous winter, she had tirelessly assailed Phoebe for wearing a vintage overcoat with a mere hint of the stuff on the collar, Phoebe's remonstrations to the effect that the mink in question had been dead for fifty years falling on deaf ears.

But, then, her sister had always had a knack for making her own contradictions seem consistent, Phoebe thought with bitterness. (No doubt this time Emily was prepared to argue that the butchering of rabbits actually forestalled global warming.) The two sisters had last seen each other the previous June, when the five of them, including Emily's currently estranged husband, Jorge Weinstein, had convened for a less than serene weekend in Lake Placid, New York. Most memorably, Emily had led Phoebe and Jorge up to a famous Adirondacks lookout point and then insisted on taking an unmarked trail back down the mountain. The situation had deteriorated from there. Thank God Jorge remembered to bring his cell phone.

"Oh, Em, you gave us some scare!" Elbows extended like bat wings, Roberta reached up to embrace her far taller daughter.

"Oh, sorry," said Emily, simpering, as if she'd felt worse about things that had happened in the past. "I thought I'd surprise you guys."

"Well, you certainly did that," said Leonard, swooping in

for his own hug, then pulling back and holding her at arm's length. "You sure don't look like a thief."

"Oh, Poppy, you're such a silly man!" squealed Emily, who had always treated her father with a combination of unconditional love and utter contempt.

When it was Phoebe's turn to say hello, she offered her sister a pointedly unenthusiastic "Hey."

"Hey, wart face!" Emily returned the greeting.

"Do you *have* to call me that?" asked Phoebe.

"You know you love it."

Emily was wrong. Though Phoebe was in some ways desperate for her sister's approval—Alex Kahn had liked to tease her that she would have jumped off the George Washington Bridge if Emily had asked her to—she found her older sister infuriating. Not to mention judgmental, sanctimonious, manipulative, and self-obsessed. For one thing, it was so like Emily just to show up without asking anyone if it was a good time to do so!

On the other hand, Phoebe conceded, it had never really mattered if she and Emily were in the same city or not. Sororal conflict was different from regular friend conflict that way. No matter how many times you screamed bloody murder— or miles apart you moved—you never properly fell out. Your sister's words would still be reverberating in your brain, reminding you (in case you'd forgotten) that you had bad knees ("I really think a longer skirt would be more flattering on you"), or made bad music ("Have you ever thought about going back to school?"), or needed to pluck your eyebrows ("Let me do them, please? I promise it won't hurt"), or improve your complexion ("Believe me, I used to have skin just like yours"), or had never really known who you were ("It just seems like you're always looking to other people to affirm your self-worth") or when to break up ("God, why don't you dump that *loser* already?").

But sisters were also the only ones who knew the answers to your stupidest childhood knock-knock jokes ("Bob who?" "Bob up and down"); who could turn to you after twenty years and say "Midget with the Ring Ding," and you alone would see the whole agonizing tableau laid out before you—the highest rung of the dusty bleachers of the local hockey rink where he once sat alone upon the game's conclusion, the midget with his after-dinner snack, methodically unfolding one triangulated tinfoil corner after another, oblivious to the way in which, for the rest of you and your sister's days, those eager hands would sum up a certain yanking, tragic, and yet ultimately hopeful feeling about the human condition, untranslatable to later-life friends and prompting you to respond "Yum-yum tree," the way you always had, and always would, though for reasons neither of you could now recall, the etymology of the phrase since lost and now irrelevant, its stranglehold attributable, finally, to the pleasures of repetition and to the fantasy of there being some kind of logic to the chaos after all.

Emily had always had an almost physical pull over Phoebe; Phoebe hated her guts, but she needed her too. She needed her to be the backboard against which she bounced all her basest fears and resentments.

Besides, if Phoebe was going to be fair about it, Emily had just as much right to come home as she did. It was even possible that Emily needed her family more just then than her family needed her. According to Phoebe and Emily's second cousin Sasha, who had given Phoebe all her best hand-me-downs growing up and now provided her with dirt about her older sister—since Sasha was the other family member living in the Bay Area and Emily wouldn't tell Phoebe anything herself and Roberta didn't want to talk about it and it wasn't clear if Leonard even remembered his son-in-law's name—Jorge was threatening to drag Emily into divorce court. This was unless they reached a settlement in which Emily (a) made no claims on his vast family fortune in Argentina and (b) agreed to split with him the paltry salary she made as a Legal Aid lawyer for the California poor and disenfranchised. (A week before hiring a lawyer, Jorge had conveniently gotten himself fired from his desk job at an Amnesty International spinoff.) What's more, since there was no no-fault divorce in New York State, and that was where the two had married—seven years earlier, in a multidenominational service (though both were Jewish) complete with chanting Tibetan monks, at St. John the Divine, the progressive cathedral on Manhattan's Upper West Side—one of them was required by law to accuse the other of something heinous (like abandonment or adultery). Which had a way of aggravating matters.

Yet, as sorry as Phoebe felt for her sister vis-à-vis her marital troubles, in truth she didn't feel *that* sorry. If Phoebe's own life loomed in her mind as a series of false starts strung together by the occasional cinematic night out on the town, Emily's had always seemed to Phoebe to work out a little too perfectly—at least until now. First, there was her National Merit Scholarship and early acceptance to Yale. Later, there was the expense-paid junior year abroad to Beirut, where Emily managed to learn fluent Arabic in nine months, founded a student organization devoted to fostering Jewish-Muslim understanding, and fell in love with a Syrian Christian war hero with one leg but (Emily never skimped when it came to certain details) an uncircumcised penis of herculean proportions.

Oh, but it wasn't just in love and politics that Emily had prevailed! To Phoebe's mind, her sister had led a perfectly strategic life that lacked even a single dangling participle, a single moment of indecisiveness or confusion. Even during her freebasing cocaine phase—somewhere between Yale and law school at Stanford—she had given the appearance of being in charge. She had stopped when she felt like it, and started again when she was so inclined. Unlike Phoebe, Emily's relationship with controlled substances had always been primarily recreational.

Which may explain why, with Roberta and Leonard now out of earshot, Roberta having gone inside to get dinner started, and Leonard having gone to see about extricating Mr. Marciano's music cabinet from the roof of his car, Phoebe felt compelled to wrinkle her nose and ask Emily, "Is that real fur?" (Phoebe was willing to admit that something about being in the presence of her older sister turned her into an equally intolerable brat.)

"You mean this?" said Emily, smoothing down her jacket collar in the hyperbolically preening fashion of a Door Number Three model on *Let's Make a Deal*.

"Yeah, that," said Phoebe.

Her eyes shifting to the Fines' oxidized birdbath, at which no bird had ever been known to bathe, possibly because it was filled with old leaves, Emily let loose a wistful sigh. "The truth is, I would *never* have bought this thing for myself, but I couldn't bear to hurt Sebastian's feelings."

"Who's Sebastian?" asked Phoebe, even though she could have guessed. (She preferred not to.) Among the idiosyncrasies she found most grating in her sister was her way of assuming that the main characters in her own life were the main ones in everyone else's too. So that explaining who they were, or even prefacing their names with an enlightening epithet such as "my new boyfriend," was unnecessary.

"Just a friend of mine," Emily answered.

"By any chance, is his last name Bach?"

"Bach?" Now it was Emily's turn to feign bewilderment. "Why would his last name be Bach?"

"Just curious." Phoebe shrugged in as bored and unimpressed a manner as she could muster, determined not to show—or feel—her annoyance at the news that her sister had already found a new man. A separated woman, she had every right and reason to be dating.

And yet, would it have killed her to remain single for all of five minutes? As far back as Phoebe could remember, Emily had always had a boyfriend, beginning in kindergarten with Thomas Munz (who, according to Roberta—who had run into someone, who had heard from someone else, who had run into Thomas's mother—was currently an Outward Bound instructor in the Canadian Rockies).

"Well, maybe you should be less curious," suggested Emily.

"Well, maybe you should stop acting like everyone's heard of your random friends, since no one has," said Phoebe.

"Are you coming in, girls?" Roberta's pale face and flaming hair appeared in the doorway.

It was less a question than a demand.

"Let me take your coats," said Leonard, coming up behind them in the foyer. "Emily, what an interesting costume you have on!"

"It's not a costume, Poppy," Emily told him, with a tight smile, clearly peeved by the comment—a fact that caused Phoebe to snicker triumphantly.

But Emily had her revenge a few moments later. After Leonard disappeared with the coats, she paused to peer at a photograph of Phoebe that had been hanging over the console for the past five years. If it wasn't particularly flattering—straw hat, outdoors, family friends' daughter's wedding—neither was it the worst one ever taken. "Funny picture," said Emily. "You look like you're about to spit up your soup." She turned back to Phoebe. "Remind me, was that during your bulimic phase?"

Phoebe raised her middle finger in her sister's face, though, in truth, she wasn't all that mad. It had been too juvenile a gibe to take personally, or seriously. Phoebe was further comforted by the thought that, in the context of 281 Douglass Street, even the great brain of the family (Emily) was susceptible to the "regression effect" that had essentially reduced her own age by half.

But as the evening progressed, Phoebe lost her ability to qualify.

"Em, you must be starving after the long flight," said Roberta, bending over the pots-and-pans cupboard.

"And I'm not?" asked Phoebe, who had never fully divested herself of the idea that Emily was her mother's favorite.

Typically, it was a self-fulfilling fantasy.

"Phoebe, I'm simply trying to put on a nice dinner here, since your sister doesn't visit us very often, and if you'd like to eat it, you're welcome to do so, and if you don't want to, that's fine too." Roberta said this more or less upside down and in her best I-gave-up-a-solo-career-in-Europe-to-be-the-selfless-mother-of-you-unappreciative-children voice.

The rebuke was followed by a percussion solo's worth of metal pot lids crashing on top of one another. Several escaped the cupboard completely, fanning out to distant outposts of the kitchen (behind haphazardly placed wicker baskets crammed with supermarket circulars and single mittens), where, drum-roll style, they ricocheted into repose. For a brief moment, the incident seemed to offer Phoebe the chance to redeem herself in her mother's eyes. But Emily somehow managed to retrieve all four lids before Phoebe had even located a second one. "Oh, thanks, Em, you're a doll," said Roberta, removing them from her hand and further convincing Phoebe that Roberta's affections lay elsewhere. "Anyway, I thought I'd whip up a nice cassoulet, since I happen to have a can of white beans in the house."

"Isn't that an oxymoron?" asked Phoebe, who was now feeling actively discriminated against. "I mean, I thought cassoulets take forever to cook."

"Maybe you should learn how to boil water before you start criticizing other people's cooking techniques," Emily interjected, before Roberta had the chance to answer for herself.

This time, Phoebe had no scathing rejoinder. Emily was even more right than she probably knew. Indeed, for Phoebe, among the greatest perks of moving back home had been the handing over of her culinary needs to her mother's care. As dicey as the outcome frequently was, there was always a meal in the works. Never mind an egg in the icebox. It was a luxury you couldn't fully appreciate until you'd lived completely alone, as Phoebe had. After she'd broken up with Alex Kahn for the last time, dinner had gone from a source of pleasure to one of stress; it was always sitting there at the end of the day, waiting to be dealt with, scheduled: What should she eat? Where should she eat? Who should she eat with? The problem was that dinner was as much a biological imperative as it was a social one. And there were only so many nights that she could rally friends to meet in restaurants. The rest of the time she was stuck cooking for one, which always seemed like a terrible waste if not a tragic joke—she didn't know how to cook anyway—or unpacking some brown paper take-out bag whose bottom had grown leaky with mango chutney sauce, or coconut milk soup, or low-sodium soy sauce, the act of which never failed to wreak havoc on her self-esteem.

The problem was that dinner was always reminding her how empty she felt on the inside.

"Well, I'm sure the best chefs *do* take their time with a cassoulet," said Roberta, as if Emily had never spoken, "but I'm not ashamed to say that I've never been much of a gourmet. Frankly, it wasn't that important to me. I had music to make and children to raise. Though in my personal experience, the very best dinners are the ones that get thrown together at the last minute anyway. I, for one, have never even been able to tell the difference between Minute Rice and the long-grain long-cooking kind. With a dash of butter . . ." Roberta disappeared into the pantry, still gabbling away.

Emily began to stroke the sleeve of Phoebe's V-neck pullover. "Ohmigod, I love your shirt," she purred. And for a split second, Phoebe was gratified by the compliment and ready to make up and be best friends again, which seemed to be her sister's intention. For a split second, Phoebe even felt sorry for her, sorry ever to have been anything less than doting and solicitous. It was one of the quirks of Emily's personality that, as unpleasant as she could be, she also invited a strange kind of loyalty.

Then Emily asked her, "Can I have it?"

"No!" cried Phoebe, taking a step away from her.

"Oh, come on, pleeeeeeeease." Tilting her head sideways, Emily fixed her with googly eyes.

"Emily, I just bought it!" This wasn't precisely true, though, having been purchased over a year and a half ago, it was still a lot newer than most of the articles in her wardrobe. Phoebe had stopped shopping retail, having convinced herself that as soon as someone like her bought something it was bound to be on its way out of fashion. It was a self-effacing paradigm but also an economical one, with rich opportunities for feeling morally superior.

"But it's designed for cleavage," whined Emily, heaving her high, luscious bosom in Phoebe's face—at least, until Phoebe turned away in agony, her own relatively minuscule breasts having been a lifelong source of agony. She imagined them to have deprived her of some essential component of feminine experience that made a woman's beauty comparable to a life jacket in a storm. Which is to say, they had deprived her of something Emily had. Unable to compete with her sister on this front, so to speak, Phoebe had cultivated sharp bones instead, but they never failed to seem like a consolation prize. More important, Emily must have known she was preying on among the sorest of Phoebe's sore points, and Phoebe couldn't understand how she dared. Was nothing too outrageous? Had the prospect of divorce not humbled her in any way? Or was it rather that, in marital strife, Emily saw not failure but merely another chance to prove the breadth and depth of her worldly weariness?

In fact, people often commented on how much the Fine sisters looked alike. But while it was true that their features appeared to have been molded in the same foundry, it was as if their sculptor had made one on a Monday morning while grappling with the difficulties of daily contentment, and the other on a Friday night as he anticipated the hijinks of the coming weekend. So Phoebe had always imagined. She thought that where her own looks could have been described as delicate and, less generously, as unassuming, Emily—who had been stamped with Roberta's curvier proportions, only on a grander scale (she was three inches taller than Phoebe)— possessed the outsized glamour of a wartime pinup girl or, less generously, a linebacker or drag queen. There was also no denying that Emily's teeth were whiter than Phoebe's, her eyes clear blue to her sister's soupy gray-blue ones. And while Phoebe's naturally etiolated complexion slipped into the realm of sallow after a single late night out without commensurate sleep, Emily sported the wind-blushed cheeks of a downhill skier all year round and regardless of lifestyle or climate.

Just then, Leonard reappeared with a bottle of sake and four clay cups. The previous spring, the flirty mother of one of his Japanese oboe students from Fort Lee had brought the set over as an Easter gift. "I thought I'd raise a glass," he said, turning the bottle on its side, "to having both my remarkable daughters home at once."

"That's so sweet of you, Pop," said Emily, but her tone of voice was less saccharine than usual, suggesting that she was still pissed at him about his "interesting costume" line.

"Oh, I shouldn't, Lenny," said Roberta, returning from the pantry with her promised can of beans.

"Not even a sip?"

"Well, maybe one."

"And this one's for you, Crump," said Leonard, handing her a cup.

"Hooray," said Phoebe, raising it in the air, though hard pressed in that moment to think of anything to celebrate.

There were *clink*s all around—except between the two sisters.

"What do you say we have a few hors d'oeuvres to tide us over until dinner's ready?" suggested Roberta. "Bebe, will you be a doll and see if there's any Château Neufchâtel in the icebox?" Though she always bought generic-brand products, Phoebe's mother had the inexplicable habit of referring to them by their famous brand-name competitors—tissues were always Kleenex, tampons Tampax, and household cleaners Babo, even though the name had been phased out in favor of Ajax at some point mid-century.

Robotically, resentfully, resignedly, Phoebe opened the refrigerator and, averting her eyes from the putrefaction to the extent that it was possible, removed from the meat and cheese drawer an orange plastic bowl encased in a clear plastic bread bag. Through it, she could just make out a semi-hard white substance that either was or wasn't Brie. (Leonard and Roberta had yet to catch on to Tupperware.) "Is this it?" she asked, handing her mother the bowl at a safe distance away from her nose.

"That looks right," said Roberta, removing it from her grip.

"Are you sure it's not the remnants of one of Dad's grout projects?"

"Well, we'll find out shortly!" Roberta pulled the bowl out of the bag.

It turned out to be a boiled chicken breast from what appeared to be the start of World War I. It turned out that Leonard had finished the cheese at lunch and the grouting at noon. The hors d'oeuvres hour began and ended there.

Phoebe wished dinner had, too.

It wasn't just the instant cassoulet. Midway through the meal, Roberta turned to her older daughter with a sprightly smile and asked, "So, Em, for how long may we expect the pleasure of your company?"

"I'm actually not sure about that," replied Emily, brushing her mane off her face, as if her life were a perpetually windswept affair. "I may be going on to Paris, and possibly Düsseldorf."

"Really?" Roberta leaned in.

Emily pursed her lips and smiled coyly. "I suppose this is as good a time as any to tell you that I have a new friend."

"A new friend—how nice!" exclaimed Roberta, beaming as she turned to Leonard for affirmation.

"Very nice, yes," Leonard muttered in agreement, his head bobbing up and down like a cuckoo atop a Swiss clock.

It was clear to Phoebe that neither of her parents dared mention Jorge's name. The secret to their consistently amicable relationship with Emily? They were terrified of offending her.

Though it was also true that, insofar as no mother wants to imagine that the daughter she brings into the world won't eventually end up, at the very least, a crude parody of herself—and this new liaison seemed to hold out a greater possibility for reproducing the species than Emily's marriage to Jorge Weinstein currently did—Roberta had every reason to be pleased by the news.

The business of antagonism was therefore left to Phoebe, who had regained enough confidence following the cleavage incident to blurt out, "So you and Jorge are finished?"

"Excuse me?" said Emily, though she had clearly heard the first time.

"I was just curious about what happened to your husband," continued Phoebe, taking the opportunity to eject a piece of bean skin that had gotten caught between her teeth, if only for purposes of demonstrating how little any of it actually mattered to her, even though, of course, it did. In fact, she could recall praying at Emily's wedding that she and Jorge would wait to have kids until it was too late. Which, by all appearances, they had done. (Phoebe supposed she had that to thank her sister for, at least.) "Now that he's gone, I actually kind of miss him."

"I can give you his number," Emily offered.

"That's all right—I didn't like him *that* much," Phoebe assured her.

Emily glared but said no more. Leonard kept eating. Roberta puckered her lips, her eyes darting from one to the other of them; divorce most definitely figured on her list of conversation topics to be avoided. At the same time, she was apparently at a loss to think of a new one with which to replace it. For several minutes, the family sat in silence.

Finally, breaking into a sanguine smile, Emily drew a deep breath through her nose, as if preparing to deliver the closing argument in a case she felt sure she had already won, and announced, "As it happens, Jorge and I have a tremendous amount of respect and compassion for each other as human beings, and I have no doubt we'll be close friends our whole lives. The current legal situation has of course been something of a strain on this intimacy, but I'm confident that that phase will be over soon."

Phoebe was left unconvinced—not just by Emily's predictions of a speedy conclusion to her divorce proceedings but by Emily's sunny description of the current state of her and Jorge's relationship. Indeed, if Jorge was the same hothead Phoebe remembered, he wasn't about to settle without a skirmish. She hadn't forgotten how he'd lost his temper at the teenage cashier of an upstate Friendly's ice-cream window who'd accidentally overcharged him for sprinkles.

"Well, we're just happy to have you back in town!" said Roberta, trying to make the best of things, as was her usual and, to Phoebe, maddening way. "It gives me my appetite back just seeing your face!" She forked a sausage round, placed it between her lips, and began to chew, then paused to reach her thumb and index finger into her open mouth.

Withdrawing them several seconds later, she declared, "Oh, dear, a little of the plastic wrap seems to have snuck into the mix."

Reconsidering the merits of take-out mango chutney sauce, Phoebe stopped eating and didn't begin again.

"I have some other news as well," said Emily, clearing her throat as she reached for her sake glass. "I'm taking a little break from the legal profession." She downed the remainder of the glass's contents.

"A break—how interesting," said Leonard, turning to his wife for guidance.

"Well, this is big news certainly," Roberta agreed, in the same superficially responsive but ultimately indifferent tone as her husband. In truth, though she and Leonard had the utmost respect for Emily's authority and were law-abiding citizens themselves, neither had ever been able to make an iota of sense out of her career. That Phoebe played the electric violin was already a stretch for them; Emily might as well have been designing nuclear plants.

In their own defense, however, their elder daughter had made it clear from an early age that their input in her life was unwelcome. The pattern had been established in the seventh grade, after Emily announced that she was giving up the cello. Naturally, Roberta and Leonard had protested that Emily wasn't giving her gift a chance to blossom. ("What gift?" Emily had griped.) Several ugly scenes involving torn sheet music and slammed doors had ensued. It wasn't until Emily's delicate-eared cello teacher, Vance Cunningham, finally admitted that it had been his idea for Emily to quit— he couldn't take the sound of her sawing away anymore, and claimed she had no ear whatsoever—that Leonard and Roberta came around to Emily's position, though not before they'd curtailed their friendship with Vance Cunningham.

After which point, they tended to believe Emily rather than not. Which meant that there had been even more pressure on Phoebe to become a member of the musical elite. At least, that was how it had always seemed to her. She suspected that her failure to have become a classical violin soloist of international standing was a matter of endless disappointment to them, especially for Roberta, who once admitted to having dreamed that the two of them (mother and daughter) were standing side by side in sequined gowns before a packed concert hall somewhere in Central Europe, performing Mozart's *Sinfonia Concertante* in E flat for viola, violin, and orchestra. To be fair, neither Roberta nor Leonard had ever uttered a direct word on the subject of Phoebe's abdication of the classical repertoire, but their idle comments about the success of certain of their musician friends' children never struck Phoebe as entirely idle. "Did you hear about Pierette Delancey? Only twenty-six, and she got hired for Mostly Mozart," they'd say. Or, "Phoebe, you remember Nancy, don't you? Travis Greenbaum's middle daughter? A very talented and *dedicated* horn player."

Then again, it was just as likely that Phoebe was projecting her own anxieties onto her parents and it was actually *she* who lamented *their* failure to have become people she could brag about—especially Leonard, whose lack of ambition she had always found somewhere between commendable and disheartening. In any event, she had grown defensive about the whole subject of her career, or, really, lack thereof, explaining how the words "Well, if you decide to become a major disappointment to your family like me, you can always get in on my Trash Night racket" found their way out of her mouth.

"Oh, Bebe, don't say things like that," protested Roberta, though Phoebe suspected that her mother's objection had less to do with the veracity of her statement than with the negative impression it made.

"It's true, Crumpet," Leonard added, only slightly more convincingly. "You know we're very proud of you."

"Thanks anyway," said Emily, turning to Phoebe with a patronizing smile, "but I have a few backup plans to exhaust before I turn into *that* serious a loser."

"I loathe you on every conceivable level," Phoebe told her.

"Girls!" cried Roberta.

But there was no stopping Phoebe. With a sensation of sizzling embers in her chest, she rose from her chair and, thinking better of stabbing her sister with a fork, instead hurled her only partly thawed French bread at Emily's face.

But her sister ducked and the bread hit Leonard smack in the eye. "Dad!" wailed Phoebe, aghast at what she'd done, as she stumbled to his aid.

"That's okay," he said, swatting the crumbs down his cheek. "Still alive here."

"Mom, can't you put her on lithium or something?" asked Emily, hands raised protectively in front of her face like boxing mitts.

"Phoebe, what's gotten into you?" asked Roberta, her lower lip trembling as she stood up, too.

"I'm sorry for everything; it's all my fault," mumbled Phoebe, her head hanging as she sat back down. She was suddenly sick with herself, sick with guilt for having upset her mother at a time like this, a time when she ought to have been comforting her. She no longer even blamed Emily for hating her. It was clear to her now that she didn't merely regress in her sister's company; she turned into a wild animal. Of course, if she were a nicer person, Phoebe also thought, Emily might take the opportunity to apologize as well, if only for that *loser* comment.

Her pride greater than her need for approval, however, Phoebe's sister merely shook her head, as if it were just her luck to have ended up in a lunatic asylum, and went back to her dinner.

"Delicious casserole," chirped Leonard, returning to his meal as well, along with his habit of radical disassociation.

In time, Roberta sat back down too, but she stared straight head, as if recognizing none of them.

Not surprisingly, there was limited conversation through the rest of dinner. Emily and Leonard bantered about the upcoming presidential election and how the "political mood" differed in San Francisco versus New York. Needless to say, Emily was voting for Ralph Nader and the rest of the family for Gore. For dessert, Roberta brought out a vanilla-on-vanilla wedding cake–style concoction that had been given to Leonard by yet another of the mothers of his music students. This one was a Korean-American kid named Ernest Park, whose family owned Whitehead's French-Korean Excellent Cake Dream bakery. Since he lived in nearby Palisades Park, he was known around the Fine household as Ernest "Palisades" Park. As for the cake, it was possibly the sweetest that had ever been baked and also, arguably, the most tasteless, with no additional identifiable flavors to offset the overpowering one of refined sugar. Even Leonard seemed hard-pressed to ignore reality. "Lovely frosting," he said, gasping for water after six bites.

The others got through no more than two apiece.

Claiming to have calls to make, and also to be short on sleep, Emily was the first to dismiss herself from the table.

Desperate to make up to her parents for her behavior at dinner in any way she could, Phoebe followed them into the den to watch a PBS documentarty on black holes. Owing to Leonard's refusal to get cable, the reception came in and out. And the narrator sounded like the devil himself as he waxed poetic about "these insatiable, matter-munching blobs of pure destructive energy." Knowing a little about destructive energy herself, Phoebe was glad when it was over and it was time to go to bed.

Alone in her childhood bedroom, however, and for the first time since moving home, she wondered what she was doing there—not in terms of the reasons she had recorded in her notebook but in the larger sense of *who were these people with whom she had been thrown together at some arbitrary date in history and directed to perform strange overinvolved relationships marked by overwhelming tenderness and blood-boiling resentment and based on no affinity other than genetic coding?* It wasn't the first time Phoebe had pondered the random quality of family, or the parallels between it and slavery, insofar as it chose you, not the other way around.

Yet, without our mortifying relations to blame for our problems and worry about dying in a plane crash, she wondered now, what would we have? Whom would we have to complain about? And how would we ever fill all forty-five minutes of therapy? As infuriating as she had found her whole family that evening, Phoebe would miss them when they were gone, assuming she didn't go first. She saw that now.

She saw that, hard as it was to believe in that moment, she would probably even pine for a last peek at Emily's beautiful cleavage.

6

But the sound of Emily prattling away on the phone the next day for what seemed like hours on end, presumably with her special friend Sebastian, had the same effect on Phoebe's eardrums as mice playing in the walls while she tried to sleep. Never mind the fact that Emily was tying up what constituted the only telecommunications line in the house, since Roberta and Leonard considered Call Waiting among the scourges of modern civilization. By Sunday night, Phoebe found herself composing a list entitled "Ten Reasons to Continue Living." It was a struggle to produce seven.

1. Not a burn victim
2. Chance to lie under warm quilts
3. Lots of good books/movies still haven't read/watched
4. Don't live in the Third World
5. Born with ten fingers and toes
6. Already made effort to quit smoking; why die now?
7. Unlikely Emily will stay in town for more than another few days. . . .

But Emily did. By midweek, Phoebe was so desperate for respite from the tensions of sibling rivalry that she was only too happy to accept her possibly insane city friends' invitation to join them for a Thursday night in Manhattan, beginning with the grand opening of a luxury leather goods boutique in Soho.

The bus to Port Authority passed through the towns of Fairview, North Bergen, Guttenberg, and West New York. Out of her window, Phoebe spotted Honduran cafés flying blue and white flags, traditional Islamic dress emporiums displaying gold chiffon scarves, five-and-dimes whose plastic merchandise had been carried out to the sidewalk in front, and countless posters with Spanish-language campaign messages from local politicians. Closer to the entrance of the Lincoln Tunnel, on Boulevard East in Weehawken, the sweeping views of the cityscape, set off against a pink and purple sky, seemed pilfered from a tourist-bureau video.

At Port Authority, Phoebe caught the subway downtown to Houston Street and walked east. No matter that she had only fled the city six months earlier. She couldn't get over how much whiter all the faces in Manhattan were! How sleek and intimidating all the young women looked in their skinny jeans and pointy shoes! And how dowdy and unkempt she felt by comparison in last season's black pants and square-toed boots. It was as if fifteen years' accumulated moxie and experience had vanished, and she had morphed back into Emily's mopey, formless, and addled kid sister, tagging after her down Broadway and across Eighth Street and St. Marks Place, with Emily playing the role of her private cicerone.

How had she always known where to go and what to

look for? Within seconds of arriving at Flip, Emily would home in on the perfect hound's-tooth raglan-sleeved overcoat. At Unique, she would make a beeline for the rubber and rhinestone bracelets. From the two- and five-dollar bins in front of Canal Jean, she would effortlessly fish up army surplus sweaters with suede shoulder and elbow patches, as if cracking open the only oysters in the sea in possession of freshwater pearls. But, for Phoebe, the aura of mystery emanating from those stores had been larger than Emily's ability to mine them. With their sulky Cleopatra-eyed sales staff, frenzied pop soundtracks, and kaleidoscopic merchandise suspended from every last inch of wall and ceiling space, they had embodied all that fascinated her and terrified her and seemed totally out of Phoebe's reach. In fact, the whole of Greenwich Village once appeared to her as a stage upon which she could reenact her favorite childhood game of dressing up and losing herself in a fresh identity.

Phoebe's mythologizing of downtown Manhattan continued into her twenties. Indeed, there was a time when every streetlamp in Soho seemed equipped with its own glittering nimbus. That was the time when Phoebe could say to herself, *I've had sex with a multimedia artist in a converted loft on Wooster Street* and it would mean something to her; it would mean she'd really arrived. And now she couldn't, and it didn't. Never mind the Pottery Barns and Victoria's Secrets and other chain stores that had colonized her old haunts—or the fact that, as crime levels had plummeted, the city had become a mecca for the upwardly mobile. The urban topography that she had once found eroticized now filled her with a nameless dread.

Halfway across Prince Street, just before Phoebe was due to meet her friends, a glistening black Town Car exhibiting a sign that read SUPERIOR #127 pulled up alongside her. Then the ostrich neck of Phoebe's friend Lisa Renfrew popped out the side window. "Hey, mall rat," she called to Phoebe.

"Hey, city snob," Phoebe called back, relieved by the sight of a familiar if not entirely friendly face. "What—are you guys following me or something?"

Lisa stepped out of the car. Nearly six feet one in stocking feet, she appeared to be wearing some kind of brocade curtain around her upper half and a pair of knee-high off-white suede boots that vaguely resembled broken-leg casts. "Didn't you know we were obsessed with you?" she barked. "Tomorrow we're going to stake out your parents' house in Paramus."

"It's in Whitehead, not Paramus," Phoebe told her.

"Same thing." The two exchanged double-cheek air kisses. Lisa was the fashion features editor of a glossy women's magazine once renowned for publishing short fiction by revered female authors; in recent years, it had shifted its focus to thigh fat and fellatio. As far as Phoebe could tell, chauffeured cars to and from the office were among the few perks of the job. "I like the outfit," Lisa went on. "Very late nineties."

"Yeah, but it's only fall two thousand," Phoebe pointed out. "Which means I'm just out of style."

Lisa shrugged. "It's never too early for retro."

"Phoeeeeebeeeeeeeeee." Chloe Berkowitz was next out of the car, her pretty head tilted at a 45-degree angle, as if she couldn't wait to borrow the nearest available shoulder. The certified mental patient of the bunch, she was both the most affectionate and the least sincere. Whoever was standing in front of her was her very best friend in the world—at least, until he or she stepped away. For the past however many years, Chloe had been writing a memoir about her battle with prescription medications vis-à-vis the passionate affair she conducted through most of her twenties with her married pharmacologist. Neither agent nor new man had yet to appear. "I've missed you so much!" she told Phoebe.

"I've missed you too," said Phoebe, trying to peel Chloe away from her neck, which Chloe was choking.

Gina Guglielmo was the last to emerge from the backseat. A publicist for independent films that few people ever saw—including the Danish satire *Whistling Past Hitler*, the Iranian feminist flick *Chador No More*, and the French erotic thriller *Les Autres Fenêtres (The Other Windows)*—she had constructed her entire identity out of being negative. In that sense, she was like the mirror image of Roberta. "Can you believe this huge zit right between my eyes?" was the first thing out of her mouth that evening. Gina's obsession with her blemishes seemed to mimic the failure rate of her films. It was as if the fewer the number of people who came to her screenings, the more she required that her face resemble a perfectly blank screen. Which, of course, it never did, since Gina was so stressed out all the time.

"Here she goes again," muttered Lisa, rolling her eyes, which were made up in the style of Kabuki theater.

"Where? I don't see anything," lied Phoebe, taking a step backward and noting to herself with a certain measure of righteousness, since she no longer engaged in those kinds of self-destructive patterns—at least not when it came to skin—that Gina had clearly been messing with whatever it was.

"You can't see *this*?" growled Gina, moving even closer.

"Well, maybe I see a tiny—"

"Gina, you look totally sexy!" insisted Chloe.

"Yeah, a sexy target practice."

"I have an idea." Lisa drowned them all out. "Why don't we stop blocking traffic with our acne show-and-tell and go get a drink."

There were no objections, especially not from Phoebe, who was starting to feel faint.

The new store was on Mercer Street. Two miniature women wearing headsets and black pantsuits stood watch outside its frosted glass doors, as if manning the pearly gates. As Phoebe and friends approached, a pack of fashion-student types with hair that appeared to have been cut with chainsaws stepped out in front. "I don't know if I can deal with this," admitted Lisa, stopping short and raising her palm like a crossing guard indicating that her children should not feel free to walk. Patience was among the behavioral modifications she was working on with her "life skills coach"—so far, apparently, without much success. She was working on other self-oriented issues with her accountant, her acupuncturist, her chiropractor, her osteopath, her facialist, and her feng shui master, respectively. Like so many professional women in New York, Lisa subscribed to the belief that success all came down to locating the right experts in the right number of fields. As if life could somehow be fixed. As if we didn't all have to die in the end.

Then again, Phoebe considered, maybe pretending otherwise was the only way to keep going.

Before Lisa had a chance to self-induce respiratory failure, the fashion students were let through and the gatekeepers lifted their eyes to the four of them. "She's with me," said Lisa, nearly giving Phoebe rotator-cuff injury as she grabbed onto her coat sleeve and yanked her forward. Two of their names identified on the master list—Gina and the store's publicist had once worked a premiere together—they were ushered inside.

Some seventy-five years earlier, the place had been a scrap-metal warehouse. More recently, it had housed a conceptual art gallery called Gluckstein Schmer. That was before a Swedish lightbulb installationist, hoping to add a few hundred extra frosted candle-tips to his already incandescent masterpiece, took it upon himself to reconfigure the gallery wiring. The place had gone up in flames. As for the artist, after reports emerged that he had sustained burns over 25 percent of his body, murmurings about an insurance scam gave way to expressions of sympathy mixed with disbelief at the man's stupidity. Meanwhile, the gallery owners moved the entire operation over to West Chelsea, leaving behind a blackened shell, of which the Italian leather goods conglomerate had taken full advantage.

The place had been stripped of all decorative accoutrements, the ceiling dropped for the sake of "warmth," the walls shellacked an antiseptic shade of white. The architect had also laid down a pink marble floor, upon which a series of Plexiglas cubes had been arranged in a tessellated pattern; each cube encased a different handbag, boot, or pair of backless loafers. "I wonder if there's anything good in the gift bags," said Chloe, as the four of them pushed past a row of diminutive violet totes with flourishes of white tissue paper poking out their tops.

"Looks like a couple of used Kleenex," said Gina, unable to conceal her disappointment.

"You guys have to get over your thing with freebies," sniffed Lisa.

"Duh, what do you think we came for?"

Not for the men, that's for sure, Phoebe thought, but refrained from saying it out loud for fear of sounding ungrateful for the invitation. Still, by her quick calculations as she made her way across the room, the female population outnumbered the male one by a ratio of six to one. Moreover, unless heterosexuals had suddenly taken to wearing skintight, short-sleeve, V-neck sweaters made of ribbed microfiber, what men were present were unlikely to be interested in the opposite sex.

With their stringy bodies, pale faces, gesticulating hands, and predominance of black clothing, meanwhile, the women reminded Phoebe of nothing so much as the mimes she had watched harassing tourists in front of the Pompidou Center in Paris during her aborted college semester abroad (she had come home two months early)—except they talked. And talked and talked. "I can't believe this," they said. And "I can't believe that," and "I'm so out of it," and "She's so into it," and "It's so great to see you," and "You're so great to say so," and "It's so frustrating . . . ridiculous . . . amazing," and "I wanted to die," and "I'm dying to know," and "I so know what you mean." Phoebe was reminded of the many times in her own life when her mood had gone from fine to lousy simply on account of being in the same company as people for whom being alive was clearly so much more vivid and ecstatic an experience than it was for her. (This was one of those times.)

Arriving, finally, at the makeshift bar—and now pining for the taste of alcohol—she was further distressed to discover several hundred martini glasses brimming with a green liquid the color of dishwashing detergent. "God, these drinks look awful. Stephen had no patience for drink sponsors," said Lisa, coming up behind Phoebe and dropping the name of the ex-boyfriend with whom Lisa was still obsessed, even though they hadn't gone out in eight years—and, what's more, he'd married someone else. "Oh, hey, Arden!"

Turning around, Phoebe found herself facing not only Lisa but one of the mime women—this one dressed in elaborate rope sandals that laced halfway up her petite tan calves, lending her the appearance of a Cornish game hen trussed up in a roasting pan. "I'm *so* recognizing your boots," she said, smirking hostilely at Lisa, one eyebrow raised.

"Glad to have jogged your memory," Lisa smiled back.

"Just so long as you return them to the shoe closet."

Lisa turned to Phoebe. "Arden is the accessories editor of the magazine, so she knows who's stolen what from the office." She turned back to Arden. "And this is my friend Phoebe."

"Hey," said Arden, her eyes now falling damningly on Phoebe's square toes.

"Hey," Phoebe mumbled back, wishing she could hide her feet behind her back.

Only then she'd be kneeling.

"I'm assuming you so don't work in fashion?" asked Arden, continuing to smirk.

"No—garbage," Phoebe informed her with a broad smile,

determined that she should have nothing to be ashamed of in front of this poultry dish, and therefore no reason to lie.

But to Phoebe's confusion, Arden's face contorted in fury. "Oh, so you're one of those really smug anti-fashion types who think they're better than people like me because they deal in recycled goods, whereas I'm just some parasite of the system, consuming natural resources and conning insecure and unsuspecting women into frivolous expenditures—is that it? If you'll excuse me . . ." Before Phoebe had a chance to defend her position—or even decide that Arden, apparently being as mentally unstable as the rest of them, wasn't so bad after all—she had disappeared.

Despite having learned the secret to her financial livelihood, Lisa showed no signs of being tempted to do the same. "If you really want to threaten the public with your outré credentials, I'd suggest going with *high-priced call girl* next time," she told Phoebe. "*Garbageman* seems a little too down-market. Not that I care what Arden thinks. She's a total cunt. Plus, she has horrible taste in shoes. It's a crime that woman is our accessories editor. Oh, look, it's Nigel Mailman! Let's go say hello—he's not in a position to pass judgment on anyone. . . ." Wondering if Lisa had thought she was kidding, and half-hoping that she did, Phoebe followed her through the crowd.

Nigel Mailman was the rare man whose face is so perfectly smooth and symmetrical and finely etched that it appears to have been constructed out of molding wax. His cheekbones jutted out like coat hooks. His jaw line resembled a sieve. His eyes were a disconcerting shade of blue. His hair was floppy and streaked blond. He was wearing a white dinner jacket with a red carnation lodged in the buttonhole, a paisley ascot, and a pair of pipe-cleaner pants emblazoned with a pink, red, and white candy-striped pattern. At the sight of Lisa, he thrust his right arm across his stomach, extended his left one out to his side, and slowly bowed. "Always a delight to see you, Ms. Renfrew," he gushed in a voice that sounded as if it had been dunked in a vat of crude oil.

"The pleasure is mine, Mr. Mailman," said Lisa, as if the pleasure were nowhere near her. (It was hard to say what, if anything, gave her pleasure aside from reminiscing about Stephen.) "And this is my friend Phoebe."

"Lovely to meet you, Phaedra," said Nigel, lids lowered to near-blindness levels as he bowed again. "Or have we met before?"

"I'm not sure," Phoebe told him. "But it's Phoebe, not Phaedra."

"Phoebe—my mistake!" He touched her arm and threw back his head. "But not for long, I hope." Flaring his nostrils suggestively, he turned back to Lisa. "Now as to you, Madame R., I'm afraid I must confess my crimes, such as they are. To wit, I've butted my bonny head into your private business and encouraged a dear friend of mine to call—"

"Nigel, if you're trying to set me up with one of your flamer friends!" cried Lisa, sounding genuinely alarmed.

"My dear, my dear!" Laying a hand on her forearm, he let loose a waggish chuckle. "I wouldn't *dream* of purporting to know what kind of young studs you fancy."

"Fine. Then what is it?" she asked him. Though she

hadn't gotten laid in what was, by most accounts, several years—and often ghostwrote her magazine's sex column ("Right before I have an orgasm, I sometimes feel like I have to pee. Is this normal?")—Lisa jettisoned all efforts to match her with an eligible mate. The general consensus was that she had sublimated her libido in pursuit of the perfect white sofa. To date, she had already bought and returned three, finding the cushions insufficiently plush, the legs too bulky, and the upholstery liable to pill, respectively.

"A strictly professional matter, I can assure you." Nigel produced a cigarette from inside his jacket, followed by a gargantuan sterling silver lighter, from which he summoned a four-inch high flame. "I've given your name to a talented writer of the kind of scurrilous prose you so specialize in at that filth factory of yours. So if a fellow named Jock"—inhaling, he redirected his gaze at the dropped ceiling—"or is it Jack?" His eyes swung down and around to the far wall. "Or maybe it's Jasper." He turned back to Lisa. "In any case, if someone claiming to know me rings looking for an honest living, be a love and say something encouraging before you slam down the receiver, would you?" His wrist flicked indolently at the cloud he'd conjured.

Lisa smiled imperiously. Though she would never have admitted it, she loved being hit up for favors, if only for the opportunities they presented to inculcate fear and indebtedness. "I'll do my best, Nigel," she told him, "on condition that you turn in your copy *on time* this month!"

"On time?" He gasped, a hand to his ascot, as if it were a radical new concept he was entertaining for the first time. "Well, it's a Faustian bargain. But I suppose I'll take it, because I'm a good person at heart." Again, he narrowed his eyes at Phoebe. "It's just on the surface that I stink of evil." Then, taking a step backward, his palm cupped beneath his chin as if he were cosseting a butterfly, he blew each woman a languorous kiss ringed in smoke. "Always a pleasure, Madam R. And lovely to have made your acquaintance, lovely PhaedraPhoebe."

"Nice to meet you too," said Phoebe, embarrassed to find herself enjoying the attention, however superficial.

"And now I'm off to circulate in the demimonde that is luxury leather goods. Ciao ciao." Pivoting on one loafer, Nigel vanished into the matrix.

"Who in the world was *that*?" Phoebe asked Lisa, intrigued enough to wonder if her mistake in love so far had been always to go for scowling he-man types.

"Oh, just this freak of nature who writes What's Hot and What's Not for us every month," Lisa shrugged. "You know, 'socks are in and sandals are out,' that kind of thing. "He's actually a nice guy—if you can get past the pathological lying. At some point, he was claiming to be a long lost member of the Windsor family. Apparently, he's a Bible salesman's son from Wichita, and the British accent is a complete fake. Go figure. Of course, the most unbelievable part is the only part that's true. I know because I've seen them together—that is, Nigel, his Greek shipping heiress, and his Greek shipping heiress's husband. Apparently, the couple portion was looking to spruce up their sex life. As for Nigel's motives, I can only assume they have mostly to do with sprucing up his bank account, though he goes around telling everyone how he's found the solution to all that petty jealousy and possessiveness garbage that plagues one-on-one relationships. Not that I can say I entirely blame him—Stephen and I definitely suffered on that account. I mean, the two of us literally had power struggles over which side of the bed we slept on! And then, of course, there was the whole issue of my male friends. He'd go absolutely *nuts* when I went out to dinner with my old college housemates, Roy and Carson. As if I hadn't already had four years to fall in love with any of them—not. I have my suspicions he was even a little jealous of my female friends, especially Betsy. Though it may simply have been that he had a little *thing* for Betsy. Once, the three of us were out in Wainscott together and I swear he was coming on to her— and right in front of me! God, it makes me insane just thinking about it. Anyway, the thing Nigel's actually most famous for is the lifestyle poster he posed for fifteen years ago, stark naked, with an infant clasped to his breast. As if he'd know what to do with a child." She laughed acerbically. "Not that I would either, but that's another issue. Back to the poster, you probably saw one in your freshman dorm at Hoover. Two million copies in print. Nigel has his mouth closed in the picture, so you can't tell, but apparently the teeth were bad enough to end his modeling career. They don't look that bad to me now, though, so he must have had work done since then. Or else he's the youngest denture wearer in New York. Or else he isn't the youngest at all. For all anyone knows, the man is seventy-five. He literally has a different answer for everyone who asks his age. If I had to put money on it, I'd place him somewhere in his mid-to-late forties. Also, he was in jail at some point in the early nineties—something white-collar, I can't remember what. Stephen would know. Anyway, that's Nigel."

"He sounds like a great guy," said Phoebe, feeling vaguely nauseated as she reconsidered her initial impulse.

After staying at the store for about an hour and consuming a half dozen green drinks between them, the four women stopped by a book-launch party at a used bookstore just around the corner from the luxury leather goods boutique. To the great excitement of the publishing world, the feted author, a friend of Chloe's named Jonathan Jacoff, had written a three-hundred-page novel from the point of view of the zoo animals at Buchenwald. Chloe swore he had a lot of cute friends, but, as far as Phoebe was concerned, Chloe had lied. Their chinos hung slack on their nonexistent behinds. Their tweed blazers failed to disguise their slumping shoulders and early middle-age spreads. Their facial expressions spoke of smugness and profound psychic discomfort. They held their cocktails close to their lips and made snide remarks about other, far more famous writers than themselves, most of whom were dead and therefore couldn't defend themselves. The women in the room, on the other hand, were dolled up like music-video extras in high boots and cleavage-centric tops and laughing too hard at lines that weren't funny. At least, this was Phoebe's impression of the party after aimlessly perambulating through the crowd for close to fifteen minutes, talking to no one. Still, she was happy to be there, if only for the open bar.

After laying her hands on a second whiskey soda, she joined Lisa and Gina in the corner, where they stood watching Chloe chat with the author. "I just think it's sad what bad taste in men Chloe has," said Gina.

"Seriously," said Lisa. "I mean, clearly I have my problems with relationships, but you can't say Stephen wasn't a good guy."

"Actually, we can say anything we want," demurred Gina, "since (a) we never met him and (b) you went out with him in high school."

"It wasn't in high school!"

"College. Whatever."

"After college."

"Right after college, which was now ten years ago."

"It wasn't right after," Lisa mumbled irritably. "We started dating in the spring after I graduated." She cleared her throat. "Our first date was on April twentieth."

"Ohmigod, I can't believe you still remember what day it was!" Gina began to moan.

"Shut up," whimpered Lisa. "It was an important day in my life, okay?"

"Just promise me you don't remember what time."

"A little past nine."

"I would have remembered what time too," Phoebe cut in, the alcohol having made her marginally more inclined to view the human condition in a sympathetic light. "I met him once. He had really nice hair."

"Did you really think so?" Lisa looked almost demented with happiness as she turned to Phoebe.

"Stop, you're hurting me!" Gina kept moaning. It was her preferred mode of communication.

For reasons of economy—of the four, only Lisa made a living wage—the gang decided to forgo dinner for more drinks, appetizers, and the free peasant bread and butter at a fashion-able faux-Parisian bistro in the far-West Village, a short cab ride away.

To someone like Phoebe, who had spent countless eve-nings in such haunts, the crowd was a familiar mix: Wall Street bankers eating hearty steaks, the sleeves of their pastel dress shirts rolled back; fledgling model-actresses whose va-cant stares were both adaptive measures to the vulture parade with which they tended nightly and blatant affectations they'd learned from movies and magazines; stray suburban couples in bulky coats who'd wandered in by mistake; and European men of a benignly sleazy cast, with neat blue jeans, narrow torsos, and indeterminate professions, who looked like they might be named Sergio, or Fabian.

Upon Phoebe and her friends' arrival, a snobbish maître d' with dreadlocked hair offered them seats at the end of the bar, as if awarding them individual Nobel Prizes. Though Gina had put a gag order on all further mention of Stephen for the rest of the night, the dinnertime conversation contin-ued down the route of bad relationships—both with men (Phoebe recounted a dream she'd had in which Alex Kahn had become a serial killer), and with medication (Gina complained about the weight she'd gained on Zoloft). Chloe managed to marry the two topics, revealing that her pharmacologist-ex-lover, Carl, had started calling again. Not surprisingly, Lisa smoked more than she said. The appearance of the check, with its tally of culinary offenses, dissipated whatever mood of camaraderie and commiseration had been established dur-ing the meal.

It turned out that the main difference between the entrées and the appetizers was the size of the plate. Divided by four, the bill came to a whopping forty-five bucks apiece. Remembering how irritated she had been at Roget Mankuvsky for divvying up their check down to the last dollar, Phoebe had to stop herself from pointing out that Lisa's soft-shell crab refried in turnip butter had been twice as expensive as Chloe's vegan medley, Gina's wilted frisse, kiwi, and Roquefort salad with prune juice reduction, or her own grilled calamari with wasabi ginger parmesan sauce. Still, it rankled her to have to pay as much as she did—and also to acknowledge that she was, perhaps, every bit as cheap as the maestro was. Chloe, meanwhile, seemed suddenly frantic as she scrounged through her purse for what she claimed was aspirin. (Her friends knew better, that it was something psychotropic.) And having excused herself to the ladies' room, Gina returned several minutes later with an even angrier-looking wound on her forehead, insisting, "Okay. Poll time. Could I be *any* uglier if I tried?"

But it was also Gina who wanted to continue the evening at a notorious coke den a few blocks north. Lisa and Chloe balked, claiming a headache and an early morning psychodrama workshop, respectively. Since the last and only time Phoebe had tried cocaine she'd been up for two days, she agreed to a brief but drug-free stopover. She didn't want to disappoint Gina. She figured it was a rare enough occasion that she made it into the city these days. It wasn't as if she had anything to wake up for the next morning, either. Also, she was drunk.

With its red-lit lanterns, faded velvet sofas losing their stuffing, and lacey netting hung from peach-painted walls, the notorious coke den reminded Phoebe of a brothel in a Belgian fishing village. Not that she had ever been to one. Far more tellingly, the line that led to the unisex rest room was far longer than the human need to urinate after imbibing large quantities of alcohol would seem to merit, and no one who disappeared in there came back for five to ten minutes. This included Gina, whose passion for controlled substances was mediated only by a recurring sinus infection that left her incapacitated for days on end and despising herself even more than usual—apparently, a matter of limited concern to her that night.

While she awaited her friend's return, Phoebe sat at the bar, sipping yet another mixed drink and listening in on the conversation taking place next to her, beneath a second ceiling of cigarette smoke, where a glassy-eyed pipsqueak stood brandishing a crisp new twenty before his half-alive-looking friends. "Andrew Jackson," he nattered on. "Tell me the dude does not bear a striking resemblance to the lead singer of the esteemed Brit pop band the Verve—Richard Whateverthefuckhisnameis."

"Ashcroft," someone muttered.

"Richard NixonAshfordSimpsonWhatever—I ask you to compare Mr. Jackson, if you will, to our main man, George." He exchanged the twenty for a single, with the first president facing out. "Nothing even *remotely* rock star-ish about the guy. Okay, the ruffled blouse has a certain Mick Jagger-esque je ne sais quoi. But check out these lips. Friends, in all seriousness, was there ever a man in greater need of collagen? I mean, we're talking about a founding fucking father here, not some used-car salesman from Duluth. But okay, you're thinking to yourself, the guy did enough impressive things in his lifetime—winning the American Revolution for our team, for instance—that it shouldn't matter how he looks. In a perfect world, yes. But here's the thing: We live in a visual culture, and in the looks category, Jackson whips George's ass by a ratio of three maybe four to one, possibly fi—"

"Jesus Christ, Lerner." A sweaty fat man in an ill-fitting navy blue suit jacket finally cut him off. "Do you ever fucking shut up?"

"At least I don't just sit there like the frigging Aga Khan, waiting to be entertained!" the pipsqueak shot back.

"You try too hard."

"At least I try."

"Well, maybe you should try not to try."

"Leave him alone, already, Morley." A muffled female voice now emerged from behind a thicket of stringy black hair, its timbre akin to a death rattle. "You're putting everyone in a bad mood."

"See, Vivian was enjoying my dead-pres riff," the pipsqueak couldn't stop himself from uttering in his own defense.

"That's because Vivian enjoys being bored and depressed," the fat man suggested, throwing back the last sip of his cocktail, a tributary of which dribbled down his double chin. "That's what makes her such a topnotch club and party publicist."

There were *oohs* from the group, a few chuckles.

"Just like you enjoy being nasty and stupid?" she asked him.

"Never said I didn't," he answered.

"Well, you know what they say," Pipsqueak interjected. "Admitting you have a problem is the first step."

"Lerner, if you admitted all your problems, you'd be institutionalized."

A lone chuckle.

"Speakingofboring," began a boozy redhead, draping her size-too-small slip dress over the fat man's vast expanse of lap, "willyoutakemesomewhereelse? Ihateithere."

"What about Club Imaguido, *where the elite meet to eat and sheet*?" he mouthed in a downbeat monotone clearly intended to parrot the stringy-haired publicist's. Then he burst into the raspy guffaws of an emphysema sufferer, clearly tickled by his own performance.

"You're such an asshole, Morley," said Pipsqueak, shaking his spiky-haired head.

But Morley kept guffawing.

"Is this guy an asshole, or what?" Pipsqueak tried again. But his friends had stopped listening, even Vivian. She lit a new cigarette and hardened her scowl at the world.

He found a new audience in Phoebe. She looked away, but it was too late. "Excuse me, you in the red shirt," he called to her. "Hey—I don't bite. I swear." She pretended to be busy examining her cocktail glass. She pretended until she couldn't pretend any more, didn't know how. It was obvious he was talking to her, and she didn't want to be rude. It was the same impulse that had gotten her into so much trouble as a young woman.

Or was it? Was it possible that she was actually attracted to this man? Found him amusing, sprightly, charismatic? Reluctantly, her eyes inched back to him. "Outside opinion requested—is this man an asshole?" he asked yet again.

"Fuck you," the fat man murmured sleepily.

Phoebe's own sweat now rose to the surface of her forehead and cheeks. She didn't know how to respond. "I'm sorry," she told him with a panicked laugh, her head wagging from side to side, her palm raised just as Lisa's had been outside the luxury leather goods boutique. "I really don't know any of you."

But her protests only seemed to fuel Pipsqueak's desire for her participation. (Wasn't it always that way? And had she not planned it to be so?) "Oh, come onnnnn," he crowed, clearly encouraged, coming toward her. "The name is Jonathan," he was saying. And then he was next to her, leaning against the side of the bar, wanting something from her, of her. (They always did.) A hand extended. An almost sugary smell emanating from it. He was tiny, really, and yet Phoebe experienced his presence as colossal, daunting.

"Go for it, Lerner," one of his friends called to him with a laugh.

"I'm Phoebe," she whispered. His hand was hot, pliable.

"You live around here?" he asked.

"I used to," she told him.

"Well, where do you live now?"

"I've been living at my parents' house in New Jersey."

"Wildwood?"

"What?"

"I said, 'Wildwood.' "

"No, Whitehead."

"Where?" She pictured her house as if from the curb, the renegade ivy, the boxy porch, the drooping elm that obscured the street number, the drooping parents who lay inside. Suddenly, she couldn't wait to go back there, to be lying there, too, trapped in her junior-sized trundle bed. At least, that was how it always felt. Since Roberta had fallen ill, Leonard had taken to making the beds himself, and he made them so tight you couldn't kick the bottom sheet out if you tried. The habit was one of the few he had retained from the two years he spent at Quantico, Virginia, drumming up patriotic fervor under the elite auspices of the Marine Corps Band. That had been Leonard's contribution to—some would say evasion of—the Vietnam War.

Roberta had been "stationed" nearby, at the Peabody Institute for Music in Baltimore. Improbably, she and Leonard had met at a military mixer in D.C.—five years before they became a couple, at a music festival in eastern Massachusetts. They were married six months after that. Emily had been born nine months later—or so they always said, though no precise chronology for this series of events had ever been offered up, owing to the fact—or was it an excuse?—of their elopement to Mexico. And was it possible, Phoebe sometimes wondered, that her parents had once lived irresponsibly, too?

She had seen a picture of her father from that period (the early sixties) dressed in the requisite white gloves and epaulets, his arm thrown jocosely over a similarly garbed chum, his facial expression unrecognizably cocky. Who had he been then? And what, precisely, had happened to lower his lids and turn him into the veritable somnambulist he became? Phoebe always returned to the same conclusion about her parents: Since she had never known them in their youth—before the disappointments and the compromises had set in, and before their bodies began to betray them, willing them to stay put and give in, as bodies always do—they would remain strangers until the end. Moreover, that cliché about no one

始ない

ever changing was simply untrue. People changed beyond recognition. At least, Leonard had.

And now so had Phoebe.

Here, through drink, she had spent the evening trying to keep up, catch up, as if she were the one who had fallen behind. With its dogged insistence on existing in the present tense, above and beyond history, or consequence, Manhattan seemed to require this kind of frenetic behavior. But what if it turned out that she was content living in the inescapable shadow of the past, and before the terrifying unknowable of the future, and New York City was the problem, the perversion, the one occupying a kind of permanently altered state?

Just then, she looked up to find Gina, returned finally from the rest room. "Can you believe what a pathetic drug addict I am?" she began. At another moment, Phoebe might have been thankful for the interference.

The rescue effort had come too late.

"Please forgive me," Phoebe announced, her coat already in her arms as she stood back up. "But I really need to go."

"But we just got here!" cried Gina.

"Yeah, what's the hurry?" asked Pipsqueak.

"God, I must be really fucking boring. Even my friends don't want to hang out with me anymore." Gina began to tear up. "I don't even know why I bother. Everyone hates me."

"I don't hate you," offered Pipsqueak.

"You don't know me!"

"Yeah, but I think you look kinda cute crying."

"You do?" More sniffles.

"Sure. And I like a woman who shows her vulnerability. You know, the thing about vulnerability is . . ."

Maybe I won't have to beg Gina's forgiveness, after all, Phoebe thought with relief as she made her way through the door.

It was a beautiful night, the air black and crisp, the city lights sparkling like gold teeth in a giant maw. Everywhere Phoebe looked there were kids—kids like Phoebe had once been, laughing and posing and imagining themselves from the outside in. Hailing a cab on the corner of Ninth Avenue and 14th Street, she directed the driver to the Port Authority. And as the streets scrolled by, one after another, she recalled having once felt as if it were all a movie. But now she realized that it starred someone else, someone who hadn't yet realized that happiness could be found offscreen. *So this is what it's like to grow old*, she thought to herself.

It wasn't such a terrible feeling, after all.

7

Phoebe spent the bus ride back to Whitehead in the seat behind the driver—which is to say, as far as possible from the two teenagers having sex in the back. By the time she got home, the house was dark and quiet, and her parents' continued vitality in question except for a copy of *Allegro* (the in-house magazine of Leonard's musicians' union, Local 802), which had been left open on the glass-covered wagon wheel that functioned as the kitchen table. (Roberta and Leonard shared a passion for found-object furniture.) Her forty-five-dollar calamari having failed to fill her up, Phoebe poured herself a bowl of Leonard's oat-bran flakes and sat down. Flipping through *Allegro*'s back pages as she ate, she found announcements for second-violin openings in faraway orchestras and advertisements for accountants and tax lawyers specializing in freelance income. The icebox's ancient cooling system buzzed and sputtered. She couldn't recall ever having had a better time.

Then again, she had always preferred staying home to

going places, her dislike of travel having been cemented at the age of thirteen during an extended summer stay in Guatemala City. The previous winter, Leonard had gone there on tour with the since-disbanded Trenton Philharmonic. He returned to Whitehead two weeks later in possession of an extra suit-case's worth of gifts, from tiny painted music boxes in the shape of guitars to wooden puppets with bulbous noses and cavernous jaws intended to satirize right-wing military dicta-tors. Phoebe found them all magical. And she was anxious to prove her independence, just as Emily had done by spending a month with an Inuit family in Alaska. Unlike the majority of their classmates, the Fine sisters had never been to sleep-away camp. Roberta thought the rigorous scheduling of chil-dren's free time stifled creative expression. She also considered South America a backward place compared to Paris, or even Anchorage. Eventually, however, she acceded to Phoebe's wishes, and Leonard arranged for her to spend June and July with wealthy German-Guatemalan patrons of the orchestra named Schwitzler.

Mr. Schwitzler owned a coffee plantation and processing plant. One afternoon, he invited Phoebe to attend a meeting at his executive offices. He and six other tan men in maroon suit jackets and gold rings were collected around a polished mahogany table covered with coffee beans. Since Phoebe lived near New York City, the men assumed she had insider knowl-edge regarding the coming trends and asked her to weigh in on which flavor bean was likely to be the best seller of the fall season. She argued vehemently against French Vanilla and strongly in favor of Hazelnut. It was the first time in her life that adults to whom she was not related had shown an interest in her opinions. She wondered if she had a future in marketing.

It was also the highlight of an otherwise trying trip.

The Schwitzler kids, at fifteen and seventeen, were stuck-up. Mrs. Schwitzler was always at the salon or pacing through the family's gated villa muttering, *"Dios mio, Dios mio."* The refried beans gave Phoebe the runs. She found the Catholic churches gaudy, the ruins unimpressive. It turned out you could buy the same bric-a-brac that Leonard had brought home to Whitehead on every street corner in Guatemala City. She was homesick, too, and cried incessantly. In this manner, she was able to convey the sentiment that she wanted desperately to leave, at which point Mr. Schwitzler drove her back to the airport in his bulletproof Mercedes. Without a boarding pass of his own, however, he could accompany her only so far. She ended up at the wrong gate, trying to board a flight to Bogotá instead of Newark. Taking pity on the weeping American girl in Bermuda shorts and a bandanna tied lasso-style around her neck, as was the current style at Whitehead Middle School, a kindly Guatemalan security guard luckily redirected her to the correct American Airlines plane.

She didn't leave home again until college.

That said, the world frequently came to Phoebe's door as she grew up in the guise of the sullen exchange students whom Leonard was always inviting into their home, usually to the chagrin of Roberta, who was far more proprietary about personal space. To Phoebe's recollection, the worst by far had been Koon, a priggish Flemish boy who had picked up the word *kitsch* and used it to describe—in reality, dismiss—every tourist attraction to which the Fines took him. He'd say, "The Statue of Liberty is pure kitsch!" One night, he used the word to describe Roberta's turkey casserole. Roberta wasn't amused. Leonard thought she was being too hard on him. They had a huge fight. Excited yet frightened—would they get divorced like so many of her classmates' parents?—Phoebe sat at the top of the stairs and listened to them going at it in the kitchen. It was clear that Roberta had won when, the next day, after a series of hushed phone calls, Leonard called Phoebe and Emily into the music room to announce that Koon was being shipped back to Ghent.

The sisters did a high five when the last of Koon's weird European travel bags with their millions of hidden pockets and Velcro fasteners disappeared out the back door, never to be seen again.

But on the morning after Phoebe's excursion into Manhattan, the waking world of New Jersey held little appeal for her, not only on account of tenebrous skies but because of the poisons she'd consumed the night before. Her head felt too heavy for her neck. She craved runny eggs. She snapped at Leonard for asking if she'd seen his reading glasses, which were perched on the top of his head.

For the better part of the day, she lost herself in cleanup and repair work on Mr. Marciano's music cabinet. She had learned how to refinish wood the summer after high school, while interning at a hippie woodworking studio in Vermont. Phoebe also found herself musing on the sociopolitical ramifications of her business plan. She had already bypassed the bulk of production and manufacturing costs by scavenging. If she were also to forgo promotion and distribution expenses by means of one of the on-line auction houses, would she not, in a certain sense, be subverting the very strictures by which the capitalist hegemony maintained itself? (And what if her great college love, tenured radical Bruce Bledstone, could see her now, toiling for the Revolution. Wouldn't he be proud?)

Her pathetic That-She-Still-Cared-What-That-Creep-Thought-of-Her fantasies were interrupted by the downstairs phone, whose ringer volume Leonard and Roberta felt somehow compelled to maintain at sonic-boom level. Regaining her equilibrium, Phoebe lifted the receiver to her ear.

"Yo, Roget Mankuvsky here," began the voice on the other end of the line.

"I'll get my father," she told him, unable to imagine that they had anything left to discuss.

But he cried, "Wait! I don't want to talk to the old man."

Phoebe was confused. It wasn't merely that she thought she'd made it clear that she hated the guy's guts. By the end of their date, she'd assumed the feeling was pretty much mutual.

And yet, at the sound of Roget's ruffian voice, she wasn't altogether sorry that he'd called, if only for the chance to tell him what he'd done wrong. She had spent her teens and most of her twenties keeping her thoughts and opinions to herself, thereby wreaking havoc on her digestive system. On the other hand, at least she'd had old friends—but no longer. She had Jackie Yee to thank for the loss. Jackie Yee, being an incompetent therapist, had encouraged Phoebe to tell each and every person in her life what was wrong with his or her personality.

"I got some serious stuff I want to talk to you about," Roget told her.

"Like what?" she asked, her tone of voice as indifferent, she hoped, as the cashiers who worked at the Whitehead CVS and didn't bat an eye no matter what you bought, from wart removal kits to lambskin condoms in bulk (assuming you did).

"I'm still waiting for my twenty-five cents," he said.

"You'll be waiting a long time."

"I thought I'd come over and get it now."

"Excuse me?"

"I happen to be in the neighborhood."

"I don't know if that's going to work." Phoebe came forth with a knowing laugh intended to imply that, while she'd heard her share of lines, she could still marvel at the most egregious of them. "We're about to sit down for dinner."

"Why don't I come for dinner then?" suggested Roget. "I could use some chow, actually—been in a frigging fundraising meeting all day. And for the record, I already know the old man, so it's not like I'd be walking in on a whole bunch of strangers or anything."

"True enough," said Phoebe, undecided as to whether to be flattered by his enthusiasm or offended by his gumption. "The only problem is that you weren't actually invited."

"Well, I'll hold on if you want to check if it's okay," he offered.

"How considerate of you."

"Don't mention it—oh, hey, nice coveralls, by the way."

"*What?*"

"I'm actually parked in front of your house. Look, I'm waving. Helloooo, Phoebe!"

At the news of Roget's proximity, Phoebe bolted from the window, crying, "Have you ever heard of calling first?"

"I did call first," he pointed out.

Having come to the end of her current line of argument, Phoebe set about weighing her options. In truth, she didn't entirely know how she felt about the prospect of Roget coming to dinner. On the one hand, just as the presence of wild-card guests had an ameliorative effect on family holidays, his presence at the table was guaranteed to break up the flow of cold war meals through which she and Emily had been suffering since the night Emily came home. On the other hand, Phoebe found the guy seriously annoying. And after all the nasty things she'd already said about him to Roberta, her credibility would be at risk. And how was it she managed to make the same mistake over and over again in life: telling too many people too many things they didn't need to know?

In the end, she decided to let her parents decide. "Hold on," she told Roget, putting down the phone and going in search of them.

She found them sitting quietly in the den, reading *The Great Composers* and *The Violin Family*, respectively. Leonard had adjusted his black leather zero-gravity BackSaver chair so far back that he appeared to be levitating. Roberta was stretched out on the divan, her feet wrapped in her favorite Aztec-pattern throw rug, a long-ago present from Barb Urdell, an eccentric old friend of Roberta's parents and Phoebe's grandparents, the now-deceased Rothenbergs. Into her late eighties, Barb continued to make the forty-seven-hour car trek alone each winter to her favorite deserted beach on the southwestern coast of Mexico, where she slept in a hammock, played the bagpipes, read Joseph Conrad novels, and cooked tropical fish on an open fire she assembled out of driftwood and other flotsam that had washed ashore. Late in life, she had also become an anti-cruise-ship activist, rallying against the floating fun houses that, with their deep-sea dumping practices, were littering her beloved coastline with things that better belonged in the toilet. In truth, Phoebe couldn't remember if Barb Urdell had died or not, though she remembered having recently heard something to this effect. And was it so terrible to say that when people reached a certain late-gerontic stage, the fact of their existence began to seem less significant than the legend that preceded them?

"Mom?" said Phoebe, wincing before she'd even begun.

"Yes, Be?" As Roberta glanced up from her book, her glasses slipped down her nose, lending it the appearance of a thumb.

"Roget Mankuvsky wants to come for dinner," Phoebe told her, in as casual a voice as she could manage—as if the situation really had very little to do with her needs or desires; she was simply relaying the news. "What should I tell him?"

Roberta laid her glasses in her lap and manipulated her mouth into a smile that wouldn't admit to being one. "Roget Mankuvsky." She repeated the name slowly, clearly delighted by the news. "Well, this is certainly a turn of events! The question is whether I have enough food to feed him. We're having coq au vin." (Read: a Perdue roasting chicken boiled in Ecuadorian table wine for ninety minutes and complemented with a few canned mushrooms, thrown in at the last minute for mainly symbolic value.)

"I could tell him another night," said Phoebe, already regretting having asked.

"No, that's ridiculous!" Roberta protested—a little too vehemently, she must have realized, because she cleared her throat and began again on a more subdued note. "I mean, I'm sure we'll be able to make do. I'm not too hungry tonight."

"Mom, I'm not having you starve yourself because Dad's stupid conductor decided to invite himself over!"

"That's not what I was saying, Phoebe! There'll be more than enough for everyone. Just tell him to come sooner rather than later. The chicken will be done in around twenty minutes."

Out of the corner of her eye, Phoebe could see her father grinning like a frog between *ribbit*s. In the week since her date with Roget, her father had done his best to avoid all mention of his conductor. But his disappointment at Phoebe's failure to have, as he would say, "hit it off" with him had been evident in the offhand way he would bring up Little Ferry for no good reason. Just the day before, he had walked into the kitchen, where Phoebe sat cracking nuts and chatting with Roberta about the Nathans' inability to shut the single shade in the death house while they were undressing, and asked, "Any of you ladies interested in accompanying me to that Asian supermarket off the *Little Ferry* traffic circle?"

"Oh, Lenny, I don't think I'm up to it right now," Roberta had told him. "But thanks."

"What about you, Crumps?" Leonard had pressed on. "I, for one, would like to try some of this boy choy stuff I keep hearing about."

"It's *bok* choy," said Phoebe.

"Bok choy. That's it."

"No, thanks."

"Well, then, I suppose I'll just have to go by myself." He sighed breezily. "You know, I've always thought *Little Ferry* was a very livable town, a sort of best-kept secret of northern New Jersey."

Phoebe had refused eye contact.

Her heart now thumping, she got back on the phone with Roget and told him, "They say you can come if you want, though you'll basically be eating my mother's dinner, since there isn't actually enough food to go around."

"All right, cool," he said. "See you in, like, thirty seconds."

"Wait!" she cried.

"What?" he asked.

"We're not ready for you yet. You'll have to drive around the block a few times."

"All right, see you in five."

"Fifteen."

"Ten."

"Twelve."

No sooner had they hung up than Phoebe went flying upstairs to her bedroom in search of a decent outfit. It wasn't for Roget's sake; she had a reputation to keep up in the world. Or so she told herself as she exchanged her overalls for the same black pants she had worn the night before (currently, her only decently fitting pair; hopefully they didn't reek too badly of cigarette smoke) and a bright pink crew-neck sweater with slightly fewer pulled threads than some of her others. Then she splashed some water on her face, ran a brush through her hair, and applied gloss to her lips and a kohl pencil beneath her eyes. She could hear a Caetano Veloso album playing in Emily's bedroom. Phoebe could never get over what poor taste her sister had in music. Emily, of course, felt the exact same way about Phoebe's taste in music, which continued to run the gamut from the melodramatic to the blatantly overproduced—that is, from Tchaikovsky's *Pathétique* symphony to late Genesis.

It had definitely *not* been twelve minutes when the doorbell rang.

"You must be Roget," Phoebe heard her mother saying. "I'm Roberta Fine. . . . Oh, thank you! I don't think I've ever had a wine cool—is that what it's called?"

"Wine cool*er*," he corrected her.

"Cool*er*, right. Well, please, come in."

"Hi," said Phoebe, catching his eye as she made her way down the stairs.

There was an unexpected excitement in meeting his clearly appreciative gaze. "Wow—you look nice!" he said, his eyes going up and down her body.

"Thanks," she mumbled, immediately embarrassed to have been recognized as having made the effort to change. "You look okay too." At least he wasn't wearing his Lee jeans but, rather, a powder-blue tracksuit zipped to the neck.

It reminded her of a Romanian gymnastics coach from the 1970s.

"Seriously, though," Roget went on, "I like the outfit a lot more than last week's—what were you wearing that night? Some kind of plaid thing?"

Roberta cleared her throat. "That was actually an old blazer of mine."

"Oh, sorry!" Roget grinned guiltily. "Didn't mean to offend you, Mrs. Fine. Just looked a little Poindexter-like on Phoebe."

"Well, hello there, Maestro." Leonard appeared before either mother or daughter had the chance to ask Roget to leave.

"Hey, Len," said Roget, meeting Phoebe's father's outstretched hand with a three-part shake that concluded with the universal gesture for smoking marijuana.

Leonard seemed both baffled and tickled by the whole routine. "You young people come up with the most elaborate greetings!" he declared. "In my day, a shake was a shake."

"By the way, nice work on the Shostakovich yesterday," Roget told him. "I only wish the French horn dogs section could keep up with you and Benson."

"You're too kind." Leonard chuckled self-effacingly.

"Well, I should go check on my bird," Roberta announced curtly and then scurried off in the direction of the kitchen.

"I can't believe this is happening," Phoebe muttered at no one in particular.

She hadn't realized how bowlegged Roget was—or how built-up his biceps were—until she watched him seesaw uninvited into the music room, his shoulders rising and falling like the piano keys he soon sat down before. "Who's the pianist?" he asked.

"I'm afraid none of us play well," Leonard told him.

With no hint of shame, Roget launched into a bangy rendition of "Chopsticks," followed by a crude approximation of Beethoven's *Appassionata* sonata. "Nice resonance, but your C sharp here is out of tune," he said, hitting the offending key again, and again, and then again, louder and more obnoxiously each time, in case there was anyone left in Whitehead who hadn't yet gotten the message, as Leonard apparently had.

A look of consternation arose on Phoebe's father's face. "Oh, dear, that *does* sound out of tune," he murmured. "You know, we had the same tuner for nearly thirty years—a Russian fellow named Igor."

Phoebe's heart swooned at the mere mention of the man's name. For almost a decade of her young life, Igor had held a center-stage position in her romantic imagination, not only on account of his fanglike incisors, which called to mind predatory mammals roaming the English moors, but because, with his statuesque posture and bald pink-egg head, he resembled nothing so much as a walking phallus—at least, insofar as she was able to picture one, having never actually seen one in the flesh. What's more, he sometimes lay horizontally beneath the piano, as if lying in wait for her, even if, in reality, he was only checking the pedal action.

"Very interesting man," Leonard went on. "Never married. A pool shark on the side, if you can believe it. I understand he made quite a bit of money that way. Always wore very expensive shirts, handmade by some tailor in Shanghai. Apparently he had them shipped here. Well, the poor man dropped dead of an aneurysm this past summer."

"Poor Igor!" gasped Phoebe. When you weren't looking, it seemed, people just vanished off the planet. That was the scariest thing about death—the quiet efficiency with which it went about its business.

"Yes, poor Igor indeed," said Leonard, in what Phoebe found to be a disconcertingly cavalier tone.

"Well, *you* sound upset!" she lashed out at him.

"Oh, I am," Leonard assured her. "As far as I'm concerned, the man was irreplaceable."

"I got someone over in Teaneck if you need him," said Roget, chin flying. "Name's Kevorkian. Good ear. For the record, no relation to the Dr. Death guy—whatever his name is; I can't remember."

"Jack," said Phoebe.

"Well, this guy's name is Bill."

"That would be super!" exclaimed Leonard. "Before you disappear, Roget, you'll have to give me his number. I mean, before you disappear for the night. I mean, assuming you *do* disappear for the night!" He began to titter in a high key, clearly frantic at the thought of derailing any forward progress on the romantic front between his daughter and his conductor.

"Don't worry, Dad, he's not sleeping over," Phoebe interjected, eager to straighten them both out.

"Oh, hey." Roget raised his chin at Phoebe. "Forgot to mention. Your father here shared with me one of your old demo tapes from your pop-band years. Cute stuff. Nice melodic sense. I even liked the fiddle interludes—in many ways more than your singing voice. What are you, a mezzo?"

Phoebe took the opportunity to shoot Leonard an unforgiving look.

"Anyone care for an aperitif?" He began to back toward the door, talking faster than usual. "I was just off for one myself."

"Probably isn't time," said Roget, squinting hostilely at Phoebe, "since, apparently, I might be *leaving* soon."

"I'm fine too," Phoebe informed her father, studiously ignoring Roget's outburst.

"Well, then." Leonard darted off.

Roget rose from the piano and walked over to Roberta's viola, which lay in its usual resting place, atop the musicology bookshelf with the glass doors. "Whose baby?" he asked, unsnapping the locks and lifting the instrument and bow from their respective cradles.

"It's my mother's," Phoebe answered guardedly, wishing he'd put them down but not wanting to antagonize him further. She felt protective these days not only of her mother's health but of her ability to make music, which seemed stamped with the same compromised quality. While Roberta regularly tuned her beloved viola's strings, believing this process to be salutary to the instrument's constitution, in truth, she hadn't practiced in months—since the "few little tests" began. (To Phoebe, the viola's case was beginning to look more and more like a coffin.)

Roget tightened the hair of the bow and tucked the instrument under his chin, as if preparing to play. Just as quickly, he flipped the the viola over and began to rub its golden-brown back in slow circular motions with the fatty padding of his palm, a look of near bliss consuming his face. "Not a bad-looking piece of wood," he purred. It was as if, in a moment's time, he had transferred the full weight of his attraction to Phoebe onto her mother's instrument. "You know what it is?"

"As far as I know, just some no-name French thing from the late nineteenth century." Phoebe shrugged, surprised to find herself so disappointed by Roget's apparent diminution of desire for her.

"Who'd she buy it from?"

"She didn't buy it from anyone. It was my great uncle Moishe's. We inherited in the mid-seventies, after Moishe died in a snorkeling incident off Montego Bay."

"I can think of worse ways to die than looking at neon fish," offered Roget.

"Yeah, well, Moishe amassed a small fortune giving abortions in the back room of his pharmacy in quotes in the black section of Pittsburgh," Phoebe continued, hoping to win back some attention with this scandalous family tale.

But he only replied, "Man's got to make a living."

"Anyway." Disappointment had become defeat.

"Viola got any papers?" Roget wanted to know.

"Not that I know of. Why?"

"Just curious."

Phoebe shrugged again. "A couple of years ago, my mother took it to that famous dealer on Fifty-seventh Street, and he told her it was a nice imitation of nothing."

"I'd be interested in getting a second opinion," said Roget.

"I don't know what the point is," she came back at him, as if it were Roberta's judgment he was calling into question. "She likes the way it sounds. That's what's important."

Just then, Roberta herself called out to them: "Break time over, orchestra members! *Le dîner est servi.*"

"Sorry," said Phoebe, now feeling responsible even for her mother's choice of words. "My mother gets really pretentious when we have people over." Then she called back: "We're coming!"

"I'll be there in a second," Roget told her, walking back over to the Fines' Yamaha baby grand, where he held the viola beneath the piano lamp and peered through its sound holes, presumably in search of its identifying ticket. "*Gasparo da Salo—en Brescia,*" he read out loud. Then he looked up at Phoebe with an enchanted smile. "Well, if it's a real da Salo, you're sitting on an approximately three- to five-million-dollar fortune."

"If it's a who?" asked Phoebe, as gratified to have Roget's gaze back upon her as she was dizzied by the sum.

"Who?" Roget released a knowing laugh of his own. "Only Gasparo da Salo, the premiere maker of violas and double basses in the world. Background as follows: Grandson of a lute player. Nickname Violino. Number in circulation—not that many. Of course, half the student cellos in the world say *Stradivarius* inside them. But, hey, you never know. Someone's got to get lucky in this world. Right?"

"Three to five million dollars." Phoebe whispered the words as she envisioned the bills stacked up before her like a deck of playing cards—the sweet susurration they'd make when she flipped through the pile. When had money become the object of her frustrated ambition, the outlet for that irksome side of her that was always aiming, angling, for *more, more, more*? Once upon a time, not that long ago, sex had been her obsession. But the green stuff, she'd found over the years, didn't talk back to you the way men did, mocking and criticizing and telling you how funny you walked and how hard you were always trying to be someone you weren't.

"Well, it's got the burnt-toast varnish, the parallel S-holes, the oversized dimensions, and the single purfling." Roget further stoked the flames of Phoebe's fantasies. "Now if there were an angel's face and a green-and-gold mermaid carved into the scroll, another mermaid on the tailpiece, a fingerboard decorated with blue and gold arabesques, and two intertwining fish etched into the bridge, I'd wager a guess it was the long-lost Cardinal Aldobrandini viola. Most famous viola da Salo ever made. Somehow ended up in Ole Bull's hands and then, upon the roaming Swedish virtuoso's death, disappeared from the public record—apparently sold off to some amateur, somewhere in the U.S. of A." The chin was at it again. "Needless to say, I'm on the lookout."

"Well, it could still be a da Salo even without the mermaids, right?" Phoebe's heart and mind raced in tandem.

"Could be." Roget turned the instrument back over and squinted through its S-holes for a second time. "Though if this ticket is from the sixteenth century, I'll eat my nuts. It's way too well preserved. To be honest, it looks like it was just printed up for a Knicks game at the Garden."

"The expression is 'I'll eat my *hat*,'" muttered Phoebe, crestfallen at the introduction of this contradictory bit of evidence. "We should go in to dinner." She started toward the door, her stomach roiling.

Roget quickly took the lead. Walking two paces ahead of her, he led Phoebe into her own dining room, where her family sat waiting.

At the sight of Roget, Emily stood up from the table and smiled the sadistic yet ingratiating smile of a cruise-ship activities director. "Hello, I'm Phoebe's sister, Emily. Welcome!" she said. It wasn't clear if she had dressed with their dinner guest in mind or not, but she was wearing a pair of black leather hipster jeans that only just obscured her pubic bone, and a low-cut ruffled blouse from which her bosom, hoisted up to some remote summit near her chin, appeared to be straining for freedom.

"Wazzup?" said Roget, checking out her sister with what Phoebe feared to be no small amount of curiosity.

"You can sit there, Roget," said Roberta, pointing at the chair next to Emily that usually went vacant.

"Please," said Emily, pulling it out for him.

"Oh, thanks," he said.

Teeth gnashing, Phoebe silently took her place on the opposite side, next to her mother.

The Fines had a long tradition of passing dishes around the table buffet style. That night, without being asked to do so, Emily took charge of the service. Crock-Pot in hand, she began to circle the table to the tune of "Boiled chicken for all! Mother?"

"Thanks, Em," mumbled Roberta. Looking somewhere between annoyed and embarrassed, she turned to the others and told them, "It's actually coq au vin."

"Any relation to Cocoa Puffs?" asked Roget.

"I'm sorry." Roberta leaned forward, brow knit. "I'm not familiar with the term."

"It's a kind of breakfast cereal," he told her.

"I see."

"What about you, Daddy?" Emily continued. "You won't mind eating the back, will you?"

"Oh, no! Wonderful. Thank you." He held out his plate with two hands, like a destitute orphan in a Broadway musical.

"And you, Maestro?" Phoebe could have sworn she saw Emily bat her lashes at him. "What's your favorite part?"

"If you got one, I'll take a breast," he replied gamely.

"Oh, but I do," said Emily, forking the meat onto his plate. (Phoebe had to fight the instinct to use her own utensils in less-civilized ways.)

At last, Emily arrived before Phoebe's plate. "And what about you, little sis?" she asked in a treacly voice an octave higher than her normal one.

"I'll serve myself, thank you," said Phoebe, yanking the pot out of her hand.

Emily turned back to Roget. "So, Roget, I hear this is your first season with the NSO. How do you like it?"

"It's a job." He shrugged. "Some days the buffoons-I-mean-bassoons sound like a herd of crapping donkeys. Other days not. We got an interesting concert coming up in a few weeks, though—an all-atonal program. You should check it out if you're in town."

"Oh, I will!"

It was Emily's distribution of the vinaigrette that transported Phoebe into realms of rage best compared to blindness. Her sister had situated herself at such a distance away from Roget that, after she asked him, "Would you like your salad with or without dressing?" and he answered, "With—definitely," she was compelled to pitch her torso at such an angle that, had Roget been so inclined to stick out his tongue, it would surely have made contact with the areola of her left breast. If this wasn't alarming enough, Phoebe could have sworn she heard Roget murmur what sounded like "Mmm-hmm" in response. Was he talking about the dressing or Emily's décolletage? Had she made the whole thing up? Was she just being paranoid? Whatever the case, Phoebe found herself pushing her chair out from under the table with a screech, throwing down her napkin, and storming out of the room, crying, "I don't have to watch this!" as she ignored her mother's plaintive pleas to return, and Leonard muttered, "Watch what?"

It wasn't just the fact that Emily was flirting with Roget; Phoebe had grown accustomed to her sister's attempts to take down and over the things she cared most about; it was that Roget appeared to reciprocate Emily's attentions, at least on some level. Even if Phoebe didn't want him for herself, she didn't want him to want Emily, either. Which meant that she must have had feelings for the guy that were more compli- cated than simple disdain, though what *kind* of feelings was hard to say. (Years of therapy aside, Phoebe was typically the last one to know her own emotions.) And why didn't anyone ever learn that the reason people storm out of rooms, cars, and bars is not because they want to be alone but because they want to be followed?

And why, oh, why, had she not waited to quit smoking on her thirtieth birthday, instead of her twenty-ninth?

After she had been standing on the screened porch for close to five minutes, watching minivans idle by and accomplishing nothing, Phoebe's fear of missing something proved greater than her need to make a point, and she returned to the dining room, still mad but resigned. If Emily and Roget wanted each other, they could have each other. What did she care?

But nothing was so clear. In fact, in Phoebe's absence the most serious bonding seemed to have taken place between Roberta and Roget. "Your mother here was just telling us some fascinating facts about the viola," he told Phoebe, as she retook her seat. She couldn't tell if he was kidding.

"I'm sorry I missed it," she said, avoiding all eye contact, even as she noted to herself that Roget's eyes were nowhere near Emily, who sat indifferently munching on her salad.

Meanwhile, Leonard had himself a good yawn, and Roberta grinned in the grandiose fashion of a teacher in the presence of her star pupil. "I was just telling Roget here," she continued, "that in the days of Stradivarius some tenor violas were produced that were so long in length as to be virtually unplayable in a horizontal position!"

"That would definitely suck," said Roget, pulling a piece of gristle out of his mouth.

"As the great violist William Primrose once said—and I'm paraphrasing here, because I don't remember the exact phrase—'The viola is a difficult enough instrument to play without the added impediment of a wrestling match.' Of course, some musicians enjoy denigrating the viola, imagining that it plays second fiddle—quite literally—to the violin. The truth is, it's a far more technically laborious instrument. Never mind its tonal capacity, which is arguably richer, as well."

"No doubt in my mind," answered the teacher's pet. "In hell, ten Suzuki students will be playing Bach partitas around my bed."

"Oh, Roget!" Roberta chuckled gaily, apparently long over the plaid blazer critique. Then she sighed audibly and began again on a more somber note. "You know, Roget, back in my prime, some thirty years ago, I was among the foremost female violists in this country."

It always made Phoebe cringe when her mother started

talking herself up. It sounded so desperate; in that sense, it reminded Phoebe a little too much of herself. But it was also untrue: Her mother had never been among the foremost anything. Nor, for that matter, had Leonard been. Yet while Roberta could comfort herself with the knowledge that she had essentially given it all up to raise kids—and had therefore never fully tested her mettle among other violists—it was she who seemed the less resigned of the two toward her own lack of recognition. Maybe it was because she loved and needed music in a way that Leonard never had; it had always been her consolation for an imperfect world and family. Leonard, on the other hand, had long treated the oboe as just another specialized trade, like dentistry or bricklaying.

"Well, thanks for the grub, Mrs. Fine." Chucking his napkin onto the table, Roget abruptly slid his chair away from the table and stood up. "I should really get going."

"So soon?" said Roberta, clearly saddened to be ending her one-man tutorial. "You haven't even had dessert!"

"Wish I could stay, but I got some programming issues I need to resolve by tomorrow." He pushed his chair back beneath the table. "See you at rehearsal, Len." He lifted his chin at Phoebe's father, then his palm at the rest of them. "Bye, everyone." And that was it. There wasn't even a special nod of recognition for Phoebe. As far as she could tell, there wasn't one for Emily either, but that didn't change the unassailable fact that the evening had ended on a very different note from the one on which it began. And was it too much to ask that, short of inviting her out for a nightcap in a dry town, Roget say a proper good night?

The embarrassed silence that came over Roberta and

Leonard after Roget had left suggested to Phoebe that her parents somehow blamed her for the rejection. She could just see her mother complaining to Leonard as they lay in bed later that night about Phoebe's need, "since she was the smallest thing, to make a scene—as if people won't notice her otherwise!" And, *If she'd only stop being so oversensitive, she'd be surprised to find that the world was actually smiling at her.* It was the message Phoebe had always gotten from her parents: to ignore her enemies and to assume the best. If only to avoid Roberta's simultaneously pitying and reproachful eyes, Phoebe jumped up from the table herself and began to clear the dishes from it. She could hear Roget's ancient sports car engine gurgling and spluttering as he drove away. The sound—and ensuing silence—made her sigh. Despite everything that had happened that night, she was sorry to see him go.

8

Or was she? As she washed the dishes, Phoebe thought back to her past relationships with men and wondered if Roget hadn't done her a favor by leaving so soon. She remembered how the smallest breach—a late-returned phone call or a perceived lack of interest in an anecdote—was capable of setting her off. What's more, she would find herself assuming new moods not organically but as one changes outfits—that is, with the sole purpose of achieving some desired external effect. She would be sullen one minute (to remind whoever it was that their love was no laughing matter) and silly and adorable the next (so that whoever it was couldn't later say that she hadn't exuded sweetness and light). All the while, she'd be keeping score, measuring the texture and consistency of his attentions and affections, whoever *he* was, just as one watches over a pot of slow-cooking lentil stew. Compared to that kind of labor, she now wondered, what was loneliness but a minor inconvenience?

And she thought back to the conversations—the endless

conversations (there was always a last remark to be uttered, it seemed, and a last one after that)—with their inevitable strings of clichés, their blatant failures of language. Their "I thought time would heal things," and "What we had was special," and "You're rewriting history," and "Try to remember the good times," and "Maybe love isn't enough," and "I wasn't just saying that," and "You're not making this any easier," and "You think I don't care about you," and "I think about you every time I open my door . . . my fly . . . my wallet . . . my in-box at work," and "I'm sorry if I misled you," and "I don't think I have," and "Neither of us was happy," and "I've never met a needier woman," and "You really got under my skin . . . deserve better . . . put me at ease," and "You're too nice . . . demanding . . . exhausting," and "If it's meant to be," and "Try to get outside yourself and on with your life," and "Only time will tell," and "The doorbell's ringing," and "I should really get this . . . can't talk about this stuff anymore but here's the thing: it really pissed me off when . . ." and "Maybe we could have coffee in a few weeks . . . months . . . years," and "If I'd met you at a different time . . . in a different place," and "If I wasn't so fucked up," and "Fuck you too."

And the parting shots:

Alex, I can't have lunch with you tomorrow. Nor do I want you to come over here and cook me bacon and eggs. I hate bacon, and this whole thing is making me ill. Please, for the last time, leave me alone! *Don't write, don't call, don't e-mail. I regret contacting you seventy-two hours ago. I just wanted to get my TV back. It was obviously a huge mistake.*

If you need to talk to someone, call my mother. We had a few great years. Please get it into your head that they are over forever. Good luck and, for the last time, good-bye.

And the final analyses that always turned out to be something less than final:

Alex, I hope you're doing okay, and I hope you don't think a letter coming at a time like this is manipulative on my part. I just wanted to say hello. I've thought about you so much in the past few weeks, and there have been more than a few times when I had to stop myself from picking up the phone—not because I had anything important to say but just because I missed the sound of your voice. (Well, except maybe when you're calling me an "acne-scarred bitch." Ha!)

Alex, I hope you don't think I'm punishing you for something you did wrong. It's true we have our differences, but most of the fault, I see now, lies with me. In fact, I feel utterly shamed by the selflessness of the love you offered me. I just didn't feel I could reciprocate it anymore—not until I figured out what I wanted. Maybe you're right and I'm involved in a serious monogamous relationship with the electric violin. But cutting off contact with you has been such a terrible shock to my system, as I'm imagining it has been for yours, unless I'm wrong and you've already found a new girlfriend and forgotten my incredibly lame middle name. (It's Ernestine.)

When I turn off the light at night, my heart races faster than it should. I've gotten about three hours of sleep per night for the past two weeks—even with the window open! I can't help but think that this all has something to do with you and the fact that you're not here, in my bed, wrapped around me like a second skin. But I can't bear to think about that right now.

On other topics, do you know the definition of "grano-blastically"? It's on the first page of this Nabokov novel, Ada, *that I started, and it's not even in the dictionary! That sort of thing annoys me about Nabokov, actually. He's always using these ridiculously big words designed to make you feel stupid . . .*

And the physical stress of it, the banging and the bucking, the swelling and the soreness, the scratch marks that had striated her back, and the rug burns that had scabbed her knees. And the pressure all the time every day and night to be ready and waiting, beautiful and bountiful, wanting and wailing, for the prodding, poking, pawing of so many fingers, tongues, pricks, always supplicant, never satisfied. (She could hear herself yelling, "Leave me alone! Wait, don't stop!") Because the desire to make a connection across the universe, to imagine that we weren't alone, even though we were, trumped everything. That was the problem. That was always the problem.

Alex, I miss you being inside me. . . .

The kitchen cleanup complete, Phoebe returned to the music room and got out her own instrument. As far as she knew, it was a factory-produced German violin from the early part of the twentieth century. She proceeded to sight-read a book of great encores from the late-nineteenth. The Paganini and Heifetz arrangements were technically beyond her, the Kreisler, Saint-Saëns, and Sarasate only slightly less so. But if it sounded pretty bad—and her performance hadn't been preceded by the requisite standing ovation, as encores were supposed to be—there was still comfort to be gained from an audience of one, she thought. You could mess up as many times as you wanted, and both your self-esteem and your reputation would still be intact. You could bring down the curtain before the show had even begun—before you ended up playing not for your own enjoyment but for other people's—people who didn't want you to stop and whom you couldn't bear to disappoint. And then, one day, you'd wake up and two years of your life would be gone and you'd wonder where they went.

9

Phoebe could still picture herself as she stood that afternoon in 1996—naked and blasély blow-drying a suspicious-looking globule on Neil Schmertz's 450-thread-count goose-down comforter, having recently applied warm water to the offending spot. Actor/bartender/cultural cliché Bo Pierce had only just left for work, while Neil would be on his way home from such in a matter of hours, on the red-eye from Los Angeles. Phoebe might have been racked with guilt. In fact, she was mostly just fascinated by the thought that the people supposedly closest to us in life quite possibly know the least about us.

But, then, what chance did happiness have in a world where everyone knew everything, she wondered self-interestedly, not just the particulars of our perfidy but the disdain we secretly harbor for the very people (Neil, for example) we claim to love the most? With that sentiment in mind, she descended to her knees to vet the floor space beneath the bed. She was concerned that Bo might accidentally have left behind a sock or stub in his ardor to extricate himself from his fashionably un-washed jeans. (In fact, he hadn't.) At which point she crum-pled the machine-washable components of her and Neil's bedding into a duffel bag and walked the lot of it over to the Chinese laundry on her corner, instructing the shopkeeper to please add bleach.

It was only later—only after emerging pink and pruned if not quite purified from a long bath—that Phoebe was able to think, *Poor Neil.* Owing to the fact of his own father having ruined all four of his marriages, the business of infidelity was among her boyfriend's chief obsessions. How many times she had been made to listen to the tale of Neil's deft espionage work in uncovering his ex-girlfriend Diane's latent whore-dom! (The case had come down to the girl's bathroom trash.) And to think now that Phoebe was no better than Diane, whom Neil, in an uncharacteristic show of strong language, had once referred to as a "lying bitch."

And yet, as bad as she felt, in truth Phoebe didn't feel all *that* bad. She wasn't married to the man, after all. And in his passive-aggressive tell-me-you'll-never-leave-me way, there was a sense in which Neil was a terrible bully. In a certain light, she was even able to convince herself that he'd been asking for it; how was she expected to remain loyal to a guy who loved Manfred Mann's Earth Band?

Moreover, lying awake that night Phoebe found herself replaying her rendezvous with Bo Pierce—the graceful way he seemed to glide on top of her and between her legs, his half-shut eyes shimmering like crescent moons, his torso hov-ering over her like the sky itself, his testes rotating like Mer-cury and Venus. Somewhat less elegantly, his navel attracted lint in the manner of the black holes she had seen a PBS documentary about on Emily's first night home. And if she didn't experience a total eclipse of her own, in Phoebe's (in truth) not so limited experience with promiscuity, you rarely did the first time. (Paradoxically, in order to feel comfortable turning into the space alien you inevitably become in the throes of sexual nirvana, you need to know the person a little better than perhaps she knew Bo.)

But as she reminded herself the next morning, after a sobering if unsettling night of sleep, her first order of business was Neil. As much as she may have loathed the taste of his mayonnaise breath, she still felt indebted to him for all he'd done—how he'd encouraged her to pursue a career as an electric violinist, taken her on holidays to Paris and the Caribbean, furnished her with a beautiful home, and hand-washed her bras. It was also true that Phoebe didn't currently have the funds with which to move into her own place—didn't know when she would. Maybe, also, there was a part of her that was wary of what, if anything, she'd find out there waiting for her. Bo Pierce, after all, was an untested entity, whereas Neil Schmertz had made it abundantly clear on multiple occasions that he wanted to be buried next to her when they were both ninety-nine.

And there *were* times when she could leave her objections to Neil behind. Admittedly, most of them took place at three in the morning when she was half asleep. There were other instances, however, when, verging on cognizant, she would wrap around his slumbering form, her breasts pressed to his back, her nose burrowed in the fleshy backside of his neck. And it would be enough—enough to be secure from the cruel winds that blew out there. Later that morning, after Neil had left for work, she called Bo and told him, albeit in her supplest bedroom voice, "I had a wonderful time yesterday, but I shouldn't see you again until I figure things out with Neil."

"You're doing the responsible thing," Bo agreed, both to Phoebe's relief and to her horror. In truth, she'd been counting on him to protest.

"I hope you don't disappear in the meantime," she muttered helplessly.

"I hope so too," he said, but in a tone of voice so measured that, in Phoebe's estimation, it bordered on impudent. How could he act so calmly about the question mark that dangled over their future after the delirium they'd shared? "But at this point, I guess I just feel like I need to protect myself."

Bo Pierce—in need of protection? Phoebe didn't understand. No everyday Don Juan, here was a guy who had finagled his own private love shack in the woods behind his progressive New England boarding school. Yet she had begun to notice how, as girls grew into women, the esteem in which they held mere coolness began to wane. They wanted greatness, too. And also candor. And compassion. And the suggestion of competence in matters as varied as changing diapers and building retirement portfolios.

And boarding school was a long time ago even then.

Phoebe, however, cared little for such practical attributes. At the age of twenty-five, while saddled with a domestic partner who preferred baby to dirty talk, she believed in passion alone. So when Bo Pierce let loose a method-actor sigh and declared, "Listen, Phoebe. You're doing the right thing. It's just that a part of me wants to say, 'Fuck it, let's just do the wrong thing anyway,' " she knew precisely what he meant.

"A part of me wants to say that too," she said, sighing with relief.

"To be perfectly honest, I can't stop thinking about you."

"I can't stop thinking about you either," Phoebe told him, her resolve and her abdominal cavity collapsing in tandem. Had a woman ever been so craven for physical comfort? Other women she knew seemed to find contentment in reading, samples sales, yoga, volunteer work, recycling, the great outdoors. . . .

"Invite me over," said Bo.

"I can't until Monday."

"Next Monday? Jesus."

"It's only a few more days."

"I miss your body already," he moaned.

"I miss yours too," she said.

"Oh, yeah?"

"Yeah."

"Tell me what you'd do if I was there."

"I'd take off all your clothes."

"And then what?" asked Bo.

"Then I'd kiss you all over."

"And then what?"

"I'd kiss you down there."

"I bet you'd like that."

"Maybe I would." It went on in this manner for a little while longer.

Finally, having run out of anticipatory chatter—and knowing better (consciously or not) than to dissipate the mood of urgency they'd spun out of inconvenience—Phoebe and Bo promised to realize the actions they'd alluded to at some date in the near future and hung up the phone.

In terms of agitation and impatience, the ten days that followed were among the longest of Phoebe's life, ranking second only to the three weeks she'd spent as a child in the
North Country of England, being shuttled from Cistercian
abbey to medieval castle. (While Roberta was a hardcore
Francophile, the ethnic bias of Leonard—though an interna-
tionalist at core—had always run more toward the Brits and,
more recently, the Japanese.) To make matters worse, Neil had
arrived home from his latest business trip in a flurry of good
cheer. Apparently, the L.A. office of his cable channel had
heaped praise on his department back east. And the new Web
site—the network's first—was receiving a record number of
hits. And some idiot who deserved to be fired finally had been
fired. And Neil had a part in it all, though Phoebe couldn't precisely say what.

In truth, she had stopped listening to her boyfriend's
work stories. Not only did they bore her, the mere mention of
Neil's boss, Jerry, made her break out in hives. Red of face,
thick of neck, Jerry Kershaw was one of those oppressively
friendly types who was always swatting everyone on the back
and was so enamored of the concept of teamwork that he had
somehow convinced himself that the inhabitants of every elevator in the nation would feel privileged to share in the tra-
vails of his workday. Only, while Neil pretended to have no
patience for Jerry's windbag ways, Phoebe could tell that her
boyfriend was actually desperate for his approval. For a short
while, she had called his attention to this glaring hypocrisy.
To Neil's claims that "Of course, Jerry was like, 'Way to

knock 'em dead, Schmertz'—God, what a loser," she'd fly back with "Obviously, you were thrilled, since you live for that man!"

But her accusations seemed to make no impression. Neil kept recounting the same dishonest tales about Jerry's blowhard ways. In the end, it just seemed easier to tune him out. When Neil accused her of not listening, she'd pretend not to feel well or to be depressed about her career—which she was in any case, since her pop-rock fusion band Schmaltz had failed to win over any recording company executives, and her financial livelihood was currently dependent on an Upper East Side animal hospital for the super-rich, where she answered the phone part-time and experienced mixed emotions about working in a place that called itself a hospital but practiced euthanasia without the full consent of its patients.

What's more, tensions were running high with Phoebe's bandmates. Her former best friend Holly Flake wanted to move the band in a more commercial direction. Her former boyfriend Kevin McFeeley, whose obsession with not selling out had led him down the path of experimental jazz, was threatening to bring in a Viennese buddy who played the homemade harp. Phoebe couldn't stop looking backward, to ocean liners and Central European hotel lobbies circa World War I. And while everybody wanted to write the songs, nobody wanted to practice them. Lyrics became their battleground.

Kevin had written a Bob Dylan knockoff that he insisted on performing in what Phoebe found to be an embarrassingly derivative rasp, and that contained the refrain:

> *You thought it was okay*
> *to shit on me*
> *after the world shit on you,*
> *well, I don't mind,*
> *I'll still be Fine.*

Except, he *had* minded—at least insofar as Phoebe had walked out on him without explanation, three years earlier, unable to admit that he'd become indistinguishable in her imagination from a con man named Arnold Allen who had touched her thighs and bilked her out of five hundred bucks.

Then there was the Holly-penned bubblegum ballad that made not-so-oblique reference to Phoebe's ill-fated college-era affair with Professor Bledstone:

> *Wanna make a bet*
> *I'm the teacher's pet,*
> *When he tells me I'm pretty*
> *I go running to the city,*
> *To my friends I act really shitty*

went the chorus. Phoebe failed to find much artistic merit in that song, either.

How was it that, without any commercial success to speak of—at that point, Schmaltz could barely get a gig at a free admission club—the four of them, including Holly's cousin, managed to stay together for *another* eighteen months? Back then, Phoebe placed a far higher premium on the inter-connectedness of everyone and everything; it made the city less overwhelming to imagine herself as part of some larger transfusion, bad blood though it may have involved.

Back then, she still considered feeling sick preferable to being alone. Then she learned better.

The water bugs only began to appear after her relationships with Neil and with her band began to falter—as if to taunt her, it seemed, with their own relative indestructability. She'd find them peering down at her from the highest point on the living room wall, defiant and implacable, and she'd wonder what sort of God had awarded such vile creatures both the speed of light *and* a coat of armor. She'd also question what kind of boyfriend advocated letting them be, rather than chasing them down with one of his Church shoes? Phoebe would have nothing of it. While Neil went into the other room to hide, she would embark on ten-, twenty-, thirty-, forty-minute staring matches, during which time, hamstrung with fear yet unable to tolerate the prospect of defeat, she would seek the courage not just to do battle but to clean up the victory parade.

But when it came to Neil, she had a lethargic streak that rendered even the prospect of upheaval daunting. In truth, she would always rather have been hiding under the covers herself. At the same time, she couldn't stop imagining hiding under Bo, his legs pinning her legs, his breath on her neck. And the more she tried to censor the image, the clearer the picture became, until it was as if her and Bo's reunion had already occurred, and she was guilty as charged and currently awaiting sentencing. And so she stepped to the bench.

She called Bo again the following Sunday evening while Neil was out *shwopping* for their *dinner-poo*. She didn't have much to say. Or maybe it was rather that she didn't have to say too much; Bo seemed to understand. She saw him the next afternoon—Neil had left for the airport an hour earlier—telling herself that this would be the last time for a long time but knowing full well that it probably wouldn't be, since, after the second time, sex has a way of becoming habit-forming. Again, she eradicated all traces of her new lover in time for the old one's return. And again, there were no suspicions on Neil's part. He had even come home with a present for her, a pair of furry dice to hang from the rearview mirror—of what? To Phoebe, those dice only proved how little thought Neil gave to the person she actually was (someone who didn't drive) versus the person he wanted her to be (someone who did), further proving that if you're looking for evidence of wrongdoing in a loved one, you can find it almost anywhere.

A cloudless sky the color of Olympic pool water dangled over that first Sunday of June, and the crystalline weather only exacerbated Phoebe's conviction that, stuck with Neil for an entire morning—at his prodding, they had climbed back in bed after breakfast to read the *Twimes* and do some *snuggle-wuggling*—she was missing out on the great party that was life. Its location was unclear. But every car that rumbled by beneath the window, stereo blasting, seemed to be headed in the right general direction. Eventually, unable to withstand another second in her boyfriend's company, she threw off the covers and announced, "I'm feeling really nauseated—I need to get some fresh air."

"Do you want me to come with you, Booboo?" asked Neil, as Phoebe stood wiggling herself into her jeans.

"That's okay," she told him, more or less slamming the door in his face.

Her main motivation for heading to Grounds for Firing, the annoying yuppie coffee bar where she and Bo had first met—and where she knew he procured his morning caffeine fix—was clearly the hope of running into him there. Their coffee was overpriced; their muffins left grease prints on the hands. What Bo was doing there that morning was somewhat harder to explain. Either he was hoping to make Phoebe jealous, or he'd simply planned poorly. In any case, she found him pressing down on a canister of low-fat milk, dressed in his usual stiff jeans and Stan Smith sneakers, a grande cup of Colombian Supreme in one hand—and an over-made-up six-foot-tall blonde with a glaciated facial expression in the other.

It was an extra second or two before Phoebe processed the implications of the sight before her. The woman's hair was still wet from the shower, and she was wearing a black pencil skirt and pair of high-heeled sandals far too dressy for a breakfast date. What's more, it wasn't a woman. The shoulders were the giveaway. "Well, good morning to you!" chimed Phoebe, in a voice so hyperbolically congenial that it could only be interpreted as a testament to the hurt and horror she was experiencing on the inside. Bo Pierce was supposed to be a walking cliché, not a source of lacerated ulcers!

"Hey," Bo mumbled back at her, with obvious discomfort, then turned away to follow the man-woman through the door to a wooden bench out front.

Phoebe skulked off in the opposite direction, toward the same faux-marble tables in back where she had first asked to see the movie clock in Bo's *Village Voice*. From her seat in back, she could just make out the back of her rival's head through the glass. She sat there watching his/her wet hair extensions dry in the sun, and when she could look no more, she went home, locked herself in her and Neil's potpourri-scented bathroom with the tinted glass canisters, and wept copious tears.

In time, Neil came knocking. "Wooboo, are you okay? Is it something Neily did?" he asked.

"Leave me alone!" she barked back at him.

"Whatever Bunny Wabby wants," came Neil's defeated reply. He had grown accustomed to having his sympathy hurled back in his face like so much projectile vomit.

A little while later—which is to say, it seemed to Phoebe as if he'd never leave—Neil left for the gym, at which point Phoebe couldn't stop herself from dialing Bo's number. Her intention was to leave him a message designed to simultaneously stoke passion and engender guilt and extreme mortification.

She was surprised to find him back at home. "I know I have no right to tell you not to see other people," she blurted into the receiver, "but at least you could decide which gender you like before you start worming your way into innocent people's lives!"

But Bo remained defiant in the face of his detection. "You're living with someone, Phoebe. How do you think I like *that*?"

"Yeah, well, I'm not having *sex* with him!"

"Yeah, but he's your boyfriend, and I hardly know Sara. I mean, I knew her when she was Sam, but that was back in boarding school, and we were on the ski team together."

"You went to *boarding school* with him!—I mean her."

In a single morning, all of Phoebe's assumptions about the world had been proven false.

"It's actually kind of a weird deal," said Bo, assuming a disconcertingly chatty tone. "I mean, she's been obsessed with me for, like, ten years. Like, she remembers all these random times when we were both in the library, and I asked her what time it was, and stuff! Now it turns out that I was one of the reasons she got the operation." He laughed warily. "I mean, that's kind of a heavy burden."

"And have you been obsessed with him-I-mean-her for, like, ten years too?" Phoebe asked him, losing sight of the weirdness factor as her jealous streak flared.

"Not really," he answered. "I mean, she's really nice and all. But—I don't know—I guess, I mean, even though she's a woman now, I still think of her as Sam. You know?" He paused. "Also, to be perfectly honest, I'm not that into blondes."

"I despise you," purred Phoebe, reflexively twirling a lock of her own decidedly brown hair around her index finger.

"You don't hate me," Bo begged to differ. "You hate yourself—for not getting rid of that lame-o boyfriend of yours!"

"I sincerely hope you die," she told him, by way of agreement.

"We all die eventually."

"How profound."

"Hey, I was a poetry major in college."

"You didn't go to college."

"For a year, I did."

"Oh, Bo!" cried Phoebe, suddenly lovesick, if only because it was a role she made better sense of than being the spurned woman in a love rectangle involving three men. "Give me a chance. I promise I'll break up with Neil soon."

"Yeah, sure," Bo replied, with a bitter edge in his voice. "In the meantime, it's possible that I might find time to fit you into my busy schedule."

Since the human capacity for rationalization knows no limits, Phoebe was able to convince herself that Bo had brought Sam/Sara to Grounds for Firing that morning as some kind of bargaining chip. Whether they had actually ever slept together was something Phoebe chose not to think about. In any event, Bo made no further mention of his ski team buddy, while at the conclusion of his and Phoebe's next rendezvous, he began to make demands on her. "I don't know how much longer I can go on with this not-sleeping-over business," he announced in a grave voice, while sprawled (yet again) on Neil's body-contouring bed, this time still clad in his windbreaker. (In their mutual war against Neil's return from work, full body nudity became the first casualty.)

"I know, I know!" Phoebe moaned, her sympathy for Bo's predicament growing in tandem with her pity for Neil, whose failure to suspect a thing only made him seem more pathetic. "It's just that—what if he kills himself, or something?"

"But you don't love him," Bo argued. "And the sooner you let him go, the better chance he'll have of meeting someone who *does*."

"I do love him, I'm just not *in love* with him," she told Bo.

"That's such a stupid cliché," he scoffed.

You're such a stupid cliché, she was about to reply but refrained, remembering Sam/Sara with a shudder and declaring, instead, "If clichés weren't true, they wouldn't have become clichés."

"That doesn't make any sense," said Bo.

"Who said things were supposed to make sense?" said Phoebe, slithering back up against him.

The subject was dropped for the time being.

But as the weeks wore on, Bo's demands became more strident. "It's either me or him, Phoebe!" he proclaimed with a jutting jaw while seated on the very bench on which he and Sam/Sara had kept company not three weeks before. (Bo and Phoebe had met up for an "emergency coffee" to discuss the current situation—yet another excuse to wind up in bed.)

It had become clear to her that the status quo was unsustainable. Bo's restiveness was threatening to become resentment. And Neil had no more plans to travel anywhere. He had announced this news over breakfast the previous Saturday—"Guess what? Neily's gonna have lots more time to take care of his special Woogoo!"—causing Phoebe to flee the room, gagging. Were she being honest with herself, she might have admitted that Bo was less the endgame than the inspiration for finally leaving Neil. But in her conscious mind, the greater imperative was to be united with the man she loved.

And so, one humid night late in June, she took a seat on the edge of the bed where Neil lay browsing through a gadgetry catalog and burst into tears, cannily establishing herself as the victim in advance of the torture she was about to inflict on him. "Doowoo, what is it?! You can tell Neily anything," he said, laying down his catalog and reaching for her cheek.

Phoebe took him at his word. "I had intercourse with someone else," she choked out, hoping that the clinical nature of her language would rob the news of some of its radioactivity. "And I just thought you should know, because you thought I'd been acting weird, and I couldn't lie to you anymore. I mean, I could have lied, but I didn't want to. I mean, I did lie, but I can't anymore." Then she held her breath, waiting for impact.

Neil didn't say anything for a few seconds. Then he covered his eyes and began to shake as if in the throes of electroshock therapy, while Phoebe sat there aghast at what she'd done and also, to be honest, a little irritated. Why did everything always have to be such a huge drama with him? "But I didn't think you were acting weird," he conceded between hyperventilated sobs. "I just—I just thought that was how you were, mean and withholding."

"But I *am* mean and withholding!" Phoebe assured him. "That's the point. I'm an awful person, and you deserve better."

"Don't tell me what I deserve!" brayed Neil. "Maybe I like mean and withholding women!"

"But they don't like you!" Phoebe told him. "I mean, they like you as much as they can. But since they're mean and withholding, they never like you that much."

But all of her attempts to rationalize her treachery only seemed to make Neil cry harder.

In time, tired and numb, Phoebe retired to the sofa, where she slept that night, and the next night after that too—never again to return to the comfort of Neil's 450-thread-count goosedown comforter. Instead, a week later, in a fit of exhilaration and with Neil standing silently in the corner, two nuclear physicists from Chernobyl turned Queens moving men carted off all her earthly possessions for an only mildly extortionist fee. They took the bulk of it to the first of many storage facilities she made use of during the period; the essentials were dropped off at a cat-sit on 64th and Park that Phoebe had arranged for herself through the animal hospital at which she worked reception.

It was her job to care for a cantankerous Abyssinian named Ondine whose owner, a septuagenarian widow by the name of Mabel La Mont, was busy circling the globe on the *Queen Elizabeth II* with a gentleman friend. The elevator opened directly into the apartment. The curtains were made of a pale yellow silk damask. The flowers were silk too. The Renoirs, on the other hand, were real. Phoebe ensconced herself in Mabel's guest bedroom, itself the size of some Manhattan minilofts, and began the rest of her life. You'd think Bo Pierce would have rushed right over—if only to check out the Renoirs. He said he had a big audition the next day, and he was working the next night and the night after that too, but he'd be "sure to stop by sometime over the weekend."

But Friday turned into Saturday, which turned into Sunday, and still there was no sign of Bo, who continued to protest work-related commitments. Just as Phoebe continued to act supportive, noting the difficult time he must be having "balancing the demands of art and commerce." (If she had learned one thing about the opposite sex over the years, it was how they consistently overestimated the significance of their professional contributions to society—and how they resented women who pointed this out to them.)

"Yeah, it's pretty much a struggle every day of my life," Bo replied.

Still, there was no sign of him.

Lonely and disoriented and becoming more suspicious with each passing day, Phoebe decided finally to surprise him at the too-cool-to-have-a-name downtown groggery where he earned his keep. Hoping to strike two things off her to-do list at once, she brought along a "duty-friend" named Karen on whom she had already canceled three drink dates.

They found Bo at the other end of the bar, shaking martinis as he chatted up—*could it really be Sam/Sara?*

"Hey, Bo!" Phoebe called out to him, confusion and outrage quickly giving way to self-pity as she contemplated the idea that, by all appearances, she had walked out on the nicest man she had ever known for a guy who was (a) seeing someone else and (b) not necessarily interested in women. The final blow: Bo's other "girlfriend," dressed that evening in a one-shouldered gold lamé minidress, stared blankly back at Phoebe, apparently failing to recognize her from that time at Grounds for Firing. Or was it Phoebe who should have been ashamed to have recognized him/her? Like all socially insecure people, she never forgot a name or a face.

Deigning, finally, to come over to where she stood, Bo smiled blankly and asked, "Hey, what are you doing here?"

"I thought I'd surprise you," Phoebe told him with a frozen smile of her own, determined at least to deprive him of the chance to see her rattled.

"I guess I'm not that into surprises," he shot back.

It was an extra few seconds before Phoebe registered the blow. Though when she finally did, it was as if she were a

neutral observer of her own quelled fortunes, looking backward at a period in her life that was memorable only insofar
as it failed to matter. She realized then that she had probably
never loved Bo or Neil. What she really wanted was to go
home and watch the latest episode of *Beverly Hills 90210*.

10

Among the groan-inducing staples of Phoebe's childhood had been the presence of young people to whom she was not related and with whom she had not been friends but who had managed to gain access to 281 Douglass Street anyway—namely, by coming for weekly instruction on the viola or oboe. Of course, Leonard and Roberta's music students were the ones who should have been embarrassed to be there. (Phoebe, after all, had had no choice in the matter.) Yet it had been she who had always felt like the interloper, her shoulders rounding, her stomach recoiling, and the ease of movement with which she otherwise traipsed through the house vanishing at the mere sight of them, Roberta and Leonard's "other kids"—or so Phoebe had thought of them, and not without a measure of ire—bowing and blowing away in the family music room.

It was in this light, however, that Phoebe had first been able to imagine her parents as people other than her parents—that is, as regular adults not unlike her own teachers (music and otherwise), who were really the only other adults she had known. This, in turn, had led her to wonder if, meeting them for the first time, she would have found them as intolerable as she had, say, Mr. and Mrs. Kosciouwicz on the first day of school. (The latter was her anal-retentive fifth-grade teacher, the former her retired husband who assisted with the class's audiovisual needs.) There had been something in particular about the way that Leonard never lost his temper but, instead, kept repeating his instructions over and over again that had tried Phoebe's patience. At some point, relentlessness had seemed like ruthlessness. Had he never heard of giving up? Moving on? Getting impatient?

Roberta, on the other hand, had been only too happy to express her agitation with her students, which had seemed to Phoebe to be a slightly preferable way to be. Against all evidence to the contrary, however, Roberta too had persisted in the lie that improvement would eventually come, which of course it wouldn't, since most of her students, like all music students everywhere in the world, failed to practice at home.

Upon her move back home nearly twenty years later, it never occurred to Phoebe that the "other kids" would still be there.

But there they were, *Still ruining my Saturdays,* she groused to herself the next morning as she stumbled downstairs after a poor night of sleep in single-minded pursuit of Leonard's nuclear winter–worthy supply of instant coffee— only to find tone-deaf Ernest "Palisades" Park seated on the music room companion chair, emitting phlegm-rich yowls with his half-sized oboe, his cheeks puffed out as if with nectarines. Leonard hovered over him, singing along in an eerie falsetto and beating his pencil against the Yamaha. Of course, Phoebe was old enough now not to feel threatened by the sight of an eleven-year-old, and especially not one with a gremlin's grin, girlish pink lips, and corduroy pants over-shooting his waist by several inches. Still, she had no particular desire to be seen by Ernest—really, by anyone right then—in her favorite pajamas with the disintegrated elastic waistband and sagging bottom. Since the music room had no door on it and you had to walk by it in order to get to the kitchen, however, she didn't have much choice (other than going back upstairs and changing, an action for which she lacked the energy).

In the end, she settled on traversing the danger zone in a half sprint and with the keen hope that Ernest was too busy concentrating on his fingering to notice her. (This was unclear.) A short while later, she sat down with the morning's headlines and was humbled by the thought that Leonard's oboe students should be her albatross when others had school shootings, suicide bombs, foreign occupiers, and famine with which to contend. Then, quickly losing her appetite for "hard news," she began an article on the migratory path of the white-bellied booby.

When, out the kitchen window, midway through the story, Phoebe caught sight of a stocky man in a red tracksuit leaving a white van proclaiming EXCELLENT CAKE DREAM along its side panel, she made the hardly brilliant deduction that it was Ernest's father. She was struck then by an even more felicitous thought than ridding the house of his son: What if she were to obtain use of his certainly spacious vehicle for purposes of her next Trash Night expedition? Surely it was of little use to the Park family in the evenings, which was exactly the time when she most needed it. And here the two families were already engaged in a successful partnership of sorts; why not expand and diversify their dealings? For his generosity, she could offer Mr. Park a percentage of all future profits.

Later that morning, after Ernest had left, Phoebe ran the idea by her father.

"Well, I don't see how it can hurt to ask," said Leonard, and he did—the very next day, when Mr. Park called to reschedule Ernest's lesson.

To Phoebe's surprise and delight, Mr. Park was amenable. Phoebe knew because she listened in on his and Leonard's conversation from the upstairs phone. "It would be great honor to loan van to member Fine family," she heard Mr. Park tell her father.

"Well, that's terrific news," exclaimed Leonard. "My daughter Phoebe will be so pleased! And she specifically told me to tell you that she'd like to pay you a commission on all future—"

Mr. Park would not hear of it. "Oh, noooooo," he said. "Not necessary!"

"Oh, but I think she wants to!" he protested.

"You know, Mr. Fine, Ernest grades improve greatly since begin oboe lesson."

"I didn't know that." Phoebe could tell that her father was tickled by this news—moreover, that he took more pride in the part he played in educating America's youth than he was ever willing to let on.

"Yes, yes," Mr. Park went on. "Also, last year, doctor says Ernest has attentive deficit. You know what this is?"

"Oh, dear, I *am* sorry!"

"Not be sorry. He better now. Last year, he laughing all

the time—*ha-ha-ha*. He has to be removed from church. He hear the word *virgin* and he laugh and laugh. Very embarrassing for Mrs. Park."

"Well, I can imagine—"

"They take Ernest outside by shirt collar. He crying—*bah-bah-bah*. But he never sit still, you know? But now, much better. So, you see—our pleasure to loan van."

"Well." Leonard chuckled gamely, as if he'd been outsmarted by a superior opponent. "If you put it that way."

"Yes, I do put it that way. This how I put that—plus also, thank you!"

"Well, on behalf of my daughter, Mr. Park, I'd like to thank you for your generosity. And of course she'll be sure to refill the tank at the end of the night."

"Tank?"

"Gas. Refill the gas. *Rum, rm-rm.*"

"Riiiight, okay." Mr. Park laughed. "Very funny sounds you make."

"Why, thank you."

"You tell your daughter: Call me anytime."

"Will do. And I'll see Ernest next Thursday afternoon at—what did we say?—four thirty, I believe."

"Four thirty. Very good. Bye-byeeeeeeeeee."

"See you then." Leonard hung up, and so did Phoebe, who went running downstairs to embrace her father, crying, "Dukes, you're a genius!"

"I'll settle for *extremely talented guy*," he said, smiling bashfully. "Now, who's going to drive this thing?"

"I hadn't thought about that," said Phoebe, taken back by this unforeseen obstacle in the road to riches. "You?"

"To be honest, Crumps, in my declining years—if I may call them that—I've grown more comfortable with smaller vehicles."

"I suppose you're thinking this is a perfect opportunity for me to finally get my license."

"And what a great opportunity it would be!" declared Leonard, who had been after her for more than a decade to get one.

Phoebe didn't answer. What she couldn't begin to explain to him, since he didn't get embarrassed like other people did, was the sense in which those STUDENT DRIVER signs tacked to the top of driving school cars rendered them the equivalent of mobile leper colonies.

Until that afternoon, Phoebe's experience with the online auction world consisted of a single fruitless sortie in search of vintage Pucci. Learning as she went along, she now posted the following announcement in cyberspace via Leonard's secondhand personal computer with the Dutch/Flemish keyboard (another story, too long to tell here):

NO RESERVE MUSIC CABINET

Currently:	First bid: $59.99
Quantity:	1
# of bids:	0
Time Left:	7 days, 23 hours, 59 minutes
Location:	Greater Metropolitan New York Area
Country/Region:	USA

Started:	Oct-1-00 16-39-41 EMT
Ends:	Oct-8-00 16-39-41 EMT
Seller:	feebeofwhitehead

Congratulations—you are bidding on a vintage flame-mahogany music cabinet in the Edwardian/Venetian style. Guaranteed to lend an aura of culture and refinement to your house, this elegant vessel with its flower detailing and wrought-iron claw feet was designed to store sheet music but easily doubles as a game cupboard or nightstand. The interior has 5 shelves, 4¾" apart. The backsplash measures 16½" long, 5" tall, and 1" thick, and features two beguiling carved rosettes. The whole cabinet measures 36¼" tall, 20" wide, and 13½" deep. Despite a microscopic chip (or two) on the top surface, wood is in excellent condition and retains original veneer. Cabinet has been in prominent Italian operatic family for generations. Will ship within the continental U.S. at a cost of $85.00. Otherwise, pick up yourself at our New York/New Jersey address. The highest bidder must make contact within 3 days of the auction's close. Please e-mail with any questions. Thank you for visiting Fine Furniture Inc., and please watch for our upcoming auctions!

It was the first foray into the world of business undertaken by a member of the Fine family since Phoebe's grandfather, Solomon Fine (né Feingold), begrudgingly sacrificed a promising career as a painter of Cubist still lifes to work in his father's dry-goods business. (He had a second baby on the way with Grandma Edith: Leonard's never-married sister, June, who went to Black Mountain College, made purple pottery decorated with interfaith religious iconography, and worked as a part-time development director for a Noh and Kyogen dance theater company in Buffalo.) It was also—as Phoebe, to her embarrassment (since she had been taught to prize culture over commerce) now discovered—really fun trying to sell things.

And while bids were slow to surface—and there was no further word from Roget—her mood remained upbeat for the entire week. The reason? Never underestimate the power of clement skies to raise morale, even the morale of the essentially despairing. Indeed, the illuminated blue splendor that blanketed northern New Jersey over the next six days gave Phoebe cause to imagine that, while she couldn't necessarily envision its outlines, a rewarding future most certainly lay ahead. Consequently, the butter on her English muffins had never tasted so sumptuous or the frozen orange juice so refreshing. What's more, she made small but tangible strides on her masterwork-in-progress, *Bored and Lonely*. And she hardly noticed Emily's presence, though to be fair Emily was hardly around, having signed on to tutor juvenile offenders at Rikers Island in reading and math. At night, Emily was conspicuously absent, as well; Phoebe could only assume she was off rubbing rabbit fur with her paramour, Sebastian.

Roberta seemed to be on an upswing as well. One afternoon, Phoebe heard her hashing out the opening bars of her favorite viola piece, Berlioz's *Harold in Italy*. It sounded a little abrasive, as if she were playing too close to the bridge. But from upstairs, if she wasn't listening too hard, Phoebe could convince herself that it was a beautiful thing, if not a small miracle.

And in the fiftieth minute of the twenty-third hour of the seventh day, someone with the user ID of chickenpotpie3 met the required opening tender on Mr. Marciano's libretto cabinet. From there on the situation resembled one of bumblebees converging on a tuna fish sandwich. Over the next ten minutes, the price ratcheted up to $176.99. The cabinet sold, finally, to an amateur songwriter and retired pipe-cleaner factory middleman in southern Jersey with the auction-land name of duckfacecharlie—though his real name, as it later emerged, was not Charlie but Ed.

Upon the man's appearance at the Fines' front door a few days later, it was his last name, Woefel, that came to seem the more incongruous. With his jolly pink face spilling out over his kelly-green polo shirt, he made his entrance to the tune of "Hey, there—I'm the music cabinet guy!" before performing a short tap dance and laughing uproariously. On the other hand, Ed Woefel had an exploded nose that suggested a complex relationship to alcohol. In fact, there was reason right then to believe that he wasn't capable of driving back to southern New Jersey. But after receiving in hand a pastel bank check emblazoned with seagulls and issued by the Toms River Savings and Loan for the agreed amount, Phoebe wasn't about to raise any objections.

By the time Ed Woefel pulled out of the Fines' mostly but not entirely gravel driveway in his silver Buick, Mr. Marciano's music cabinet wedged into the backseat, she was feeling positively euphoric. By her quick estimations, it was the first time in her life she had gotten something for nothing, with the possible exception of the gratification (oral and otherwise) that Neil Schmertz had bestowed upon her on a semiregular basis, even though she treated him like shit. Though—as was so refreshingly *not* the case with this purely commercial interaction—a feeling of indebtedness, followed by regret and revulsion, typically followed whatever smatterings of pleasure Neil had provided.

With the start of the new week, however, Phoebe felt listless and exhausted in ways she associated with visits home during the earlier portion of her twenties. Back then, within seconds of walking in the door, she had been overcome by the desire to lie down. More recently, her tiredness took the form of a lack of interest in sustained activities. How, then, did she fill her days? It turned out that, if you really set your mind to it, you could be incredibly busy doing almost nothing. For example, there was no limit on the number of times you could check to see if the mailman had come, or if you had any new messages in your in-box, or if your head was still screwed onto your neck. And having climbed the stairs, you would eventually find the need to come back down them. Just as there were freshness stickers to peel off fruit and also eyebrows to tweeze and random drawers to open and close whose contents you hadn't browsed through in a long time.

There were also, sometimes, mothers to take care of. Thursday morning, Leonard took Roberta to the hospital for her usual "little tests," but having dropped her back at the house, he immediately headed back out to Newark to rehearse Hindemith's *Mathis der Maler* (*Matthew the Painter*) with the NSO. Emily, meanwhile, had conveniently set off for Rikers moments before Roberta was due home and didn't plan on returning there until after dinner. Here, Phoebe had feared that her sister would usurp her role as their mother's chief caregiver! It turned out she could have used the extra help—or, at least, that day she would have liked it. (That night was also Trash Night, which she would now be missing.) And—was this terrible to say?—she had grown envious of Roberta's cheekbones, which now projected out like cornices on an Italianate house, while Phoebe's own were busy disappearing behind a wall of pudge. Next to opening and closing drawers, eating, Phoebe had found, was still the most enjoyable thing to do, when you didn't feel like doing anything else.

And the clouds were so heavy it looked like the sky might fall, after all.

And sometimes the disconnect between Phoebe's old and new lives seemed to her so vast that she felt like an imposter sitting there nodding her head in agreement while, propped up on her poly-fill pillows, Roberta declaimed about the truths of this world: the "if you're going to raise children with good values . . . to appreciate good music . . . to be a good neighbor . . . citizen . . . mother, then you'd better (a) . . . (b) . . . (c). . . ." As if Phoebe hadn't already taken this same class over and over again as she grew up! And as if it had prevented her from letting Arnold Allen touch her thighs and take her money. Which is why she tried to avoid all use of the "t-word" in her own sentences. Because the only truth, as Phoebe saw it, was that there was none so big as the human capacity to learn nothing and keep erring.

She just didn't feel it was right, under the circumstances, to express this dissenting worldview to her mother. Though even before she became ill, Roberta had had a fragile quality about her that made the adult Phoebe prone to sarcasm in her company but rarely anything more scabrous—for fear that she might really upset her.

At the same time, Phoebe's silence and complicity nagged at her insides, spewing resentment in all directions—not just at her mother, for maintaining such a pat view of the world against all evidence to the contrary, but at the people (Arnold Allen, for instance) who had made it impossible for her to believe the lies her mother propagated. But since Arnold Allen had vanished and her mother was sick, she transferred the brunt of her fury onto her sister. (There was no one else to blame; Leonard was already too dutiful.) "Speaking of the importance of families sticking together," she said, interrupting Roberta's sermon, "I have to say I think Emily is being a little selfish about her time. I mean, she came all the way back east—for what? All she seems to care about is criminal rehabilitation. What about us?"

But to Phoebe's irritation, Roberta replied without a trace of bitterness. "Em has always done what she wants, when she wants. I accepted that long ago. She's a free spirit, your sister!"

"Well, what does that make *me*?" asked Phoebe.

"You've always been much more susceptible to others' influence," Roberta explained to her.

"Thanks a lot."

"It's not an insult, Phoebe. It makes you a more open person as well."

"Whatever that means," she muttered in disgust—mostly

with herself. Why did she always have to set herself up for comparison with her older sister?

For that matter, who wanted to be an *open person*? Phoebe pictured a tin of sardines left out on the counter overnight, its contents filmy and congealed and buzzing with flies. Her mother was right, of course: She had led her young adult life like a smashed window in an abandoned building. Any bum who'd wanted to could climb right in, she had been that eager for attention. Now, the image of it—the image of her spastic, freewheeling desire—caused a full body shudder.

Now, it seemed to Phoebe that *she,* not Arnold Allen, had become the bum, the hustler, the opportunist, the squatter with a suitcase, the con man who'd come calling under the guise of offering succor but who was really only looking for a warm place to spend the night.

On Saturday morning, to compensate for her crimes, Phoebe brought her mother breakfast in bed—her usual: two slices of rye toast and a soft-boiled egg. "Well, look at this!" exclaimed Roberta, seeming genuinely touched by the gesture as she sat up to accommodate the tray. "Tell me what your mother did to deserve such treatment."

"It's nothing." Phoebe shrugged uncomfortably. "I just want to thank you for putting up with me all these months."

"Putting up with *you*? I should be thanking you for putting up with *me*! I don't think Dad and I would have gotten this far without you." Phoebe's heart swelled; she had never known love this gratifying. "Of course, I still worry that we're keeping you from seeing friends and meeting new—"

"Mom!"

"Fine, fine." She raised her palm defensively.

After breakfast, since Roberta was in the rare mood to get behind the wheel, and Phoebe now had money in the bank, the two set off for a couple of garage sales in the neighborhood. If only for nostalgia's sake, Phoebe bought a copy of the famous 1976 red-bathing-suit poster of Farrah Fawcett, for seventy-five cents. From there, they headed to a silent auction of storage locker remains at the same facility in Pringle where Phoebe had deposited her own belongings six months earlier. (She was relieved to find her own effects not yet on sale.)

The town of Pringle, meanwhile, had undergone a substantial demographic shift in the twelve years since Phoebe had gone to high school there, at Pringle Prep. While there was still a railroad track dividing rich from poor and white from black, Orthodox Jews now comprised a sizable portion of the former population. It wasn't hard to figure out who they were, either, since nobody else in the suburbs walked who didn't have to, and the OJs did so in the middle of the street—at least, on Saturdays—since Pringle didn't have proper sidewalks. Moreover, observing their movements out the window of the Yugo that afternoon, Phoebe marveled that people always pinned Catholics with the ribbon of hollow ritual when it was so clearly their Jewish forebears, with all their funny rules about food touching and when you could and couldn't turn on electrical switches, who were the true obsessive-compulsives of the bunch. This, in turn, gave her cause to imagine that her connection to the Jewish religion, to which she had been born but in which she had been purposefully deprived of an education—her parents worshiping at the altar of Steinway, not Yahweh—was, in fact, far more involved than she might have imagined.

From Pringle, it was on to the armory-sized Red White and Blue store in Paterson, with its giant rolling carts and color-sorted clothing (all sweaters in the blue family here; all pants with connections to the beige clan there). Phoebe nabbed a few fuzzy sweaters and a Steuben glass bowl for $5.99. The Hadassah thrift shop in Teaneck would have been next, but it was closed for the Sabbath. So mother and daughter continued on to Goodwill in Bergenfield, with its mixture of new and old merchandise.

On the new end:

1. Humidifier filters
2. Easter grass
3. Golf tees
4. Action dolls

And, on the old:

1. 78 rpm records
2. Bowling trophies
3. Damaged breadboxes
4. Vinyl suitcases
5. Communion dresses
6. Jumpsuits
7. Ski pants
8. Fruit accent pots
9. Shell lamps

10. Coffee mugs (I'D RATHER BE DRINKING TEQUILA;
    WOMEN'S BANKERS ASSOCIATION OF NEW JERSEY)
11. Commemorative glasses ("ALWAYS SOMETHING THERE
    TO REMIND ME"—*Tenafly JS Senior Prom '87;*
    SONOMA COUNTY CONVENTION AND VISITORS
    BUREAU; DELTA ZETA KILARNEY ROSE BALL—
    April 24, '92; SHARON'S 58TH—*November '96;*
    PARENTS WITHOUT PARENTS—*36th International
    Convention—July 4–8, New Orleans, LA*)

Phoebe purchased two shell lamps, at $1.59 apiece. In short, buying things, as she kept discovering, over and over again in life, could be really fun, too.

11

At 1:30 A.M. the next morning, Phoebe was still awake, sitting up in her trundle bed, thumbing through an old yearbook from Pringle Prep and trying to decide who the biggest bitch in her class was. (Jennifer Weinfelt, probably.) *And wasn't that just typical,* she thought with a renewed sense of outrage as she read the Grateful Dead lyrics that Jennifer had included on her senior page:

> *Time there was and plenty*
> *but from that cup no more.*

With her 42DD bosom, what had *Jennifer* ever known about cups running out?

Even more sickening, somehow, was Jennifer's sign-off, with its gleeful cataloging of the six most popular girls' initials, at the clear expense of the rest of the girls in the grade, including PFs:

> To the whole posse, S.C., G.K., C.M., E.R., J.S., and
> A.A.—friends 4-ever.

Phoebe knew it was a little worrisome that she was still getting worked up about this stuff at her age. It was just that—

The telephone rescued her from any more traumatic memories of having to get undressed in her high school locker room. Curious as to who could be calling so late, she climbed off her bed and walked the fifteen feet to her parents' bedroom door, behind which the upstairs phone was kept. "What happened?" she heard Leonard croak into the receiver. It was clear he thought someone had died, as he always did whenever anyone called past eleven.

And also that he'd been sound asleep.

"Roget—I mean, Maestro! Always a pleasure to hear from you," was the next thing out of his mouth. Phoebe felt her body stiffening, her mind agitating. It wasn't merely that Roget's name was now synonymous in her mind with rejection; it was that her father always deferred to authority (maybe he had learned that at Quantico as well), even when the authority was so obviously a sham, as in the case of his conductor. And why couldn't he have said, "Jesus, Roget, it's nearly two in the morning; have a little respect for my family!" instead? And was he calling for Leonard, or for her—or, God forbid, for Emily? "Phoebe? Well, I'd be delighted to get her, if you'll just hold the line for one moment," Leonard told him, thereby solving the mystery.

Only, what if she didn't want to be got? What if she wanted nothing more to do with him? Cracking open the door, she stage-whispered, "Dad, I'm right here," unable to resist the opportunity.

"Who's there?" Leonard called into the darkness. Next to him, Roberta lay facedown and motionless, suggesting that she was either dead or not holding back on the painkillers any more than she needed to.

"It's me!" Phoebe said testily. "Who do you think it is?"

But still he squinted through her, her voice and form apparently failing to come together for him, making her wonder how soon the day would come before her father failed to recognize her during daylight hours as well.

Eventually, the puzzle pieces must have fit together, as he held out the receiver. "Phone for you, Crumps," he told her, in a hoarse voice.

"I'll get it downstairs," she told him.

He mumbled something unintelligible and fell backward onto his pillow with the phone still in his grip and the cord extended diagonally across his torso like a beauty pageant sash.

Phoebe correctly assumed that her father would be fast asleep again by the time she got to the kitchen. *"Dad, I've got it!"* she bellowed into the receiver, hoping to rouse him into hanging up, just as she had done so many times as she grew up, while she had been upstairs pretending to do her homework and he and Roberta had been downstairs watching the *MacNeil/Lehrer NewsHour*. Back then, Leonard would pick up the phone even if it had stopped ringing. Even if it was clear that someone else had already gotten it. He wasn't purposefully snooping; it was just a reflex, if a completely maddening one.

Through a series of clangs, bangs, and scratches—presumably Leonard trying to locate the receiver bed—Phoebe could just make out the words, "Christ, you're gonna blow my fucking eardrums out!"

When silence had been restored, Roget continued with, "Dude—what time do your parents go to bed anyway? You'd think I'd called at four in the frigging morning."

"It's one-thirty, actually," Phoebe replied, surprised to find herself so enraged by the sound of his voice.

"Exactly my point," he said. "The night is young."

"Are you sure you're not looking for Emily?" The whole vinaigrette incident had come throttling back at her.

"Who?" he asked.

"My sister," she answered.

"Oh, you mean the tall chick with the big tits at dinner that night. Why would I be looking for her?"

"Never mind," she hissed, though secretly pleased by his apparently diminished assessment of Emily's attractiveness. (Phoebe never tired of compliments, even indirect ones that existed mainly by implied comparison, however insulting in the other direction.)

Or was Roget being rhetorical, having just named two big reasons why he might like to see her sister again?

"So listen," he went on. "I got a friend in the Bronx I'd like to show your mother's viola to. Transylvanian by birth. Deals, repairs, appraises, the whole nine inches—I mean, yards. What do you say?"

"Let me get this straight," said Phoebe, determined to keep her priorities in order this time. "You flirt with my sister. You leave without saying good-bye. You never even call to thank my mother for dinner. And then, one day, two weeks later, you suddenly feel the need to wake my entire family at two in the morning because Dracula wants to see my mother's viola?"

"Funny. I got the feeling your mother slept right through the ring," said Roget.

"That's not the point!"

"Also, as you pointed out just moments ago, it's closer to one-thirty than two."

"That's not the point, either!"

"Then what is the point?"

"The point is—"

Just then, Emily appeared in the doorway of the kitchen, looking like a sexpot ghost in a see-through white nightgown. "Hey," she said, opening the refrigerator.

"Hold on," Phoebe told Roget, pressing the receiver into her stomach, as she waited for her sister to get her milk and go away.

But it seemed that Emily had a few questions first. "Who's the phone for?" she asked, squinting at the date on the carton.

"It's Roget," Phoebe told her.

"What does he want?" Emily snapped back, without skipping a beat.

"What do you mean, *What does he want?*" said Phoebe, taken back by her sister's proprietary attitude toward Roget's rudeness. She was the only one who got to hate the guy's guts! "He called *me.*"

"Fine—God." Emily assumed her favorite *excuse-me-for-living* face and disappeared back up the stairs.

Phoebe got back on the phone with Roget and, momentarily flustered and straining to recall where she left off in her argument, announced, with a minimum of conviction, "Well, you should be ashamed of yourself."

"I am—deeply," Roget assured her. "Anyway, I'm not

promising you it's an authentic sixteenth-century da Salo. But I will say this: I've seen my share of varnish before, and that grease on your old lady's viola isn't any candy-apple glaze. Also, I can guarantee that, if it comes to it, my guy'll pay top dollar. Or he'll find you someone who can."

"There's only one problem," said Phoebe.

"What's that?" asked Roget.

"My mother isn't interested in selling."

"Yeah, well, she might *get* interested when she finds out what kind of dollar sum she's looking at." A jaded laugh escaped his lips. "You'd be surprised at how *unpossessive* people get about material goods when you dangle a fat wad of hundreds in front of them."

"Yeah, well, you don't know anything about my parents," Phoebe told him with a knowing laugh of her own, confident in her superior knowledge of her family's retrograde ways. "They're not interested in material wealth. They don't even know what the NASDAQ is."

"Yeah, well, they're not getting any younger either," offered Roget. "To be honest, your mother looks like hell."

The nerve of him to invoke Roberta's illness as a motive, as opposed to a mission unto itself! "For your information," Phoebe nearly spat on the receiver, "my mother is fighting off breast cancer. Which may explain why she looks like shit!"

"I said hell. But you're right," said Roget, "she looks like shit too—under the circumstances, who wouldn't? Just don't tell me your old man can afford the cost of her care. I know what they pay him at the NSO 'cause I sign off on all the checks. And let me tell you, *it ain't much.*"

"He gives lessons too!" A tender nerve had been hit.

"For what? Fifty bucks a pop? Maybe the Koreans pay sixty. As an immigrant group—I have to say—they've done very well. But back to the fiduciary angle. You guys should give some serious thought to how you're planning to make ends meet in the next few years and beyond. Of course, there's always a chance your little Dumpster-diving expeditions might reap some choice fruits, though it seems unlikely."

"How did you know about Trash Night?" Phoebe gasped. Was there nothing she could keep from this man?

"Drove by you the night after I took you home," Roget explained. "I would have stopped to say hello, but I was running late. Dinner date and stuff. But back to the NSO. Fact is, your father could be cut loose at any moment. On the other hand, I've always found Old Len the Hen amusing—livens things up backstage with his gambling ways. Also, the orchestra's bankrupt and we can't afford to hire anyone who can actually play his instrument. To be honest, your old man can barely blow through a straw at this point. *My* point being, if you know what's good for your family, you'll sneak the viola out of the house for a few hours next week and let me find out what kind of nest egg you're keeping warm for no reason."

Phoebe was now courting collapse, her wet eyes and strained breathing finding cause not only in the harsh way in which Roget had summed up her parents' slim chances for survival (musically and otherwise), but in the sensation of having failed to notice that the world was a far crueler place than she had ever imagined.

"Okay, look," he continued, sounding vaguely exasperated even as his voice had grown gentler. "We'll come to you. That way, no one has to know we've even seen the thing. What do you say?"

It had become a difficult offer to refuse. "Maybe you could come over Thursday morning, while my mother's at chemo," she told him in a trembling voice she tried not to hear.

"Fine with me," said Roget.

"Don't you have to check with your friend first?" Phoebe asked through sniffles.

"I'm sure he'll be fine with it," he answered. "The man doesn't exactly have a busy social calendar. So what time does your old lady leave for the bio warfare lab?"

"She'll be gone by ten."

"Then we'll swing by at ten fifteen."

"Who were you having dinner with the night you saw me going through the trash?" In the final analysis of Phoebe Fine, jealousy and curiosity still trumped pride.

"Oh, just this cellist from out of town," Roget tossed off. "We didn't do the nasty or anything."

"I didn't ask you if you slept with her!"

"Well, I told you anyway. See you on Thursday."

"Bye." Her head spinning, Phoebe hung up the phone and went back upstairs to continue perusing her high school yearbook, which suddenly didn't seem half as threatening as it once had, if only because the people in it were all young and stupid. That included Phoebe.

12

Among the curious aspects of intelligent life is its ability to juggle competing crises, turning them on and off as if a light switch. By Sunday night, Phoebe's ongoing conflict with her sister, which seemed to have grown even worse since their kitchen run-in, had momentarily eviscerated from her mind all traces of the one concerning Roget and her mother's viola. As usual, the trouble began again over dinner.

Roberta had invited over their neighbors Bill and Carol Ann Breakstone for a potluck supper. The Breakstones contributed a veal stew. The Fines supplied wine, salad, bread, and dessert. Other than grown children the same approximate age (though the Breakstones' kids, unlike the Fines', had homes, intact marriages, children, and jobs), and comparable old-fashioned Liberal Democrat politics (both had campaigned for McGovern in the sixties, Carter in the seventies, Mondale in the eighties, and Clinton in the nineties), it was hard to say what the two couples had in common. Bill Breakstone was an engineer for an aerodynamics company. Carol Ann worked three days a week as an administrator at Whitehead's shelter for abused women. He was extremely fat and told the kind of stories that had punch lines. She was stickly thin and seemed to find her husband hilarious, even after thirty-seven years of marriage. They were the Fines' closest nonmusical friends in Whitehead. And while Phoebe mocked them behind their backs, calling them the Breakmirrors, she had always enjoyed their company too.

That night, however, Emily made pleasure difficult. "Could you move your chair over?" she asked Phoebe through gritted teeth, hunching her shoulder away from her sister, as if Phoebe were a veritable supply closet of communicable diseases. "You're all the way over on my side."

"Actually, I'm not," Phoebe grumbled back at her.

"Thanks for being so accommodating."

"You're welcome."

"So I was down at Lou's Hardware the other day," said Mr. Breakstone. "And the funniest thing happened. I was standing there looking for two frosted candle-tip bulbs for Carol Ann's chandelier, and this bald guy with a really narrow head comes up to me. And I do this double take, and say, 'Hey, you're just what I'm looking for!' And he says, 'Excuse me?' "

"Oh, Bill!" squawked Carol Ann, her laughter seeming to belong to a much larger person than herself. "You're too much!"

"A very amusing anecdote, Bill," said Leonard. "I'll give you that."

"Some more chardonnay, Carol Ann?" asked Roberta.

"Oh, yes, please, thank you," she said, holding out her

wine glass with one hand as she dabbed her eyes with the other.

"Princess," muttered Emily, striking Phoebe's ankle beneath the table.

"Prima donna." Phoebe kicked back.

"So, girls," said Carol Ann, oblivious to their subterranean conflict as she turned to face them with her gummy smile. "What's new in your lives these days?"

"Nothing much," they answered nearly in unison. Both then proceeded to relay artificial news, since, in truth, nothing suitable for public consumption had happened to either of them lately.

But an unexpected rapprochement came about between the two sisters the next morning, as they stood pushing and shoving each other in an attempt to remove the other from the family's single bathroom, just as they had been doing for the past twenty-odd years. (Following a prison-wide riot, Emily's students had been placed in lockdown, so she had the week off work.)

"Hey, I've been meaning to ask you something," said Phoebe—for the sake of experimentation, releasing the door and allowing herself to be ejected from the premises.

"What?" Emily yelled from the other side of it, while Phoebe stood listening to her sister pee and registering to herself with surprise and maybe even a little shame that, in fact, Emily *had* had to go far worse than she had.

"I was wondering if, next Trash Night, you'd be willing to drive Ernest 'Palisades' Park's family's bakery van?" Phoebe asked her. "I mean, assuming you're still in town. The next one's on the twenty-sixth."

"Sure," said Emily, who had made no further mention of jetting off to Paris or Düsseldorf—or, for that matter, of ever leaving Whitehead again.

Then again, neither had Phoebe.

"Cool!" exclaimed Phoebe. "I mean, thanks."

How did this sea change from cold war to cooperation come about between the two? Phoebe had noted in the past how the difference between success and failure sometimes seemed to come down to the difference between asking and not asking: "Will you sleep with me? . . . sign my band? . . . surrender your arms?" (By the laws of statistics, sometimes the answer had to be yes.)

And also, Phoebe and Emily were sisters. Which is to say that they were capable of reverting from loathing and competitiveness to charity and affection in the space of a single second.

Phoebe suspected that Emily might have a financial motive for wanting to get in on her trash-hunting racket, as well. One day the previous week, while Emily was off tutoring at Rikers, Phoebe had succumbed to curiosity and tradition and wandered uninvited into Emily's bedroom, where she came across two scraps of newsprint sticking out from beneath her NO NUKES mug. One was a traditional help-wanted ad for phonathon fund-raisers for a well-known philanthropic organization that was even better known for its questionable allocation practices. The other was an open call for paid volunteers for a clinical trial of some promising new anti-eczema medication with questionable side effects. Phoebe began to wonder if, between the Palo Alto divorce lawyer she was keeping on retainer and her unpaid leave from her Legal Aid job, Emily may have been in as dire economic straits as the rest of the family, and possibly even worse.

Phoebe was also struck by the radical thought that perhaps her sister's life wasn't so charmed, after all.

At the very least, Phoebe's sale of the Marcianos' music cabinet had left Emily if not outright jealous then visibly piqued. In fact, she had harangued Phoebe for most of the previous weekend. "You sold someone garbage for nearly two hundred dollars! That's really outrageous. Did you at least tell him you found the thing in the trash? . . . You didn't?" Caustic laughter. "God, someone should call the Better Business Bureau on you. A hundred and seventy-seven dollars. I can't fucking believe it."

"A hundred and seventy-six—and ninety-nine cents," Phoebe had corrected her.

"Same thing."

Finally, even though Emily had assured Phoebe at dinner that first night that she'd pretty much rather be dead than participate in any trash-hunting party, Phoebe had seen on more than one occasion how her sister's most cherished opinions were all ultimately open to revision—depending on what was in it for her.

As it turned out, Emily had more than just her skills behind the wheel to offer Phoebe. "About Trash Night," she began, the day after agreeing to drive, while the two raked leaves in the backyard. "I have to say I don't really see the point of tooling around Whitehead. I mean, the success rate of this kind of venture is going to hinge on both the density and the wealth of the residential population. And frankly, I don't see Whitehead ranking particularly high on either scale. Now, if you're talking about certain areas of Manhattan—"

"Well, if you'd be willing to drive us into the city," Phoebe cut in, impressed by Emily's reasoning.

"Anything to get out of this pit for a few hours—shit, what was that?" she said, jerking backward as she broke a tooth of her rake on the semiexposed surface of a smooth white stone.

"Probably the remnants of Dad's Japanese rock garden project," offered Phoebe, who was tempted to ask her sister what she was still doing in Whitehead if she hated it so much there, but refrained, not wanting to alienate her new designated driver. "Anyway, I could call my old cat-sit lady, Mabel, and find out what night they put out household trash on the Upper East Side."

And she did.

"Well, hello, my dear, what a lovely surprise!" began Phoebe's former employer, in the strangulated pseudo-British accent endemic to all theatrical types of her generation. "As a matter of fact, I've just arrived home from a *divine* excursion to the South Seas! Can't recommend the area enough. Such friendly people. And, of course, Ondine just adored . . . A what? A scavenger hunt? The games you children play these days! . . . Not a clue, my dear, but happy to transfer you to Charlie in the lobby. Oh, and by the by, I don't think I ever got around to reprimanding you for the terrible mess you left in my home. Thumb and lipstick prints literally all over my silk furniture! . . . Well, thank you for saying so, but it's a little late for apologies. The cleaning crew have already come and gone. Transferring! . . ."

As Phoebe soon learned, the NYC Department of Sanitation provided free removal of up to three large or six small items at a time (with a combined total of no more than six pieces) from every residential address in New York. Just as in Whitehead, residents were asked to drag their so-called regular bulk (items composed of less than 50 percent metal) to the curb on the night before collection. In Manhattan, however, that ritual was reenacted three times a week, on Mondays, Wednesdays, and Fridays, and was conducted in conjunction with regular (fermentable) garbage removal. Which meant that there were treasures to be hunted that very night—the fact of which Phoebe soon informed her sister.

At the news, Emily pressed her teeth together like a Halloween pumpkin and sucked in, as if the problem of being wanted in too many places at the same time was one that plagued her. "The thing is, I was supposed to see Sebby tonight," she said slowly, as if problem-solving as she spoke. "I mean, I *guess* if I had to I could put him off until tomorrow." It was the first mention Emily had made of her mystery beau in over a month.

"How long is he in town for?" asked Phoebe, hungry for more details about the man who potentially stood to replace Jorge as her brother-in-law.

"Oh, just a few days this time." Emily shrugged. "He comes back and forth a lot—from Europe."

"Right." Phoebe nodded a few times, while her sister smiled impassively, as if lost in tender thoughts. Or were they troubling ones? "Well, would you be willing to go in after dinner?"

Emily shrugged yet again, as if the whole escapade had really nothing to do with her—she was simply being helpful—and said, "Sure—whatever you want."

"Hey, I really appreciate you volunteering to drive, especially on such short notice," Phoebe told her, registering how much less energy it took getting along than getting pissed all the time.

"Don't worry about it," Emily told Phoebe. "But thanks for saying so." It was almost, suddenly, as if they liked each other.

At some point later that afternoon, Leonard placed a call to Mr. Park, advising him that his daughters were ready to take him up on his kind offer to loan his van—assuming, of course, it was a good night. And it was. Everything seemed set to go—until Phoebe remembered that they had no way to get to the Parks'. Defying all reason, except maybe the reason of her father's life, Leonard had come out of NSO rehearsal several nights earlier to find his Yugo vanished. Not seeing any broken glass on the street, he at first assumed that he'd simply forgotten where he parked, as he occasionally did. But after wandering the streets of downtown Newark for three quarters of an hour and finding nothing, he resigned himself to flagging down a couple of cops, who drove him to the local precinct, where, with rapidly diminishing hopes that his car had merely been towed, he filed a missing vehicle report. The clerks on duty, far from offering hope for his vehicle's retrieval or even sympathy for his loss, amused themselves by cracking jokes about Yugo owners begging strangers to take their cars off their hands. (His good nature apparently having its limits, after all, Leonard failed to find it amusing.)

Now Phoebe turned to Emily and asked, "Wait. How are we going to get to the Parks'?"

"You're going to call us a taxi," Emily informed her. "That's how."

"Oh, right. Good idea," said Phoebe, who proceeded to look up the name of a taxi service in the yellow pages, rather than ask her father for a recommendation and risk making him feel even worse about his lack of wheels than he probably already did.

Sometime between the hours of seven and eight that brisk October eve, a wood-paneled station wagon pulled up in front of the Fines' bungalow and honked.

Emily got in first, Phoebe after her. The car smelled of burnt plastic. It wasn't until they arrived at the Park family's new-construction two-family white-and-pink brick-composite house in Palisades Park that the man behind the wheel revealed himself to be one of Phoebe's old junior high classmates. He did this without ever turning around, making eye contact via his rearview mirror from behind a pair of oversized yellow-tinted shades. As Phoebe recalled it, the so-named Vincent La Vroux had been painfully shy as a child, too. He had also been mercilessly teased and yet had been seemingly indifferent to all but his Swiss Army knife and his leather knuckle cuffs. (Phoebe got out of the car as quickly as she could without being rude.)

With its paucity both of windows and of surrounding

vegetation—it had a cemented-in front yard—the Park property looked like nothing so much as a white-collar prison. Only the barbed-wire fence appeared to be missing, though to the left of the house there was a shoulder-high green chain-link one sporting a sign that read KEEP AWAY FROM DOG. Unsure as to which door the Parks lived behind, Phoebe naturally chose to ring the right-hand bell first. (Emily stood on the sidewalk, smoking another of her clandestine cigarettes.) There was no answer on that side, however, so Phoebe tiptoed over to the other, whereupon a snarling pit bull tried to jump the fence and, as far as she could tell, kill her. (Visions of Alex Kahn in her head, she angled herself into the side of the doorway and wondered whose cockamamie idea it had been to borrow the bakery van. Her own?)

Mr. Park appeared in the door, finally, in a striped bathrobe and fuzzy slippers. He was sipping through a straw attached to a giant plastic tumbler.

"Hi, Mr. Park, I'm Phoebe Fine," she shouted to be heard over a cacophony of murderous noises coming out of the dog. "And that's my sister, Emily." She motioned at the sidewalk.

"Hello, yes, very well." He nodded perfunctorily, taking his time stepping away from the entrance.

"Thank you so much—Emily, come on," Phoebe called to her sister, who flung her cigarette into the street and started up the cement path, whereupon, to Phoebe's irritation and incomprehension, the Park family pit bull lay down and purred.

"Cute dog," Emily told Mr. Park, as she passed through the door.

"Yes, very well." He continued to nod, but this time with an expansive smile. "Say hello, Wolfgang!"

He led the Fine sisters down an internal staircase that opened onto a two-car garage, where his bakery van sat dwarfing a lime-green Hyundai. "At least we know we won't be stranding you," said Phoebe, trying to be conversational.

"Stranding you?" said Mr. Park, looking at her like she was insane.

Phoebe tried again: "Leaving you with no transportation."

"You from England?"

"No, just from right here." Phoebe tried to drown out her sister's snickering with some of her own light laughter.

But again, Mr. Park stuck his neck forward, his eyes crinkled, as if he had no idea what she was talking about.

"The same place as my father, Leonard Fine!" she found herself bellowing in her desperation to be understood.

Mr. Park took another long sip from his tumbler. "Well, you talk real funny. Hard to understand. Also very loud. You know." With his free hand, he covered one ear and assumed the traumatized facial expression of the man in Edvard Munch's painting *The Scream*.

At which point Emily's laughter achieved the voltage of a shriek.

"Sorry, I'll try to talk softer," mumbled Phoebe, resigned now to her estrangement from Mr. Park, even as she mused to herself that—in her own defense—the world would be a lot easier place to navigate if everyone spoke the same language, preferably English.

Though if it had to be Korean, then so be it; she would simply learn.

"So—who drive?" Mr. Park's eyes darted from one sister to the other.

"I do," said Emily, stepping forward.

"Then I show you first." Again, he smiled warmly at Phoebe's sister, who joined him in the front seat of the van in order to review the vehicle's basic operational functions. Shooting Phoebe's language theory to hell, Mr. Park and Emily seemed to understand each other perfectly. Or, at least, Phoebe could hear them giggling in there, as she stood helplessly in the corner studying a wildlife poster of two elephants linking trunks.

Five minutes later, Mr. Park exited the passenger seat and motioned for Phoebe to replace him, which she did. Then he pressed his thumb against a button on the wall that raised the door to the garage, sipping all the while at his seemingly bottomless soda. She could hear Wolfgang yapping and hissing in the background as they pulled out.

"I drive, I control the radio," Emily declared, before they'd even made it up the roller-coaster incline of Boulevard East, to the apex of the Palisades. (Phoebe had reached for the dial, only to have Emily slap away her hand.)

Already irked by her sister's power grab yet only too aware of her own compromised position—Emily, after all, could turn the car around at any moment—Phoebe told her, "Fine."

"So, where are we going?" Emily projected to be heard over the house music from Soweto.

"The Upper East Side, I thought," Phoebe shouted back.

Emily lowered the volume as they turned onto Anderson Avenue. "I mean, *where* on the Upper East Side? It's a big neighborhood."

"I don't know." Phoebe shrugged. "What about Sixty-fourth between Madison and Fifth? Isn't that where all the billionaires live?"

Emily laughed her ironic laugh. "As if I would know? In case you haven't noticed, my life doesn't exactly bring me in close contact with the moneyed set." Phoebe stopped herself from pointing out that, until further notice, she was married to a member of this group.

However, she did feel entitled to point out, "Well, it was your suggestion that we—"

"Are you trying to tell me I'm to blame for not knowing where Manhattan's billionaires live?" Emily shot back, with an accusatory glance in her sister's direction.

"No, but I think it's a little disingenuous of you to suddenly act like you have nothing to do with this plan," said Phoebe, "when it was actually your idea to—"

With a sudden jerk of the wheel, Emily yanked the van off the road and into the parking lot of an office supply and copying store, where she brought it to a full stop, then turned to her sister with laser-beam eyes, and asked, "Are you calling me a liar?"

"I said *in*genuous, not *dis*ingenuous," lied Phoebe, remembering the lesson she'd learned earlier in the day about the advantages of appeasement. "Hey, that's a really great color on you! It really picks up the blue in your eyes."

"Thank you," sniffed Emily, unable to keep from looking down at her sweater. Flattery might not get you far in life, but it propelled the Parks' EXCELLENT CAKE DREAM van back onto Anderson Avenue.

The sparring that took place later that evening over, first, a balloon chair with no seat ("Oh, look, a new toilet for you!")

Phoebe busted Emily), and then, a cracked mirror ("Too bad you had to look in it," Emily busted Phoebe) was in the spirit of roasting, not rancor. It was also, quite possibly, the best time the Fine sisters had had together since fitting Leonard into the stocks at Colonial Williamsburg in the late 1970s. And while the stated goal of their trip remained the accumulation of material goods, the one of doing the job without getting caught—by the police for illegal parking, but most of all by friends and acquaintances for engaging in socially unacceptable behavior—became the more immediate. "Quick!" was their mantra. For a while, they went unnoticed.

Then, since modern man (or woman) is fated to bump into the one person out of however many million to whom he (or she) most desperately owes a phone call, Phoebe found herself staring into the face of Lisa Renfrew on the corner of Lexington and 72nd, while pushing a wheelbarrow containing a shadeless boudoir lamp. In her beige pashmina scarf, Lisa looked like nothing so much as a giant wrap sandwich. Even so, Phoebe recoiled in shame at the sight of her, not merely because, after the third day of going unreturned, phone messages have a way of breeding excessive levels of guilt akin to infidelity and never-purchased wedding gifts, but because there could no longer be any mistaking Phoebe's current occupation.

To her continued surprise, however, Lisa greeted her far more warmly than, say, Mr. Park had, complete with the usual double-cheek air kisses. "Fabulous costume," she said, taking in Phoebe's boiler suit. "Where's the party?"

"It's actually not a costume," Phoebe began, determined to end the pattern of deception.

"Ohmigod, I'm such an idiot." Lisa bumped the fatty

part of her hand against her giant light-reflective forehead. "Halloween isn't for another two weeks, is it?"

"Well, no—"

"And that's from the new Helmut Lang collection."

"It's actually—"

"And they call me fashion features editor! Well, to my credit, I've been calling for the return of the jumpsuit for a whole decade now. In any case, you look fabulous, my dear, and I hope, someday, you can forgive me the gaffe. I'm really so mortified. By the way, I like the gardening gloves, too. Nice accessorizing." She sighed heavily. "I only wish you'd take over from Evil Arden." There was no mention of the wheelbarrow or the boudoir lamp with no shade.

Maybe there was something to be said for not telling everyone everything, Phoebe thought; maybe not everyone wanted to know. (Maybe Roberta's euphemisms had their merits, after all.) "Yeah, sure" was all Phoebe finally said.

"I'm serious!" cried Lisa.

"So where are you off to tonight?" asked Phoebe.

"Just a quick meeting with my breathing coach."

"Well, I won't keep you. I just want to say that I know I've been a terrible friend lately. And I—"

"Please, it's nothing," Lisa interrupted her, slapping at the air, as if it had been misbehaving. "You have a lot going on. How's your mother?"

"She's doing okay, actually," Phoebe told her. "Thanks for asking. How's Stephen?"

"Oh, he's fine." She shrugged. "I mean"—she paused, as if seeing the madness of it for the first time—"God, how should I fucking know? It's only been *seven years*!"

"Well, that's not *so* long."

"Not if you're a stalker. Listen, I really should run—before I forget how to breathe—but let's talk soon. Miss you. *Mwuh*." Lisa proffered another few air kisses, turned her back, and disappeared around the corner.

Uplifted by their meeting—maybe she had real friends, after all!—Phoebe deposited her wheelbarrow and its contents in the back of the van and then rejoined Emily in the front seat. "I just ran into my friend Lisa," she hesitated to tell her, recalling how, seemingly at every stage of her life, her sister had made it clear that she disapproved of Phoebe's friends.

"She looks like an ostrich," said Emily.

"She's sweet, actually."

"Speaking of old friends, whatever happened to that psycho roommate of yours from college, Holly something?"

"She married a preppy business guy named Chad and moved to Houston. We're not really friends anymore."

"People grow apart." Phoebe thought Emily might take the opportunity to riff on her separation from Jorge—in essence, to shed light on a heart that Phoebe had always imagined as being, if not more durable than her own, then certainly better known to its host body.

Unlike most women Phoebe knew, however, her sister had never been the confessional type. This night proved no exception. "So, where to next, Midget with the Ring Ding?" Emily asked next.

"Why don't we make a left on Lexington, and come back across Seventy-ninth?" Phoebe suggested.

No sooner did she exit the van than Phoebe found herself before her high school boyfriend-for-one-day.

"Phoebe Fine from Pringle Prep?" he said, his index finger in her face.

It took her a few seconds to figure out who it was. Then she died, came back to life as a friendly person, and exclaimed, "Ohmigod, Jason! How *are* you?"

He was still handsome enough, if in a prematurely middle-aged way, having grown out of his hairline just as he seemed, finally, to be growing *into* his nose. The dominant impression, however, had to do with money. In his pinstripe suit, violet dress shirt, and purple silk tie, there was no doubt in Phoebe's mind that Jason Barry Gold was making a killing somewhere, somehow. "Been worse," he said, nodding rhythmically, a half smile on his plump lips. Then he pointed at the bar stool in her arms. "You liked a strawberry daiquiri now and then—I remember that."

"Oh, right!" Phoebe chuckled with entirely performed amusement at the ancient Sweet Sixteen party reference, as she set the stool down on the sidewalk. Were she living in a lawless society, she might instead have chosen to bash the thing over his head. "So what are you doing these days?" she asked Jason Barry Gold.

"You know, a little management, a little consulting," he answered. "Been a tough year, with the dot-com crash and all. Otherwise, things are pretty good." He nodded some more.

Phoebe nodded back. That's when she noticed the wedding band. "Hey, remember how you and I were going to get married in fifteen years if we didn't meet anyone else?" She couldn't stop herself from reminding him.

Or from feeling betrayed—even though she would no

sooner have married Jason Barry Gold in his present incarnation than she would Vincent La Vroux.

"Oh, yeah, that's so funny," he said, throwing back his head. "Unfortunately—well, fortunately for me!—I met Dina."

"Dina. That's great!" said Phoebe, pretending not to be insulted by the insinuation that this new woman had saved him from a far worse fate—with her.

"And I got my first kid on the way."

"Wow, sounds like you got it made!" The bitterness was now oozing from each and every one of her pores. If there was one thing Phoebe resented about her generation, it was the smug pride with which they seemed to turn their backs on the rest of the world and retreat to the safe havens (and sanctimony) of their own young marriages. As if there was something so noble about reproducing the family unit. As if they all deserved medals. Or was shutting doors simply the only way to survive the cold? And, in a way, had she not done the very same thing by going home to Whitehead?

"So, what about you?" asked Jason.

"You know, drinking heavily. Taking the occasional magic carpet ride." Phoebe tugged on the hooked rug that lay draped over her left shoulder. And how was it that the world's most *random* sentences had always managed to exit her mouth in the company of this man? She laughed to mask her misery.

He laughed too—as if she were a danger not just to society but to herself. "Well, nice running into you," he said, slowly backing away.

"You, too!" Phoebe told him. "And good luck with the

wife and kid. I mean, when it's born, assuming it's born. I mean, not stillborn!" She laughed some more.

"Thank you." Jason's smile had turned suspicious, his voice sharp. He scampered off, breaking into a run as he reached the corner.

Phoebe could only hope that it would be another twelve years before they met again.

In the meantime, she and Emily covered a few more blocks, a few more piles. By midnight Tuesday the EXCELLENT CAKE DREAM van could be found rumbling back across the lower level (aka Martha) of the George Washington Bridge, in possession of the following undervalued treasures:

1. Two walnut bookcases
2. An oak bureau missing three out of its six wrought-iron knobs
3. A floral tub chair with some upholstering issues
4. Three broken Venetian blinds
5. A Persian rug
6. A kidney-shaped vanity table with a filthy lace skirt tacked to its bottom half
7. A stack of *Life* magazines from the early 1960s
8. An old backgammon set with an untold number of missing pieces
9. The aforementioned walnut balloon chair with no seat, wheelbarrow, shadeless boudoir lamp, hooked rug, and bar stool
10. A cease-fire on the sibling rivalry front

13

Ever since she was a small child, Phoebe had carried around with her the sound and image of a ticking clock. On the plus side, this meant that she was rarely late. On the negative side, it meant that she was forever being made aware of the paltry few minutes she had left on this planet in which (among other things) to feel guilty about all the time she'd wasted. If only you could occasionally put time on PAUSE, as you did a rental movie when you had to go to the bathroom, she sometimes thought. For Phoebe, sitting immobilized in a plane on the tarmac, unable either to get off or to go forward, was among the cruelest forms of punishment, second only to being trapped in an elevator.

As much as she hated wasting time, however, what really made Phoebe crazy was the collapse of her carefully made plans. At eleven minutes past ten on that Thursday morning, Leonard and Roberta had yet to depart for the hospital and Roget and his Rumanian appraiser friend were due to arrive in another four minutes (Emily wasn't due back from Rikers until two). "You're going to be late, Mom!" Phoebe kept telling her.

But Roberta didn't seem the slightest bit worried. (Phoebe couldn't really blame her.) "Late for the torture chamber," she said. "Big deal."

There was also the fact that, were Roget and company to ring the bell before Roberta had left, Phoebe would have to make up an excuse for their presence, thereby forcing her to confront the fact of her deception. And what if it turned out that her motives for going behind Roberta's back had as much to do with personal enrichment as with her mother's welfare?

"Well, you look pretty this morning!" Roberta paused at the door to admire—or was it eye suspiciously?—her daughter's made-up face.

"Oh, thanks," said Phoebe, for once in her life repelled by a compliment. It wasn't just that she feared being found out; her discomfort also had something to do with the recognition of her own continued ambition and striving for more than she already had. She liked to think that she had left those impulses behind in New York, but it wasn't true. Now she imagined herself as she must have looked from the inside out—all pumping blood and crackling synapses and quivering nerves—and wondered if nothing would quiet her but death itself. (Maybe the "d-word" wasn't such a detrimental force, after all.) "Only three visits left after today and then you're home free!" she called after her mother, trying to distract them both from weightier thoughts.

It wasn't clear if Roberta had heard or not; she was already out the door, headed for the mustard jar that Leonard had leased at Rent-a-Lemon in the wake of the Yugo theft. A minute later, Phoebe watched it shoot out of the driveway, trailing a column of fetid gray exhaust. Only then did she feel her breath returning, her body relaxing. Finally, she had the house all to herself.

The bell rang three minutes later, a minute earlier than scheduled. Her back straightening, Phoebe went to the door.

She found Roget rocking from one sneakered foot to the other. He looked different from the last time she'd seen him, his eyes darker, his body more robust, his beard beginning to grow in. She had forgotten how much color he had in his cheeks. "Wazzup?" he said, jiggling the change in his pocket.

"Nothing," she told him, realizing, just then, that he too was alone. "Where's your friend?"

"Georgiu? Overslept." He shrugged. "I dunno. Went by to pick him up, and there was no answer." He glanced nonchalantly at the Nathans' hedge and snapped his gum.

"So, after all that, he's not coming?" Phoebe felt her chest deflating like a pool raft at the end of summer. Not that Georgiu's failure to show up meant anything more than that she would have to wait for her answer about whether her mother's viola was an authentic da Salo. But that she could feel so disappointed about a mere delay made her realize how, in her suggestible mind, fantasies so often took on the quality of reality. She thought back to how, at Hoover, she'd kidded herself into thinking that she didn't care about whether or not she got into Tri Pi sorority; later, about whether Professor Bledstone loved her or was simply looking to get laid; still later, about whether her rock band got signed by a major recording label or not—only to experience each rejection as a terrible shock, a devastating blow.

"Sorry for the mix-up," offered Roget, sounding marginally more humble than usual.

"It's all right," said Phoebe, trying to be adult about it.

"By the way, are you going to invite me in, or do I have to stand outside talking to you all morning?"

"Oh, sorry." She stepped away from the door.

As usual, Roget made a bee line for the Fines' music room, where he ran his hand down Roberta's waterproofed viola case as if it were a favorite cat. "I know Georgiu was looking forward to seeing it," he said. Then, just like last time, and without asking permission, he unsnapped the locks and removed the instrument and bow, which he tightened with two flicks of his wrist and pulled across the viola's highest two strings in a spine tingling double-stop.

"Stop it!" cried Phoebe, her palms flattened over her ears.

Letting his bowing arm fall to his side, Roget walked over to the hi-fi and hit PLAY. "Wagner's *The Siegfried Idyll*," he announced, after listening to no more than five bars. "Maybe I'll play along." After he fit the instrument under his chin for a second time, Phoebe lunged for his bow, which she immobilized in his clasp. He lowered it with her hand still on it, then released his own, so the stick belonged to Phoebe alone. Then he laid the viola down on Roberta's practice chair and reached for Phoebe's face. He pushed the hair off her forehead and stared into her eyes; and she stared back, transfixed by his touch, and ran a finger down the length of his rosy cheek. Roget returned the favor by running his hands over the hump of her shoulders, down the side of her arms, and around the curvature of her waist and hips, concluding around her backside. "I've wanted to bang your brains out since the moment I saw you backstage," he told her in a throaty whisper, his usually muddy eyes illuminated like loose diamonds.

"How romantic," she whispered back, disappearing into his cold, soft lips. From that point onward, the strained history of their acquaintance ceased to matter, at least to Phoebe, for whom it was replaced by a flood of longing, the dramatic tension of which, after so many men, so many performances, so many curtains falling in her face before Act Three had ever been resolved, took her by surprise. So did the words that now emerged from her mouth: "Make love to me." Alas, there was a time when the very phrase—another euphemism, wasn't it?—had summed up for her all that was diseased and dishonest and therefore dangerous to literate society. Back then, she preferred conjugations of the f-word.

Back then, Phoebe had been on a campaign to rid the world of its niceties, of "You shouldn't have" and "My pleasure," and "Don't worry . . . flatter me . . . spend another moment's thought on the matter," and "That's great" and "I'm fine"—when she was so clearly anything but. (She had preferred "How much?" and "How could you?" and "Who cares?") She had seen things for what they were, and she didn't see the point in pretending otherwise. But now she did: Now she wanted to remove herself from everything she knew to be true, to disappear into Wagner's undulating violins and climaxing cellos, and to feel the *ka-boom, ka-boom* of Roget's beating heart beating against her own, so she could imagine, if only for one fleeting moment, that the music existed just for them.

Phoebe let him wrestle her down to Grandma Lettie's

hooked rug with the dancing apples. And there, like domestic cats reverting to jungle behavior in the too-long absence of their owners, they began to make good on her wishes, clawing and mauling each other until their flesh was an indistinguishable muddle. At some point mid-delirium, however unfortunately, Roget had the inspired idea of hoisting her into his lap so he could have her that way, as he seemed to want her every which way (and as she seemed to want to be had). Crouching, he grabbed her around the knees and lifted her into the air. But the celerity of his movements caught her off balance, and she fell toward him, then on him, knocking him backward, the two of them transformed into a ballistic missile in search of an enemy target.

They found one in Roberta's practice chair, which fell sideways and away from them, while Roberta's viola, which had been lying on its vinyl seat, landed directly beneath Roget's behind.

A terrible crunching sound was audible even over Siegfried.

Glancing down, Phoebe found herself naked except for a faded purple brassiere, and sprawled diagonally atop a man she wasn't sure she was even attracted to (it was hard in that moment to say), possibly because he was clad in nothing but a pair of knee-high tube socks with green stripes. As far as she could tell, neither of them was injured. But what about her mother's viola? After sliding her thigh off Roget's face, then Roget off the instrument, Phoebe inspected the damage. The viola's upper sphere and scroll seemed to be in respectable shape. However, the bridge and tailpiece had punctured the soundboard, leaving behind a gaping hole in the viola's lower half.

"Looks like we're going to the Bronx after all," said Roget, reaching for his pants.

No longer able to come up with an argument against it—and too aghast to speak, anyway—Phoebe began to dress as well.

Georgiu Ceausescu (no known relation to the late Communist dictator of Romania) oversaw his fiefdom from a desolate street hidden between the Third and Willis Avenue bridges, on the South Bronx side of the East River. It contained a car wash, a couple of body shops, and numerous semiabandoned warehouses and tenement buildings. Georgiu's instrument dealership was based in a two-story brick garage toward the southern end of the block. Roget parked his Corvette out front, and he and Phoebe got out, Phoebe clutching her mother's viola to her breast as if nursing a baby.

The sign on the front door read CEAUSESCU FINE VIOLINS. As Roget pushed the buzzer, Phoebe looked around her in bewilderment that a dealer in rare and valuable instruments would be located on a block like this. The buildings were covered with graffiti. The sidewalk was awash in the remnants of long-forgotten fast-food dinners. Although it was the middle of the day, there was no sign of human life. What's more, the din from the two bridges and the two major highways on either side of them—the Major Deegan and the Harlem River Drive—was deafening. Judging from a set of dappled yellow curtains in the second-floor window of Georgiu's garage, however, it was a live/work situation.

On the first floor, there was a bay window hung with a

cheap plastic blind. Just then, Phoebe saw an aging finger pull back one of the slats. Vermiculated white hair projected out of the joint. About twenty seconds later, the finger's owner pulled open the door, if only to the extent allowed by the safety chain. A great honker of a nose appeared, then retreated from the resulting air column. "Geo, it's me," Roget called out.

Finally the door opened fully, revealing Geo in his entirety. He was dressed in a white butcher's apron stained brown. His narrow face was totally dominated by his nose, which was so long and bulbous that his eyes, which were tiny and squinty and set back in his head, seemed more like ornaments than organs, as in the overhangs of the letter *T*. The fifty silver hairs left on his dome had been combed up and backward in a way that suggested what, in heartier days, may well have been a pompadour. The decrepitude factor aside, there was a masculine energy about the man that spoke of seductions and betrayals enacted over fried pork lunches at art deco cafés, in Velvet Revolution–era Bucharest. "Ah, my morning expedition conveniently arrived for lunch," he began, in a Central European accent as thick as cornmeal.

"Yeah, thanks for answering the frigging door this morning when I came by!" Roget pushed past him into his shop, his coat already off.

Phoebe hovered in the doorway, her confidence flagging as she took in her surroundings. In fact, it was a total sty in there. Sawdust, wood chips, and scraps of newspaper littered the floor. On one wall, hanging from hooks, were every imaginable size of pliers and chain saws. On another wall, there was a long metal rack with a series of disassembled instruments dangling off it, like carcasses drying in a meat locker. Extended across the ceiling was a fish wire strung with hundreds of violin bridges. In the middle of the room, on a giant worktable, a cello back lay saddled with a half dozen clamps. The instrument was surrounded by several years' accumulation of junk mail, concert programs, and potato-chip bags. In the far corner there was an ancient gas furnace, which had yet to be turned on. Georgiu's luthier diploma from Mittenwald, Germany—the Harvard of instrument-making schools—was prominently displayed on the wall above it, next to a reproduction of the famously smutty Man Ray photograph of a naked woman with S-holes drawn on both sides of her hourglass-shaped back.

The place reeked, too. Phoebe couldn't make out the precise smell, but it resonated with traces of wood glue, resin, tobacco smoke, and stale tuna fish.

"I must have been in the middle of a beautiful dream," said Georgiu, catching sight of Phoebe for the first time.

"Hi," she said, hoping he'd wake up soon.

"Yeah, well, time to rise and shine," Roget told him. "We got an emergency on our hands." He tossed his coat over a dusty double-bass case.

"Could it be of such a dire nature that there remains no time to introduce me to the lovely lady?" asked Georgiu, his reptilian eyes flickering with unrepentant lust.

"This is the chick with the viola I was telling you about." Roget motioned with his chin. "Phoebe—Georgiu. Georgiu—Phoebe. And keep your dirty paws off her!" He pointed an admonishing finger in Georgiu's direction.

Phoebe rolled her eyes at this display of bravado, though

it was mostly just for show. In truth, she had always been far less concerned about male possessiveness than she had been about the absence of it. In certain respects, she had yet to recover fully from Professor Bledstone's failure, a decade earlier, to express even a modicum of jealousy at her announcement that she'd slept with an aspiring Hegelian from Massapequa. (He'd told her, "Well, that sounds fun.")

Meanwhile, blatantly ignoring Roget's directive, and with the sinewy limbs of a ballet dancer, Georgiu bent over Phoebe's hand and pressed his clammy lips to the back of it.

After he'd kept them there for a second longer than he needed to, Roget wailed, "Georgiu, what did I tell you?"

"I am but introducing myself!" he cried, in his own defense, as he backed away, hands raised.

"Yeah, sure." Roget turned to Phoebe. "Georgiu's a talented luthier. Unfortunately, he's also a grade-A lech."

"Ah, but you underestimate me," he demurred, with a self-satisfied smile. "A lech is one whose libido finds fulfillment in looking and pestering. A lover, on the other hand, is one who extends to women the gift of his passions." Again, he gazed hungrily at Phoebe.

"Spare me the crap, Geo. No one wants to make love to that old leather suitcase of yours anymore!" Roget informed him.

"That's your opinion." Georgiu harrumphed, with an elevated neck that lent his Adam's apple the distended appearance of a softball. "There are others with differing points of view." He nodded slowly at Phoebe. "In any event, it is a pleasure to make your acquaintance, mademoiselle."

"Nice to meet you too," she mumbled back at him, wishing she could go wash her hands.

"And what type of favor may I assist you with today?"

"I was hoping you could fix this," Phoebe told him, her voice cracking as she handed him the case—and recalled her reason for being there.

"Now, now, let's see what the damage is before we start crying over spelt melk," said Georgiu, laying the case down on his worktable. He flicked open its locks and lifted the instrument up and over his head, the better to inspect it in an exposed bulb at the end of a twisted wire attached to a ceiling fan missing one of its three propellers. Then, frowning like a sad clown, he stuck his giant nose down the offending hole. Finally, he flipped over what was left of the instrument. "An attractive-looking back," he murmured, a mischievous glint in his eye suggesting that he was done with his favorite-uncle routine. "Of course, a back doesn't do much good without a front."

"Geo, I'm warning you!" cried Roget, taking a step toward him.

"Fine, fine!" Again, Georgiu lifted his palms into the air. "The reconstruction will take at least six months, possibly more."

"Six months!" croaked Phoebe, realizing for the first time that there was no way she could keep the accident a secret from her mother.

"It's got a da Salo ticket under there somewhere," added Roget.

"And perhaps one for the New York Knicks," Georgiu sniffed. "Well, my children, I will do my best!"

"Do you need some kind of down payment?" asked Phoebe, anxious to get the process started.

"We are all friends, no? And some of us, perhaps, more

than friends?" His eyes traveled from Roget to Phoebe and back again, accompanied by a sleazy smile. "Besides, we will be billing the insurance gods. Yes?"

"I should probably get back to you about that." She wasn't even sure if Roberta *had* insurance!

"Alternatively, mademoiselle might simply get *on* her back," suggested the luthier.

Fists raised, Roget lunged for Georgiu's throat.

"Roget—stop! It's fine!" said Phoebe, trying to wedge herself between the two men. She was far more upset about her mother than she was about some horny old violin maker making a ridiculous pass at her.

"Forgive me, I am helpless before the female sex!" Georgiu squealed as Roget rode him piggyback across the room, nearly knocking over the double-bass case on which Roget's jacket lay draped. (It swung to and fro.) No sooner had he been released from between Roget's knees, however, than the appraiser straightened his apron and announced, "I'll be billing in the vicinity of twenty thousand dollars, possibly more. It is of no great interest to me who writes the check, so long as the check gets written."

Phoebe thought back to a time when she still believed in wizards, fairies, and superheroes—figures who, with a touch of a scythe or a wand or a net, could make all the problems in the world go away. Just as to look at Georgiu now was to realize that you were on your own in life pretty much from start to finish. Though, on occasion, you might come across a willing accomplice.

The price was usually steep.

And were Georgiu's numbers even to be trusted? The degree from Mittenwald was some comfort. But what did she really know about this man beyond Roget's recommendation? Would it make sense to come clean with her mother first and ask *her* to recommend a repairman? "Do you have a card or something?" Phoebe asked him, suddenly in doubt as to whether she should even leave the viola with him.

With a protracted sigh, as if the very asking were an imposition, Georgiu reached into the drawer beneath his worktable and methodically removed two staplers, six plastic forks, a pair of scissors, and a hundred-odd unsharpened pencils wrapped in rubber bands. After laboriously folding back his cuff, he extended the full length of his bare forearm into the opening; he emerged five seconds later with an ink-stained square of card stock that he handed over to Phoebe with a burp.

GEORGIU CEAUSESCU—VIOLINS, VIOLAS, CELLOS—BOUGHT, SOLD, AND REPAIRED, it read. There was a phone number listed but no address. It wasn't hard to see why.

At the same time, she wondered, was it even possible to live without trusting strangers? And didn't we all start out that way?

"Well, I guess that's it for now," said Roget, dusting off his jacket and heading for the door. "We'll be in touch. Thanks for everything, man. Oh, and I got the name of that hematologist at Mount Sinai if you need it."

"If I don't bleed to death first," Georgiu muttered, from the metal stool on which he now sat slumped, his head hanging over his worktable like a potato attached to a stick. "Good-bye, young people in love."

Could that really be the way it looked? And if it *looked*

that way, might it *be* that way? Or were appearances every bit as deceiving as Phoebe had convinced herself they were—even the appearance of love?

And should men of Transylvanian descent beset with blood disorders be considered innocent until proven guilty? Mulling over his parting words, Phoebe thanked Georgiu for his help and followed Roget back out to the street.

In the twenty-odd minutes they had been inside, the clouds had coalesced into an impenetrable fortress of gray. The wind had picked up, too. It lifted the French fry and hot-dog pockets into the air, where they twirled like flamenco dancers.

Back in the Corvette, Roget flipped on the radio, which was tuned to the same classical station that Roberta and Leonard listened to at home. The mighty theme of Beethoven's *Ode to Joy,* from his *Ninth Symphony,* soon filled the car, making Phoebe feel as if their lives were significant in some way she hadn't realized until now. Roget must have felt it, too. As they turned north in the direction of New Jersey, he shot a bluff glance in her direction, and said, "So anyway, back to an earlier topic. I'd be interested in continuing where we left off this morning—before the accident, that is."

"Thanks for letting me know," she quipped sarcastically. It seemed sacrilegious even to be *thinking* about pleasure at a time like this!

Except her thoughts kept returning to the possibility of it, and to the possibility that Roget wasn't such a bad guy after all. At the very least, he seemed to spend a lot of time connecting his friends to people who stood to help them, whether they were doctors, piano tuners, or overweight tenors—to cheer up the grandmother of the Unibrow at the pizza ristorante that night—never mind stringed-instrument dealers, repairers, and appraisers. And why was it that the most hopeful times always coincided with the most harrowing ones, so that you never got to wallow in either one completely?

The sky had begun to shed fat droplets of water like a leaky faucet; now they splattered on the windshield like ink blots. For the next fifteen minutes, Phoebe and Roget sat without speaking. "You need to follow the signs for Route Four," she told him on the bridge, trying to be helpful, as the high-rises of Fort Lee began to take shape through the glass.

But he only laughed. "What, you think I don't know how to get to Whitehead? I only frigging grew up there!"

"You what?" said Phoebe, her hand flying to the volume control, which she promptly turned down to zero.

"I said, I only grew up there," Roget said again. "On the other hand, whether I ever actually grew up is a point of debate. Though it's a medical fact that, at a certain point along the way, my balls *did* drop." He puffed out his chest and smiled broadly.

But Phoebe was too preoccupied with his earlier statement to find his last one amusing or distasteful. "Would you please tell me what you're talking about?" she demanded to know.

"You mean about my balls or my upbringing?" he asked.

"Your upbringing."

"I said I grew up in Whitehead. Which isn't technically true, since I was only there for a few years."

"But why didn't you tell me before?" That Phoebe had

plenty of her own secrets seemed beside the point; that Roget had kept such an elemental one from her struck her as somehow unforgivable.

"I guess it just never came up before." He shrugged. "To be honest, I'm not really the sentimental type. I mean, I'm not the same person I was then, so what does it matter where I lived? I don't even have the same name."

"You don't what?"

"I had it legally changed when I was eighteen."

She couldn't help herself. "You willingly renamed yourself after a thesaurus?"

"Yeah, I got a lot of synonyms," Roget replied. "Among them: *handsome, cool, virile, dashing,* and *debonair.* Jean-Pierre was just too sissy for me."

"You went from Jean-Pierre to Roget?" Phoebe asked in disbelief.

"I'm kidding," he said. "It was actually Roger."

"And what about your last name, *Roger*?"

"It used to be Mancuso. Hey, I'm a total fraud, I admit it! But that's just the business I'm in. Some people think we just stand up there and wave our hands around. They have a point, of course. But if you're going to be a successful conductor, you can't have the name of a petty Mafioso. You gotta sound exotic. Think Kurt Masur, Seiji Ozawa, Herbert von Karajan. Besides, there's a precedent for my name change. Ever heard of Leopold Stokowski, the old conductor of the Philadelphia Orchestra? The man began life as *Leo Stokes.* And Erich Leinsdorf of Boston Symphony fame? Born with the last name *Blau.* Sounds like Yiddish for *boink.*" His chest shook as he chortled. "Then there's that famous cellist chic, Zara Nelsova, who began life as—check this out—*Sara Nel-*

son. Sounds like a frigging cake company or something. I mean, can you blame the dame? The conductor formerly known as Roger Mancuso yawned loudly as he merged onto Route 4. "Anyway—yikes, this has been a tiring morning!— the profession has a lot of crossover with Hollywood. Or so I like to think."

Phoebe couldn't believe what she was hearing. Or seeing, suddenly, as if for the first time. Except, it wasn't; she would know those bug eyes anywhere. A moment of silence passed between them before she found the wherewithal to repeat his real name. "Roger Mancuso," she began in a shaky voice. "As in Roger Mancuso, the Stink Bomb King of Whitehead Middle School?"

"Jesus!" he said. "How'd you know I used to set off stink bombs? God, I was a real troublemaker growing up." He shook his head.

"I was in your class," Phoebe told him quietly, too stunned for theatrics.

"You're kidding," he went on. "Wow, that's a really weird coincidence. Well, I don't remember you, so I guess we didn't know each other very well. As I was saying, I was only there for a few years. Then, it was on to the next place. Life of an orphan. Know what I mean?"

"Do I know what you mean?" she asked, her breathing becoming strained. "We only *went out*! I mean, practically."

"Oh, yeah?" he said.

"Yeah. We went roller-skating together at the recreation center, and then afterward we went out back to the Veterans' Memorial statue and kissed, and you asked me if I wanted to be your girlfriend."

"Wow, some things never change!" declared Roger/Roget. "Though I can't say any of it rings a bell."

"But you used to circle me with your mountain bike on my way to my violin teacher's house after school!" said Phoebe, her tone turning from plaintive to pleading. "How can you not remember?"

"I'm sorry."

"And you were always trying to get me to play 'The Devil Went Down to Georgia' on the violin. And then, one day, you showed up at my house after school, and we went in the backyard and lay in the hammock and"—the thought of it further amazed and confused her—"you told me you wanted to change your name to Keith Richards."

"That's right, I was really into the Stones back then," he said, nodding slowly. "Hey, wait. Did we go to some Sadie Hawkins dance together? Was that you?"

"I don't remember any Sadie Hawkins dance," she muttered inconsolably. That he could mistake her for another woman, even another ten-year-old woman! "Do you even remember Mrs. K?"

"Mrs. who?"

"Our fifth-grade homeroom teacher who made us memorize the dictionary. She was really old, and she was always out sick. And one day, we had that crazy sub with the plaid pants and you set off that stink bomb and got suspended."

"I could have sworn that happened in New Rochelle."

"No, it happened in Whitehead!" Phoebe was nearly screaming now.

Meanwhile, a smile of bemused pity crossed Roger/Roget's face. "I'm sorry to tell you, Phoebe," he told her, while merging into the exit lane for Whitehead, "but I think you have the wrong guy."

"But I don't have the wrong guy!" she cried, her sense of betrayal now verging on epic. Here she had recorded Roger "Stinky" Mancuso's abrupt disappearance from her life and town at the age of ten as not merely a defining moment but as her first encounter with romantic loss. Just as she had spent the subsequent twenty years wondering *what if*, his peanut-shaped face framing the chaos in the manner of the North, East, South, and West putti who once decorated Renaissance maps.

It turned out that the events that had seared a hole through her stomach had failed even to register in his universe. "After your grandmother died, you went to live with your uncle in New Rochelle. I read it in the local paper," she continued, determined to honor her memories.

But at this revelation, his eyes expanded to the size of half-dollars and he laughed. "God, you must have been, like, obsessed with me. I mean, you seem to know even more about my life than I do. What, d'you hire a private detective or something?"

The question wounded her. In fact, Phoebe hated Roger/Roget more in that second than she could ever remember hating anyone. She had grown accustomed to regarding her childhood as the first and last time that her emotional responses had been authentic, and here he'd made her feel like Lisa Renfrew on the subject of Stephen! But she hated herself even more; she felt suddenly foolish and pathetic for even remembering Roger/Roget's name. Other people seemed to forgive and forget, especially what happened in fifth grade: Why couldn't she do the same? "I have one of those scary memories. I mean, I remember everything," she mumbled, ashamed and embarrassed and doubtful that he would even want to be with her now. Even so, she couldn't stop herself from adding, "For the record, after you asked me if I wanted to go out with you, I told you that I'd let you know on Monday. And you left town before I ever got to give you my answer. And you didn't say good-bye either." Then she looked up, hungry for any shard of solace or contrition he had to offer her.

"Jeez, sorry." Roger/Roget laughed some more, but this time as if things were more sad than funny. "If it makes you feel any better, I probably didn't even know I was moving. No one told me anything back then. One second I was here, and the next second I wasn't." He elbowed her in the side and raised one eyebrow. "In any case, I assume the answer was *yes*?" How many years, how many times, Phoebe had pictured this day, this confrontation!

"I can't remember," she lied. In all her dreams, it had never occurred to her that the perpetrator would have no defense to offer.

For a few minutes, they drove in silence. Phoebe couldn't of anything else to say. Neither, apparently, could Roger—until Beachmont Avenue, when he turned to her again and asked, "Wait, did your mother play the violin back then?"

Phoebe's lungs filled with fresh air; color returned to her cheeks. In fact, he had made a similar mistake twenty years earlier—mistaking Roberta's viola for what he had then termed a "big violin." And yet, like all of life's great ironies, it seemed less ironic upon review than it did inevitable. "No, but you *mistook* it for a violin," she told him excitedly. "And then you tried to play it, and I showed you how. But you lost interest pretty quickly and wanted to play air guitar."

"Yeah, I think I might remember that." He nodded faster than before.

If it wasn't quite an admission of fond memories, it was enough to convince Phoebe that history still mattered, and we weren't all strangers to the end, after all. And she cried, "I didn't think I'd ever see you again!"

"Well, here I am," said Roger/Roget, rounding the corner of Douglass Street. "And here I go, I guess. Hey, fun morning! I mean, until the accident. Oh and by the way, do me a favor and don't spread that stuff around about my humble beginnings. I have a reputation to maintain, even with your profligate father. Also, don't take it personally that I didn't remember you. At a certain point, I just kind of blocked out everything that happened to me before the age of twenty-five. Didn't see the point of dwelling. Gotta keep moving forward, even if you end up in the same place, just like the earth does every three hundred sixty-five days."

Phoebe had Roger/Roget stop his car a house away, so as to avoid any questions that their being seen together might provoke. "Well, I guess I'll talk to you soon," she said, before she slammed the door shut. Now, as she made her way up the sidewalk she had once scrupulously vetted for cracks—"Step on a crack; break your mother's back," went the saying—she wondered if it weren't time she left her *own* past behind, not just her Stink Bomb King but her pit bull, Alex, and her nice guy, Neil, and her pretty boy bartender, Bo, and her artists and her anarchists and her East German pen pal whom she waited two years to write back, and her critical theorist, and her cabbies, and her cocky assholes, and her con man. (Maybe she could forget Arnold Allen's greasy hands, after all.)

Pausing in front of her house, she watched Roger/Roget's Corvette slow to a crawl as he neared the corner, whereupon the passenger door appeared to swing open, suggesting that she hadn't slammed it, after all. Memories, even recent memories, it seemed, could be deceptive—contrived and embellished after the fact to represent not only what we meant to do but what we wish we had done, insofar as having done it better helps us justify what we failed to do afterward. Which meant that it was impossible to say for sure what had really happened between her and Roger Mancuso in fifth grade anyway—or maybe even in the music room, earlier that day.

14

Phoebe found Leonard standing over the kitchen sink, knife in hand, paring one of his oboe reeds. Every oboist has his own preference in terms of dimensions; Leonard liked them long and fluted. "Hey, Dad," she said, as if it were just another day in the week. How inconsistent time could be that way! So many hours came and went without anything to remember them by, while others seemed to encompass a lifetime's worth of raw emotion and significant events.

"Hello, apple pumpkin cake," he muttered, without looking up.

"How'd Mom do this morning?"

"Fine enough. She's upstairs resting. Been out with your little friends?"

"They're not so little anymore," Phoebe told him, wondering why she even bothered trying to dispel the myth of her agelessness. "But yeah—just out for a coffee."

"That sounds nice."

By all appearances, and to her immense relief, the absence of her mother's viola had so far gone unnoted.

Phoebe walked over to the kitchen table, where the classified-ad section sat open to the used-car page. "You're not going to buy another Yugo, are you?" she asked her father, mostly for the purposes of turning the conversation away from herself—another first in her life.

"We haven't decided yet," he replied, lifting his hand-fashioned reed to his mouth and testing its airflow. "When Mom is feeling better, I thought we might drive out to Gasoline Alley, on Route Forty-six, and take a look at the *carros barratos,* as they're known in those parts."

"Aren't those the kind of places that prey on poor immigrants?" said Phoebe.

"Well, let's not condescend to the poor now," Leonard snapped back at her, in a tone of voice as prickly as it was prosaic, and it made Phoebe question the regard in which she was accustomed to holding her father. Indeed, his outer demeanor was so blithe that she often imagined him to be a neutral force in her family, innocent by nature of his impishness, less a grown man who had lived through the usual panoply of hard truths than a clueless child who was still oblivious to the existence of evil. Because of it, there were times when her love for him felt almost maternal in nature. (Sometimes, Phoebe loved him so much her heart physically ached at the thought of his orangutan gait.)

And yet, there was a way in which Leonard could be just as harsh in his judgments as Roberta or Emily was, the main difference being his approach. Where Phoebe's mother changed the subject, and Emily thrust her points down everyone's throats, her father cloaked his barbs in jocularity. The older Phoebe grew, however, the more it seemed to her that Roberta's standoffishness was the most preferable of the three approaches; in the end, it seemed most honest about the ways of the world and the land mines that lurk at every crossing. But rather than call Leonard on his critical streak just then, Phoebe decided to let it go. It didn't seem like the right time to be causing trouble; there was already enough of it in the house.

In time, Leonard wandered off to try his new reeds on his oboe, and Emily wandered in, returned from Rikers and apparently en route to yoga, her skin aglow, her hair up, her body just about perfect, except where it wasn't. Even so, the same distortions, the same pangs of envy and inadequacy welled up inside Phoebe, and she found herself unable to stop staring and comparing. That wealth should be distributed so unequally in the world! Not just in terms of beauty, but in terms of poverty, health, sheer luck! Americans were always going on about *freedom* and *liberty*. Why wasn't *equality* just as important?

And what if, instead of being jealous and competitive all the time, interspersed by flare-ups of self-interested flattery, Phoebe decided simply to be proud to be related to Emily? It followed that, rather than constantly deride her sister's talents, she might use them to her advantage—in particular, her experience in conflict resolution. "Can I talk to you for a few minutes?" she found herself asking. "I need your advice about something."

A short while later, on the same screened porch where Phoebe had gone to sulk on the night that Roget came to dinner, she regaled her sister with the story of her morning, give or take a few details, such as the facts that (a) their former dinner guest was actually Roger Mancuso from Whitehead Middle School and (b) she and Roger/Roget had sex in the music room earlier that day. (*Making out* was the phrase she opted for, modesty—in this particular case—trumping her desire for revenge.)

Even so, and to Phoebe's surprise, Emily visibly flinched at the news of her and Roger/Roget's romantic coming together. "I thought you hated him," she shot back.

"Well, I do," Phoebe assured her. "I mean, sort of."

"And you were *making out*?" Emily raised one expertly plucked eyebrow, reverting to the role of experienced litigator trained to sniff out inconsistencies in the narrative. "That's not an activity that's generally associated with knocking over furniture and damaging fine musical instruments."

"Well, we were doing a little more than making out," conceded Phoebe, caught and now squirming in her lies.

"Well, if you're planning on telling Mom you destroyed her viola, I suggest you come up with a more convincing explanation for how it happened than 'It just fell off the bookcase.' "

"But it did just fall off! I mean, sort of."

"Then how come you're blushing?"

"I'm not!"

"I guess it depends what's more important to you"—Emily sighed—"telling the correct version of the story or the version that's least likely to piss off Mom."

"Well, what else could I say happened?" asked Phoebe, cringing at the sound of her own question.

"I don't know—dizzy spell, seizure, earthquake, meteor shower, mental retardation."

"Ha-ha."

A hint of a smile flashed across Emily's face. "Of course, you could always blame the whole thing on your friend Roget. For instance, you could tell Mom that since you wouldn't let him take her viola out of the house, he devised an elaborate plan by which you'd be forced to do exactly that." Her smile grew wider. "Who knows? Maybe it's not actually that far from the truth."

"What are you trying to imply?" said Phoebe, her heart throbbing in her throat at this startling new reading of events: Could Roger/Roget really have planned the accident?

"Only that in life people find ways of achieving what they need," replied Emily.

"But I was the one who fell on him!"

"I thought you said it fell by itself."

Phoebe opened her mouth—to speak, to explain—but nothing came out.

"You know," Emily went on in a breezy tone, "Dad once told me that instrument dealers award a finder's fee to the middlemen who bring them the instruments they refurbish for resale."

"Georgiu was going to come anyway. . . ." Phoebe trailed off, her conviction disappearing as she realized that he hadn't come.

"How do you know?" asked Emily, fueling Phoebe's suspicions. "That's what Roget *says*. Frankly, I've never heard of a dealer making house calls before." And what if it *had* been greed, not lust, motivating Roger/Roget's amorous advances that morning? The thought of it—of her body being a mere vehicle in his quest for material wealth—made Phoebe feel filthy and used.

But, then, had she not ordered her own priorities in precisely this way (with lucre first and love a distant second)? If so, why should she have expected any more or less from Roger/Roget? Maybe they were both guilty of the same heinous crime. Or should she consider her reprioritization of money over men a positive development in her life?

"Anyway, if I were you, I'd think of something to tell Mom sooner rather than later," Emily concluded. "By which I mean, before she wanders into the music room and finds her viola missing. Which will probably be in the next few hours—assuming the radiologists didn't nuke her this time."

Phoebe left her sister convinced of the need for immediate action—if only she knew what to do! Feeling as if each of her legs weighed a thousand pounds, she started up the stairs to her parents' bedroom.

She found Roberta sitting up in bed, with the shades drawn and her wig off, gazing through the artificial dusk at the Audubon print of three western warblers that hung over her antique Singer sewing machine. She had never sewed a single hem on it, her relationship to distaff and the domestic arts always having been more about appearances than actuality. There was no soft music playing in the background, as there usually was—no Bach or Berlioz to add gravitas to her pain. "I'm dying, Bebe," she announced, just like that.

It was such an un-Roberta-like thing to say in its unassailable negativity that Phoebe fell speechless. Then she looked up at her mother, at her bald head, and wondered when she had become somebody else. She didn't even look completely human anymore—more like a space alien or a very old baby. The strangeness of the sight contributed to a growing feeling inside Phoebe that life had raced on ahead when she hadn't been looking. And now it was too late; the train had already left for the next station, stranding her on the platform, powerless to bring it back. "Why are you saying that?" was the best she finally came up with, and she added in a similarly badgering tone, "What did the doctor say?"

"That I should enjoy life," replied Roberta. "Which is medical speak, if I've ever heard it, for *Your days are numbered, pal.*"

"But you don't know that!" Phoebe protested. "Maybe he really meant it. Not everything everyone says is a euphemism. I mean, sometimes an expression is just an expression—"

"Expression, my ass."

"Mom, your language!"

"They can wash my mouth out with soap when I'm in the funeral parlor."

"Mom, *please*!"

"Please, what?" asked Roberta. It was becoming increasingly clear to Phoebe that the woman currently occupying her mother's bed was not the same one who had raised her.

"You're not going to any funeral parlor," Phoebe told her. "I mean, not anytime soon."

"You don't have to lie to make me feel better, Bebe."

Roberta's declaration both startled Phoebe and had the immediate if unintended effect of empowering her to tell her own tale of woe. "I know I don't have to," she began, "and that's why I'm about to tell you what I'm about to tell you"— she took a deep breath—"which is that, when Roget Mankuvsky came over for dinner a few weeks ago, he thought your viola might be worth more than—"

But Roberta cut her off with "What does this have to do with anything?"

"It—" Phoebe stopped herself, realizing, suddenly, that she had done the very thing to her mother that she was always complaining about her mother doing to her—namely, changing the topic rather than dealing with the unpleasantness at hand. "I'm sorry for interrupting you," she mumbled instead.

"Well, now that you've started, you might as well finish," Roberta came back at her.

Shamed, Phoebe said nothing.

"Fine, we'll talk about me. Tell me this. Have you ever seen an uglier mother?"

It was an impossible question to answer, and Phoebe paused before deciding on "Yes."

"Well, you must have seen a lot of mothers then," said Roberta.

"But I only have one."

Now it was Roberta who fell silent, her bony knuckles stabbing at the corners of her eyes. Had Phoebe finally found the right words—words not just to distract but to comfort? Or had she only succeeded in upsetting her mother more? Phoebe's heart beat violently as she awaited Roberta's response. "For better and for worse, I suppose," she eventually answered in a trembling voice. "Well, I've tried to be a good role model for you and Emily."

"And you have been!" said Phoebe.

"You're nice to say so. But sometimes—well, I fear I made both of you too ambitious for your own good and didn't teach you to enjoy life enough, especially while you're young and healthy."

"Enjoy life enough?" Phoebe cried incredulously. "I thought you were disappointed I hadn't grown up to become the next Midori!"

"Midori?" Roberta sneered. "Hardly. The woman has more problems than Bangladesh. Now, what is this about my viola?"

Her own eyes now threatening to explode both with joy and with apprehension, Phoebe took another deep breath and told her, "Roget thought it might be a genuine Gasparo da Salo, and—"

But, again, Roberta interrupted her in mid-sentence. "Please," she scoffed. "There are only about a dozen da Salo violas left in the world, and they're all accounted for, with the possible exception of the Cardinal Aldobrandini viola, which has a mermaid carved into the scroll."

The news hit Phoebe like a lightning bolt. What if in addition to wanting to make a buck off her, and knowing full well that the provenance was an impossibility, Roger/Roget had dropped the da Salo name simply to excite her into submission? It would make him not just opportunistic but crooked. And how was it that she allowed herself to be taken in, over and over again? Had she learned nothing in thirty years? Was she still so vain and needy and greedy that any show of attention was enough for her to prostrate herself? (Phoebe had the weakness of believing absolutely the last person to whom she'd spoken.) Little wonder that when she got to the part of the story where she and Roger/Roget tore off each other's clothing, she found herself explaining, "And then Roget started fooling around with your viola. I don't know what he was thinking, but he was sort of throwing it up in the air and trying to catch it.

"But if you're going to be mad at anyone, you should be mad at me, since I'm the one who gave him access to it. And I'm committed to paying you back the full cost of the repair, or whatever your insurer doesn't cover—for however long it takes me," Phoebe added—a bit disingenuously, it should be said, since she must have known that Roberta would blame Roger/Roget absolutely. Or maybe that was the point. Convinced now of his innate malevolence, Phoebe was as keen to tar his name as she was to avoid her mother's wrath.

"My viola" was Roberta's initial response. She said it in a near whisper, her eyes as distant as the northern lights, while Phoebe stood there, waiting for Steinway/Yahweh to strike her down (and her mother's tears to flow). "Well, this is certainly unexpected news," she continued in an unexpectedly stolid voice. "Of course, I could tell you that my life was over. Well, it may be over soon. In the meantime, and in case you haven't noticed, your old mother hasn't exactly been getting much use out of her strings lately. And I can't say for sure if or when that situation is likely to change. They may be tightening the screws on me before I get the chance to tighten another bow!" A not entirely unhappy-looking smile passed across her thin lips. Was it possible, Phoebe wondered, that she was actually relieved to be spared the pressure of her viola sitting dormant, day after day, waiting for a player who almost never appeared?

Phoebe might have been relieved as well, but Roberta's failure to express greater alarm over the demise of her for-

merly beloved instrument had the unexpected effect of further traumatizing her. She saw it as final proof that her mother
had abandoned her. Who was this "other woman" who no
longer needed to drown out all the problems of the world
(and most of her own, as well) with beautiful music? It was in
Phoebe's eyes that tears stockpiled and then burst forth.
"Don't say that, Mom!" she wept, her voice splintering like a
windshield after a head-on collision with a deer. "You'll play
again!" That she didn't necessarily believe what she was saying seemed beside the point. Since escaping the clutches of
Jackie Yee, Phoebe had come to believe that delusion had its
benefits, after all.

It was Roberta who was refusing now to play along.
"That remains to be seen," she said, sliding herself farther
down the bed, whereupon she began to kick. "Jesus and
Mary—Dad tucks these sheets in so tightly I feel like I'm in
prison! Of course, certain members of this family who shall
go unnamed prefer to spend their time locked up, especially
on small islands in the East River. But not I."

"I love you, Mom," Phoebe told her, straining this time
for words to comfort herself as much as her mother, as she
helped yank the bottom sheet out from beneath the mattress.

"I love you too," Roberta mouthed into her pillow.
"Though your choice of men over the years has really stunk."

"I know, it's true," said Phoebe, her sobs multiplying as
she closed the door behind her. "I only date assholes."

"Your language, Be!" she could have sworn she heard her
mother call after her, but maybe it was only wishful thinking.

Phoebe's outrage at Roger/Roget's deceitful ways and determination never to speak to him again lasted through dinner. Toward bedtime, however, she found herself dialing his number, albeit with the ostensible aim of hurling vitriol at him. But there was also clearly a part of Phoebe that wanted to make sure he was still there, just in case his motives didn't turn out to be as nefarious as they seemed.

He picked up after the first ring. "Mankuvsky here." Phoebe could hear his television going in the background. Could he really be watching game shows?

"It's me," she said.

"Hey, *Me*," he said. "How's it hanging?"

He found out soon enough. "You staged the whole accident, didn't you?" Phoebe lit into him with all the bile she could muster.

"I what?"

"I was just too upset and disoriented this morning to see the situation for what it was: a big fat moneymaking venture for you! Georgiu was never planning to come over here, was he? Meanwhile, my sister assures me that, for your efforts, you'll wind up with a nice little commission for bringing in the instrument." She laughed ruefully. "God, I've been so naive—here I thought you were actually interested in me. Well, maybe this was the lesson I needed to learn before I could let go of the past once and for all—including you."

There was silence on the other end of the phone, followed by a gelid, "I'm going to assume you're high on crack cocaine. On the chance that you aren't, I'd like to point out that it was *you* who knocked *me* over in your haste to get in my pants. Furthermore, you only learned we went to fifth grade together about an hour ago, so your 'hanging on to the past argument' falls flat on its frigging face too. Anything else?"

"You fell on purpose!" blurted Phoebe, taken aback by Roger/Roget's decidedly nonconciliatory manner.

"And you need your brain examined," he told her. "Jesus—leave it to me to always get involved with the psychos. Oh, hey, I know a good Freudian shrink in Fort Lee—an Indian guy. Name's Atul. On the expensive side—nickname, Capitalist Atul—but apparently well worth it. Let me know if you need his number."

"How'd you know I saw an Indian Freudian in Fort Lee during college?" she asked him in a mousey voice, bluster giving way to awe at Roger/Roget's prophetic talents.

"I didn't—I just guessed." He laughed scathingly.

"Well, I just hope the next time you sleep with a woman for money, you're more up-front about your motives!" she told him, trying to regain some of her indignation.

"None of the hookers I've visited in the past have ever complained about being misled," he replied.

"I'm not talking about prostitutes!"

"Then, what *are* you talking about?"

"I'm talking about—about you wanting to be with me only so you could have access to my mother's viola!"

"Hey, just because you're too paranoid, or insecure, or damaged, or whatever to believe that a guy might actually enjoy spending time with you, horizontally or otherwise, doesn't mean I did anything wrong," Roger/Roget yelled back.

"So you're telling me my sister's wrong, and you're not getting a commission from Georgiu?" Phoebe's heart thumped with confusion and excitement as she awaited his answer.

"Damn right I'm taking the commission," he told her, with a quick snort.

"So, it's true!" she yelped.

"I know a lucky break when I see one—no pun intended."

"I'm sure."

"Tell you what. If the check is fat, I'll take you out for a nice dinner with a cut of it."

"Oh, I can't wait," Phoebe said, seething at him. "Another greasy pizza joint with reheated spaghetti. Your generosity never ceases to amaze me."

"Fine, be a food snob, but don't say I didn't ask."

"Believe me, I won't."

"Hey, listen." Roger/Roget's voice had turned suddenly cold. "If you want me to leave you alone, I'd be happy to do so. To be honest, I'm getting a little tired of being insulted by you. Maybe it's because I never had a family to blame all my problems on, but I've always taken responsibility for my own fuckups. Some of them I'm even proud of. Whereas you seem to feel the need to turn everyone else into the villain all the time—me, your sister, every guy you ever swapped spit with. I mean, shit, we were doing the nasty, and we broke the frigging viola *together*! So deal with it already. Or don't." He made another nose-based noise. "What do I fucking care?"

The truth, of course, is the most maddening thing we ever hear. So it was for Phoebe, who recognized herself in Roger/Roget's monologue in a way she never had before. Though her rage found further ammunition in the fact that, if only for purposes of his argument, he had chosen to align himself with Emily. *"I'll deal with what I want to deal with!"* she exploded, having arrived in a place that bore little relation to reason or civility.

But Roger/Roget's response stopped her in mid-tantrum. *"Exactly my point!"* he screamed back. *"It's always about you, Phoebe! What about my needs?"*

In Phoebe's experience to date, the only people even *capable* of articulating such a phrase as *my needs* had had at least some experience lying horizontally on a distressed-leather sofa from the Door Store. "Are you in therapy?" she found herself inquiring.

"I see this guy in Teaneck once a week," he told her matter-of-factly, apparently over his tantrum as well.

"But you don't have a family, so what do you talk about?"

"That's just the point. My man in Teaneck thinks that, 'cause I grew up more or less on my own, I never learned to negotiate—not just with women but with the orchestra, too. And—here's the thing—life's a compromise. Also, things aren't always black or white, so sometimes what you want is contradictory. Like, say there's a guy in the wind section who's literally destroying your ears, he's that bad. And you really want to fire him and hire someone new. But then it turns out he's got this pain-in-the-ass but admittedly hot daughter who—well, not only do you want to impress her but you know it would mean a lot to her if you kept the guy on. Plus, if she's in a good mood, she'll probably be a lot nicer to you. Which means she'll be that much more likely to put out and you'll be that much more likely to get laid. So you figure—well, there are eighty-some people in this ensemble. Chances are, even if you upgrade one, the orchestra is still gonna suck, because the other seventy-nine aren't that great, either. Because we're still talking about a regional orchestra here, not the New York Philharmonic but the Newark Fucking Symphony Orchestra. So you decide to re-sign the guy's contract for another three years, hoping—well, *praying* is more the word—that he'll retire before then and join the Polar Bear Society or something. And if he doesn't, well, at least you made a few people happy along the way. Me and Teaneck talk about some other stuff, too."

Whether his story was apocryphal or literally about Leonard Fine, Phoebe didn't in that moment care to know. Nor did she wish to interrogate too deeply the sexual blackmail angle of his tale. Instead, she seized on the image of Roger/Roget supine on the couch, talking about his struggles with the wind section. It left her deeply moved and, what's more, suddenly aching to be next to him, stroking his hair, cradling his face, kissing his lips, negotiating his needs, and, just as Roger/Roget had suggested in the car that morning, continuing where they left off before the accident.

Just as quickly, panic gripped her at the thought of their never seeing each other again. Sure, they might cross paths at some future NSO concert. If twenty-year-old history was any indication, he'd pretend not to know her. And then, one day, he'd simply disappear—to a new orchestra, a new appointment, a new city—with no forwarding address. Or had she already antagonized him past the point of his even bothering to keep Leonard on? Maybe he'd already decided she was too difficult, semi-hysterical, not worth the effort. "Roger/Roget/whatever the hell your name is, please let's not fight anymore," she heard herself pleading. "I think I might be falling in—in love with you."

"Well, since you raised the subject," he began, before Phoebe had the chance to regret having revealed herself to have a heart, "I'm fairly into you myself. Or, at least, I was—quite literally—this morning."

"You're hilarious," she said, joyous to find her feelings reciprocated at least on some level.

"So I'm told," said Roger/Roget. "So, hey, maybe I'll come say hello after rehearsal tomorrow. I could even give Len a lift home. I heard his car got picked off or something?"

"Oh, that's okay, he already got a Rent-a-Lemon," Phoebe told him, as it dawned on her what a terrible mistake she'd made ratting on him to her mother. Who was to say Leonard would even accept a ride with him now?

But the thought of any more interpersonal drama was too much for Phoebe to bear just then. Instead, she bid her new love a good night, swallowed the equivalent of a horse tranquilizer, and collapsed on her junior-sized trundle bed without opening either her yearbook or her notebook.

15

Non-pharmaceutically stimulated REM only became more difficult for Phoebe to achieve as the days wore on. She was far too wound up; she felt vaguely out of her mind. She figured there wasn't much she could do about it. If her past experience had taught her anything, it was that there was no halting passion; it had a will and a momentum all its own. Phoebe had also learned it was much easier being involved with someone you didn't really care about than with someone you did. It was even easier being alone.

She also knew enough to know that all able-bodied people newly in love tend to behave in a similar manner, feeding each other spoonfuls of creamy desserts, and occasionally the lobes of each other's ears, and giggling like maniacs at the smallest of ironies—one napkin folded, another in disarray, imagine!—while the rest of us skulk about the crawl spaces of our shriveled hearts, titillated by mere pornography and worrying ourselves sick over next year's tax returns or the appearance of new (precancerous?) moles. Let the record state, however, that over the next ten days, so massive an amount of nibbling and tittering was achieved by Phoebe and Roger/Roget, some of it in his Corvette, most of it in his bed, that a combined twelve pounds of weight was lost.

But since even the sexually obsessive need occasionally to eat whole food, to use their legs, and to feast their eyes and minds on new sights, so they have something to talk about between lovemaking sessions, there was also one guided canoe ride down the Hackensack River, through the pungent morass of the Meadowlands; a thwarted excursion to a girly bar called the Navel Base on the North Bergen/Secaucus border, which turned out to have gone out of business; a brief but rollicking ride on the kiddy steam train in Van Saun Park, in Paramus; and a tour of the Aviation Museum at Teterboro Airport, including a perusal of the authentic Korean War M.A.S.H. unit that had been transplanted to the museum's rear yard. The two watched several brain-dead action films on Roger/Roget's hideous purple-chenille sectional in his Little Ferry living room, as well. As in a teenager's bedroom, concert posters took up nearly every available inch of wall space. But rather than paying homage to Keith Richards or Jimi Hendrix, the featured deities were the composers Beethoven and Mahler and the famously tyrannical early-twentieth-century maestro, Arturo Toscanini.

Meanwhile, both neglected practical duties to such an extent that an e-mail sent to or phone message left for either one of them during the period would have gone unreturned for days. That Roger/Roget even made it to rehearsal—never mind found time to study his orchestral scores—rates as a small miracle. The same goes for Phoebe refurbishing and reselling another two items (a chair and a bookcase) from the stockpiles of Fine Furniture Inc., and for a considerable profit both times. On the downside, she had become a consistent enough presence in the world of virtual junk dealing that rivals began to surface. Making use of the "rate this seller" function, they cast aspersions on the quality of her products and the cost-efficiency of her shipping and insurance policies—all, of course, from behind the protective guises of their user IDs. It was in Phoebe's nature to take all criticism personally. This time around, however, she was too delirious to care.

As with any couple, of course, there were "issues."

"Rogie Rooster, I feel so close to you!" Phoebe, in her newfound romanticism, had taken to announcing—or something equally annoying—at least once every ten minutes.

"Well, before he goes home, Rogie Rooster would like to get close to Foxy Phoebe as well—and preferably all the way inside her foxhole," he replied the following Sunday afternoon, with a pinch to her rear, as they made their way across the parking lot of a local shopping plaza, ice cream cones in hand.

At which point, exasperated by what she felt to be his prioritization of the physical realm of their relationship over all others, she turned him and said, "Do you have to reduce everything to sex?"

"I thought you liked being objectified!" he cried.

"I do," Phoebe assured him. "It's just that—well, what about focusing on something having to do with my *person-*

ality once in a while? For instance, you could say you enjoy spending time with me."

Roger/Roget grimaced and turned away, clearly uncomfortable with what was being asked of him. "Okay, how's this?" he said, with his back still to her. "I like you a lot but I'd rather not talk about it because everyone I've ever gotten close to has ended up dying."

"Better," she told him.

She found it difficult to stay mad.

There was also the fact that he hadn't told her he loved her. Well, to be fair, it was early yet.

More immediately, there was the unresolved matter of the broken viola. After it became evident that she wasn't on her deathbed quite yet, Roberta had grown somewhat less blasé about the matter. Which meant that her anger at Roger/Roget, whom she understood to be the agent of its destruction, had only become more intense. Phoebe had tried to rectify the situation by confessing that she too had been "joshing around" with her instrument that day. But the blame, once assigned, proved intractable: Roberta simply assumed that Phoebe was trying to take the heat off Roger/Roget. As things currently stood, Roberta could scarcely bring herself to open the door for him. "I'll get Phoebe," she'd say, her nose twitching at the sight of his leather bomber on the steps.

One evening, she'd hung up on him when he called and then pretended to have dropped the phone.

Owing both to his personality and his professional obligations, Leonard was more cordial than Roberta was, if only to a point. The following Friday evening was the NSO's third concert of the fall season, an all-organ extravaganza featuring Saint-Saëns' "Organ Symphony" that put half the audience members, who totaled about thirty, including Phoebe, straight to sleep. Backstage, after the show, Leonard didn't depart his timpanist bookie friend's side until his oboe was all packed up and he was ready to go home. Then, walking directly past Roger/Roget, and without complimenting him on the performance, he tapped Phoebe on the shoulder and asked, "Care for a ride?" in a clipped voice.

"Oh, thanks, Dad," she began, "but I think I'm going to hang out with Roget for a while. It was a great concert, though. Didn't you think?"

"As you like," he said, ignoring her question, and disappeared.

And on those occasions when Leonard found it necessary to address Roger/Roget at all, he now opted for the impersonal "You" instead of his usual, "Maestro." On the one hand, Phoebe was pleased to see her father's obsequious streak in decline. On the other, considering what she now assumed to be true about Leonard's status at the NSO, it seemed pretty ungrateful. But, then, he couldn't very well know that, and she couldn't very well tell him without humiliating him and getting herself in trouble too. Besides, she felt she had only herself to blame for her parents' negative feelings toward Roger/Roget. Here she had always dreamed of bringing home a man they approved of!

Well, she nearly had.

Emily's antipathy was harder to explain. At the mere mention of Roger/Roget's name, she made a face that suggested recent contact with curdled milk. Phoebe chalked it up to a displacement of the guilt she surely felt about her systematic neglect of their mother. But with relations between the two sisters so much improved, Phoebe was reluctant to accuse her of anything right now—other than taking too long in the bathroom.

As for Roger/Roget, he seemed less concerned about Phoebe's parents hating him than about Phoebe deriving a valuable lesson on personal responsibility. She had admitted to having incriminated him soon after they'd come together, complete with an apology, which Roger/Roget had refused. "What do I care if your parents like me?" He'd shrugged as they sat astride adjacent kiddy swings at a nearby park. "At least they're alive, which is more than I can say for my parents, who'll never like you either, since they'll never get the chance to meet you, except maybe at the pearly gates, if you believe in that crap. I really don't."

It had been hard to argue with his logic.

As the days grew shorter, they provided Leonard with new opportunities for preparing and applying caulk, as he set about putting the cracked storm windows back up. One day, Phoebe saw him in the bathroom, going at a gap between the window and its casement, his finger stabbing and twisting, and she thought he looked like a madman. Maybe *he* thought that if he could keep out the cold, he could forestall death, as well.

Meanwhile, Phoebe suspected that things were over between Emily and Sebastian. Her sister seemed sulkier than usual, and she was home more and more (and on the phone less and less). She had even begun to make noises about heading back to San Francisco. Despite everything, Phoebe wondered if, in a funny way, she would end up missing her.

On Halloween, while Roberta rested up for her penultimate visit to the "bio warfare lab," Phoebe took charge of the front door, doling out the same granola bars that had made the Fines' house so unpopular while she was growing up. They seemed to cast an equal pall on the next generation of trick-or-treaters. Some kids didn't even bother saying thank you, instead watching in disgruntled silence as the wholegrains fell into their satchels. Still, the number of callers far exceeded Phoebe's expectations, not merely on account of the damp chill that cut through the air that afternoon, but because she had wrongly assumed that the hidden razor blade and cyanide scares of earlier seasons had zapped the holiday of its acquisitive zeal. In fact, the doorbell rang so often that she kept losing her place in the Henry James novel she had begun and having to start all over again at the top of the page (and the beginning of an interminable tea party description). The informal tally she found herself keeping of the children's costumes didn't help her concentration level, either.

By six o'clock, she had counted, on the male side:

Five Supermen
Three Batmen
Two Spider-men
One pirate
Two ghosts
Four rubber-mask men who either were or weren't
supposed to resemble horror film mainstay Freddy
Krueger

    One grandfather clock constructed out of three RCA
        TV boxes stacked vertically (Phoebe's favorite)
    Six Ninja Turtles

And on the female side:

    Four Spice Girls
    Three pussycats
    One Cleopatra
    One cross-dresser with a mustache
    Fourteen variations on the ballerina-princess theme

Though he'd patronized the local costume shop in order
to purchase the fake blood he used to terrorize their substi-
tute teachers, pretending to have been shot, and so on, Roger
"Stinky" Mancuso had been too cool to dress up for Halloween.

Emily and Phoebe, on the other hand, had celebrated the
holiday by engaging in what Roberta called "creative cos-
tuming," constructing their outfits out of clothing and everyday objects they found around the house. Moreover, where
their classmates had dressed up as Luke Skywalker or
Princess Leia from *Star Wars,* the Fine sisters had found inspiration in cultural and political history. Always the more
eager of the two to please their parents, Phoebe usually chose
a famous figure from the classical music world. One year, she
went as Mozart, in white tights, tan gauchos, embroidered
vest, velvet blazer, and her mother's 1970s hippie-chic blouse
with the lace jabot. She even dumped a can of talcum powder
over her hair, which she pulled back in a ponytail with a pur-

ple ribbon. But when the neighbors mistook her for George Washington, she didn't bother correcting them. It seemed like too much work. She was more interested in the candy anyway, since Roberta—an advocate of wheat germ from early on—wouldn't allow the other stuff in the house.

Emily had always had other priorities. That same year, Phoebe's sister wrapped a white bedsheet around her waist and between her legs in the style of a giant diaper, which she paired with shower flip-flops and one of Leonard's ancient black concert tuxedo jackets, the collar of which she turned up and fastened with a silver brooch. After circling her eyes with a black pencil and drawing up a few anti-imperialist placards decrying the British Empire, she anointed herself the modern incarnation of Mahatma Gandhi. But when the old school nurse who lived around the corner confused her with the Penguin from *Batman*, Emily hurled her basket of treats in the woman's face and then stormed off to the public library, insurrectionist placards in tow, to read more books about the Indian caste system.

Halloween wasn't the only time of year that the sisters went incognito. When not fighting, they could often be found fishing through a giant packing crate filled with the serendipitous costumes of the family's deceased relatives and eccentric friends. It was stored in the ladder-only attic.

Its choice offerings included:

1. A navy-blue admiral's jacket with gold buttons
2. A Colonial American mobcap
3. A pale pink straw cloche
4. A ruffled Spanish-dancer blouse

5. A plaid petticoat
6. A blue flowered full slip
7. A pioneer-lady poke bonnet
8. A Mexican wraparound skirt with an orange-and-purple geometric pattern
9. A Count Dracula–style black velvet cape
10. Black spider beads
11. A pair of sparkly shoes with metal heels
12. A pair of cowhide chaps with rhinestone insets
13. A Liberty print hoop skirt made out of straightened hangers
14. A suede fringe vest with patch pockets found lying in a field on a family trip to Indiana to visit the remnants of an early utopian community
15. An ancient mink *ushanka* with one missing ear flap that either had or had not belonged to Leonard's long-deceased uncle (by marriage) Moses "the Menshevik" Moscowitz

To this effect, the Fine family living room would become a stage set for dungeon scenes and Wild West shoot-outs, hippie tea parties and pas de deux performed to Tchaikovsky's *Swan Lake*. (Naturally, Emily got to play Rudolf Nureyev to Phoebe's Margot Fonteyn, stripping off her shirt and stuffing a banana in the front of her tights.) In a similar vein, when the sisters decided to stage a church wedding, Emily got to dress up as the groom, in one of Leonard's extra-wide floral-pattern ties, while Phoebe was left to pin an old lace brassiere of Roberta's to the top of her head, then extend a chiffon scarf out from under the cups, in a crude imitation of a bridal veil. But if the opportunity to cross-dress typically fell to Emily, in scenarios where both roles were reserved for men, Emily always insisted that Phoebe play the oppressor—tying on the chaps and acting bloodthirstily, for instance, while Emily got to sport feathers and a loincloth, arrange stones from the backyard in circular formations that hinted at spiritual concerns, chant "Hiawatha," and die a dramatic heart-clutching death.

The costume box, of course, achieved obsolescence when the girls reached adolescence. The fashion wars, on the other hand, continued through their teens, with Phoebe and Emily's ugliest battles waged not over boys or politics or secrets not kept but over articles of clothing they either had or had not stolen from each other, or copied the style of, or borrowed without asking permission, or failed to return in the condition lent, or were simply insanely jealous of, such as Emily's motorcycle boots or Phoebe's vintage baby-blue London Fog raincoat with the tie belt. From an early age, both intuitively grasped how much of life came down simply to dressing the part. Just as, when Phoebe wanted to break out of a mold that had her paying what she felt to be a fulsome level of deference toward her sister—for years, Emily had made Phoebe sign a written form of consent every time she checked a book out of her big sister's personal library, and responded only to the epithet *Your Royal Highness*—she began refusing all Emily's clothing-related requests.

The day after Halloween, just over a week before General Election Day, Emily's estranged husband, Jorge Weinstein, showed up unexpectedly at the Fines' front door. It was evident to Phoebe from the moment she answered it—she was the only one home at the time—that he had come to Whitehead to explore the possibility of reconciliation. She could tell by his slumping posture, which had caused his horn-rim glasses to slide halfway down his nose, which, were it a ski slope, would certainly have been labeled an EXPERT TRAIL. That small defect aside, Jorge—with his bronzed skin, white teeth, sculpted jaw, and lean yet muscular build—was generally regarded as a handsome man. His fashion sense, on the other hand, rivaled Roger/Roget's for appalling taste, if in a completely different manner; he appeared always to have just stepped out of a cologne advertisement. He was dressed that afternoon in his signature medley of browns. On the top, he wore a mocha-colored cashmere turtleneck and camel-hair overcoat—on the bottom, a pair of mustard-toned corduroy pants and dark brown snakeskin loafers. "Hello, Phoebe," he began, in a voice as stuffy as it was desperate-sounding.

"Jorge—wow! What are you doing here?" Phoebe asked him, if only to see what he'd say.

"I was hoping to speak with Emily," he said.

"Oh, she's still at Rikers."

His eyes bugged out.

"Tutoring juvenile offenders."

"Of course." He cleared his throat, embarrassed. "So she informed me." Phoebe had always understood her brother-in-law's bizarre speaking manner to be a product of his chichi South American upbringing combined with a serious "English as a Second Language" problem.

But, then, how to explain the fact that he had lived in the

United States since the age of ten? "She'll probably be back soon, if you want to come in and hang out," she offered, feeling slightly more charitable than usual, if only because her distaste for Jorge had as much to do with the fact of his being with Emily as it did with his personality.

It followed that, since by all appearances he and Emily were no longer involved, he wasn't such a bad guy after all.

"Thank you," he replied, his head bowed as he stepped through the door. "I would be pleased to pay my respects to the extended Fine family as well."

"Well, I hate to disappoint you further," said Phoebe as she led him into the den, "but it's just me right now. My parents are out shopping for a new car. I mean, new to them."

"I see." Jorge seated himself in Leonard's BackSaver chair, which had been raised to the upright position, and scanned the room, saying, "The house appears precisely as I recall it."

"That's because we didn't redecorate," she told him, recalling why she had always found her brother-in-law so tedious.

Just then, she happened to catch sight of Jorge's cuticles, at least two of which were bubbling up with fresh blood. "Do you want a Band-Aid or something?" she asked him, her stomach rebelling at the image.

"This will not be necessary," he told her, "but I thank you for asking."

"Yeah, but you're about to drip blood on the carpet."

After a brief glance southward, Jorge popped the errant fingers into his mouth and began to suck, while Phoebe turned away in horror. Behind the well-oiled façade—she had always felt—was a deeply disturbed individual.

Eventually, to her relief, he conceded, "Maybe one Band-Aid."

"Why don't I show you to the bathroom," she suggested.

Jorge stood up. "I recall its location. Thank you."

"There's a whole box of them on the bottom shelf of the medicine cabinet," she called after him. "Don't be scared off by the ADHESIVE STRIP label. My parents buy everything generic."

"Yes, I am aware," he called back.

To Phoebe's distress, he returned from the bathroom several minutes later with just one finger bandaged. Keen for distraction, she was about to ask him how work was going when she remembered he was unemployed. "So what's up with you these days?" she said instead, opting for neutrality.

"I have prepared an independent report on sweatshop conditions in Malaysia," he answered gloomily, "which I intend to present to the human rights commission of the United Nations at some point in the coming calendar year."

"Oh, cool!" Phoebe exclaimed, her head moving up and down in the way people waggle when they care very little about a conversation but hope to imply otherwise. "That sounds really interesting."

"Thank you. And yourself?"

"No big news, really. So, about you and my sister." Unable to control her curiosity (or her agenda) for a moment longer—who knew when she'd have Jorge all to herself again?—Phoebe leaned forward in her seat, on Roberta's divan, and began to grill him. "So what really happened with you two? Did she just bail on you, just like that? We don't know anything because Emily doesn't tell us. She's never had much need for her family—or really, for that matter, for loved ones of any kind. Jorge, I have to tell you—I'm sure what you're going through right now is hard, but I honestly think you had a lucky escape. I mean, I would really think twice about trying to win her back. She's just not a very nice person. Fun, yes. Supportive? I don't think so. . . ." While Phoebe clucked away, her brother-in-law constructed a basket out of his hands. Now he collapsed his head into it and released a high-pitched noise that stopped her mid-sentence and sounded to her ears like what a hyena might sound like if it were in labor. "Oh, no. Jorge! I didn't mean to upset you!" she cried, with genuine remorse for the misery she'd wrought, as she rushed over to lay a comforting hand on his shoulder. "I have such a big mouth sometimes. You shouldn't take any notice of me. I'm a complete idiot."

But the man kept mewling and puling, at some point choking out the words, "Your sister was so cruel!"

"You don't have to tell me," Phoebe told him with bitter laughter. "She tortured me the entire time we were growing up. And the abuse continues. For twenty years I've been 'wart face.' Imagine having to answer to that every day of your life!"

"I conducted an extramarital affair," wept Jorge.

"You what?" Phoebe withdrew her hand and began to back away.

"With the director of the clitorectomy commission," he whimpered, as he wiped his tears. "A woman of Sudanese origin."

"Oh, Jorge." She shook her head in amazement and disgust as she transferred her loyalties to Emily. Even so, Phoebe had to admit there was something vaguely thrilling about the idea of her sister being cheated on. She was used to imagining her inflicting damage. "You've got to be kidding."

"I was eager to give her pleasure," Jorge went on to explain, "as she had no clitoris of her own." He covered his eyes and again began to vibrate.

"And you're wondering why my sister was a bitch to you?" squealed Phoebe. "I would have beat the crap out of you if you were my husband. Frankly, you're lucky to be alive."

"She did accost me"—he continued to tremble—"with some force."

"Well, that's good at least," she told him, feeling marginally more sympathetic. "So, did you guys try counseling?"

Phoebe averted her eyes while Jorge wiped his nose on the sleeve of his mocha turtleneck. "Your sister believed there was little to be gained from such a course of action. Rather, she suggested that my behavior had caused her to lose faith in the very concept of public service, since the people who had made it their mission in life to impart goodness were, in fact, causing the most harm." (So that was why Emily had taken a leave of absence from her job, Phoebe registered with interest.)

In the meantime, Jorge had burst into tears all over again, severely trying Phoebe's patience. Since when had crying become acceptable for men? "Would you shut up already?" she finally barked at him. "You sound like a girl."

"I'm so alone!" he moaned.

"Everybody's alone—except when they're with someone."

That meaningless little axiom seemed to silence him for

the moment, and he went back to transforming his sweater sleeve into a repository for extraneous bodily fluids. Then he gazed up at Phoebe with a frantic look on his face. "Do you think she'll ever take me back?"

"I'd say the odds were slim," she told him. "But I guess you never know how desperate people are until you try."

Too caught up in his own malaise to register the insult implicit in Phoebe's reply, Jorge sighed heavily and tipped backward in Leonard's chair. "Recently, I have been made aware of the fact that she has become romantically entangled with a new man," he announced, with his feet higher than his head. "Comfortable chair."

"You mean the mysterious Sebastian?" she asked.

"Sebastian?" His brow furled, he plunged back down to earth. "No, I do not believe that was his name. Perhaps there is more than one suitor on the scene." Seeming even more distraught than before, Jorge cased the room, as if expecting to find one of his rivals hidden behind the sofa.

"Well, maybe she was seeing one guy before, and now she's seeing another guy," suggested Phoebe.

"The only one of whom I am aware is the maestro of an orchestra in which your father participates."

"A *what*?"

"A maestro. Do you know anything of him? . . . Phoebe— are you not well?" She had abruptly turned her back, the better to hide her burning face. Now it was Jorge's turn to jump up from his seat and attempt to comfort an injured party.

Unlike her brother-in-law, however, Phoebe wanted no outside aid. "I think you should go now," she told him in an extraterrestrial voice, after tossing off his hand. She felt the walls closing in around her and there wasn't room for two.

"But I recall your having said that Emily was on her way home shortly," mumbled Jorge, sounding somewhere between guilty and peeved.

"I did say that, and now I'm saying something else." Under the circumstances, Phoebe also felt it was her right to act like a banana republic dictator.

It wasn't just Emily's leave of absence from the legal profession that was starting to make sense; it was Roger/Roget's hot and cold behavior toward Phoebe during the early stages of their courtship, followed by Emily's sudden turn against him. And while Phoebe had been out on the screened porch sulking that night, had he and Emily exchanged numbers or otherwise orchestrated plans to meet up? Or might Emily have made up the whole liaison simply to make Jorge jealous? And if she hadn't made it up, would Phoebe ever be able to make up with Roger/Roget, to get past the knowledge that he had made love to her sister first? (Anyone but her sister! Why, oh why?) Her secret glee at finding out that Emily had been cheated on had all but evaporated, replaced now by utter despair and unanswered questions. For one thing, who the heck was Sebastian?

Just then, Roberta's raspy voice came sailing through the kitchen. "We're home!"

Seconds later, Phoebe found herself staring into her mother's gaunt yet gleeful face. "Why, Jorge—what a wonderful surprise!" she declared.

"Hello there, young man," said Leonard.

"Sir. Ma'am." Jorge had never gotten comfortable calling his in-laws by their first names, as most American husbands do. He kissed Roberta hello—on the left cheek and on the right, another time on the left, and then, having apparently lost track of the count, another time on the right.

He and Leonard shook hands.

"I feel nauseated and I'm going out for a walk," Phoebe announced to the group, just as, on another watershed day, she had announced to Neil Schmertz.

"Okay, Be, see you in a bit." Her mother waved her away without a second glance, indifferent to all but the vision before her and what it might mean for future Thanksgivings and Jewish Christmases (presents, no tree). But, then, who could blame her? These were important issues, after all.

Grabbing her pea coat—and a bright orange New Jersey Devils ski hat that Leonard had gotten for free at Happy Gas the last time he ever filled up the Yugo—Phoebe let herself out the back door. She composed a list as she went.

Ten Reasons Why Sex Is Overrated

1. Endless laundry
2. Too tiring
3. Sleep better alone
4. Have to worry about how you look naked
5. Most men uninspiring in bed anyway, with their predictable and hackneyed moves, like blowing in your ear
6. Have to make conversation at breakfast
7. Totally unoriginal pastime (everyone does it)

8. Have to act like you've shared meaningful experience
9. Without realizing it, you actually start to believe you have
10. Only after you've been hoodwinked into thinking you've made deep connection do you realize that he's also trying to bed your sister

The trees had begun to resemble old scarecrows, just without the bowler hats. And the air had a bite to it, a little time-delayed, like the sting of a chili pepper. There was no mistaking the coming thaw. Yet it seemed to Phoebe that winters in New Jersey weren't like they used to be, before global warming melted all the ice in Antarctica. She could still remember skiing down Upper Oak, Whitehead's own bunny slope, the streets empty and eerie but for the occasional property-tax-supported snowblower, its groaning shovel-snout clearing a determined swath up the center of each block. She would never forget the agony and anticipation of unsnapping boot buckles with a frozen mitten, either. Or the simple joy of standing in sock feet on the living room heat grate, its emission made all the more wonderful because of its rarity. An adherent of the British boarding school model, Leonard considered cold air to be character building.

To Phoebe's mind, her father was simply cheap. Growing up, it had been a running complaint: "Mom, it's freezing in here!" How many times she had uttered those words. And how many times Roberta had suggested that she put on another sweater and see if she were still cold. *Why don't you put on another sweater and see if you're still cold?* Phoebe could still hear her saying that, sprightly, with her simple-solutionsto-simple-problems smile. Her parents had been so madden-ingly sensible all the time!—so maddeningly satisfied with so little and uninterested in ever trying new methods or ma-chines. Most maddening of all was their refusal to engage with the fact that we're all helpless in the end. They had a per-fectly good solution, it seemed, to everything, even death: Don't mention it.

At some point along the way, however, Phoebe began to find their stubbornness attractive. If Leonard and Roberta re-fused to change with the times, maybe Phoebe could refuse to grow up. Now, as she passed by the patch of clover where she and her first best friend, Brenda Cuddihy, had once found a lucky four-leaf variant, Phoebe saw that she was always liv-ing someplace other than *right here*. Moreover, she had come back to Whitehead not so much to care for her mother as to have her mother care for her. So she could imagine that she was still someone's daughter, still young and sweet and un-tarnished and in need of protection, when it simply wasn't true anymore.

In New York City, on the other hand, Phoebe had been living mainly in the future, constantly delaying the possibility of happiness until she had achieved a certain level of success, attained a certain body and fashionability, grown far enough away from certain bad memories that they no longer seemed to be her own. She preferred to imagine herself in the Greek Revival town house in Greenwich Village in which she might someday live, than in the modest Murray Hill studio in which she hadn't yet unpacked. In the same way that half the stars one sees in the sky no longer exist, having imploded in the years it took for their light to reach the earth, she pictured time as a continuum. But human life didn't work that way. She saw that now, too. There could be no skipping ahead, no return to anything. Wherever you were in life, the baggage simply followed you there—if not on your own flight, then on the next one in.

16

Returning from her walk, Phoebe was confronted with the improbable and alarming sight of her sister and Jorge holding hands on the sofa, a Second Empire rosewood and red velvet two-seater that was the Fine family's one good antique. "Hey, Feebs," began Emily, in a sickly sweet voice that Phoebe had never before heard her use (and hoped never to hear again).

"Been out for a nice walk?" asked Roberta, who sat across from the happy couple, beaming.

"Wow, things sure change fast around here," muttered Phoebe, ignoring her mother's question. It was pathetic, she knew, but the part that annoyed her most about Emily and Jorge getting back together was that her sister was rich again.

"I could have sworn there was a bottle of sparkling wine somewhere in here," came a muffled voice from inside the oak buffet: Leonard. "Well, I can offer you all some tequila, though I don't know I'd recommend it. It looks a little on the old side. Ow!"

He emerged several seconds later with a trickle of blood

running down the side of his ear and a bottle of booze pressed to his chest.

"Oh, Lenny!" cried Roberta. "Your ear!"

"Not to worry," he said, reaching for his hankie with his free hand and holding it against the wound. "Now, in lieu of sprinkling rice on the happy couple, as I believe we've already done, may I suggest some celebratory rice wine?"

Phoebe found herself wishing she'd kept walking, preferably beyond the town limits, never to return again. Only where would she have gone after that? Until further notice, this was still her home. "I'll get it," she shrieked at the sound of the phone ringing, delighted for the temporary out it promised to provide.

But despite having no more free hands, Leonard shooed her away with "I'm right here."

He reappeared ten seconds later with the receiver held out in front of him at the farthest distance away from his body, as if he thought it might bite. "It's the juggler," he told Phoebe in a snide voice.

"Tell him I don't want to speak to him," Phoebe told Leonard.

"Gladly," he said.

"God, what happened with you two?" snorted Emily.

"Maybe the better question is, What happened with *you two*?" said Phoebe, adrenaline suddenly rushing.

"I have no idea what you're talking about," Emily answered.

"Well, I'd be happy to explain," Phoebe offered.

"Um, can it wait till later?" she asked. "Jorge and I haven't seen each other in, like, two months?"

"It's actually kind of important."

"Fine." Sighing in an exaggerated fashion, Emily turned to Jorge and told him, "I'll be right back, baby. Be good."

"And I shall be waiting," said Jorge, "for my true love to return."

For the second time in an hour, Phoebe felt like vomiting. Instead, she led her sister to their usual boxing ring, on the screened porch, where, once out of Jorge's sight, Emily quickly reclaimed the bulldozer-like personality that Phoebe knew her to possess. "What?" she said. It had always been her favorite question.

"Did you sleep with Roget?" Phoebe asked her, as upset as she was secretly elated to be, for once in her life, speaking to her sister from a position of righteousness.

But Emily came back at her with a vehement and outraged, "What? No!"

"Then, who, precisely, is this maestro you told Jorge you were seeing?"

Emily let loose another bored sigh, as if she had more important things to talk about with more important people somewhere else. Then she said, "Okay, we went to second."

"You what?" said Phoebe.

"We went to second base."

"You let Roget feel you up?" Phoebe could barely get the sentence out; the words kept disappearing down her throat. After nuclear war, it was her worst nightmare come to life. She would almost have preferred to hear the word *sodomy* on Emily's lips—well, maybe not quite.

"It was a few nights after he came over for dinner that time," Emily continued in a flat voice, as if dictating a story to a court reporter that she had told many times before, her eyes everywhere except on Phoebe. "He slipped me his number while you were off pouting. I was lonely and seeking revenge on Jorge." She glanced up at the ceiling. "God, this house is like Cobweb Central!"

"What do cobwebs have to do with anything!" cried Phoebe, rage mounting.

"My God! Sorry," said Emily. But still she sounded as if she'd felt sorrier about things that had happened in the past. And then, as she finally made eye contact with her sister, she broke into a giddy smile far more inappropriate than any facial expression that Phoebe had ever come up with at the wrong time. "To be honest, I didn't think you guys were that into each other. At least, not back then."

"You could have asked me!" Phoebe now exploded, furious enough for her lips to be quivering.

"Look, I think you're overreacting here." Emily began to laugh, if uneasily, as if realizing that her own argument wasn't all that convincing. "I mean, judging from what you just told Dad, it doesn't even seem like you guys are together anymore."

"And why do you think that is?" Phoebe asked quietly, trying to regain her cool.

"You had a bad fight?"

"I found out he'd been fooling around with my sister!"

"I told you we only went to second!"

"I don't care if you went to forty-third!"

"Jeez, I don't even know what that is. Foot fetishism?"

"It's just a fucking metaphor, *okay*?"

Outside, a neighbor's car alarm let loose its psychotic yo-yoing wail, drowning both of them out. Emily shifted her posture from one foot to the other. It was pretty clear she couldn't wait to be dismissed, and that she would have preferred to have been standing almost anywhere but right there. But Phoebe wasn't finished with her yet. She waited until the alarm sputtered into silence. "My whole life, you've been cutting down the things I care about," she told her sister, feeling as if she'd waited thirty years to get out those words, slight overstatement though they may have been.

Emily made a face at the floor. "Okay, I admit that I occasionally enjoy torturing you." She looked back up at Phoebe. "But you were always the pretty and talented one!"

"*Me* the pretty and talented one?" cried Phoebe. "Give me a break. You were always the big shot in this family. And you still are."

Now Emily shook her head from side to side and laughed. "God, you and I have been living on separate planets. As far as I can remember, you were always the cute and fashionable one—and musically gifted, too, so Mom and Dad loved you without you even having to try. And so did your teachers. I still can't believe you got that hegemony guy at Hoover to sleep with you! My gov and law profs wouldn't even take me out to coffee. All I was ever good at was debating and starting action coalitions. And I was so bad at the cello, Mr. Cunningham literally *begged* me to quit. Poor Mom and Dad. Imagine two musicians having a daughter who can't even carry a tune! It must have been so humiliating for them."

"Yeah, and you had a serious boyfriend since the day you started preschool," Phoebe fired back. "And you won so many academic prizes at Pringle they had to invent new ones to make the other kids feel better!"

"Yeah, well, that was also, like, *eighteen years* ago! And in case you hadn't noticed, I'm currently *unemployed* and in the middle of a *divorce* proceeding!" Emily cleared her throat and looked away in the direction of Jorge, evidently embarrassed by her outburst. "At least I was until a few moments ago. It's not clear what's happening now. We may or may not try and work things out." Her pearly teeth grinding, she turned back to Phoebe. "You know that prick cheated on me with a fucking clitorectomy activist?"

"I heard," said Phoebe, not feeling particularly sympathetic in that moment to either of them.

Emily looked confused. "How did you know?"

"I was the only one who was home when he showed up here looking for you, forty-five minutes ago."

Emily brushed her hair off her face defensively. "Well, I guess it's a little late in the day for secrets."

"I guess so," said Phoebe, becoming enraged all over again.

Then Emily told her, "On that note, you'll be delighted to hear that your darling friend Roget Mankuvsky blew me off like a dust bunny! Which did nothing for my ego, by the way. It was actually kind of humiliating. He was just like, 'Your sister is so much hotter than you. So, like, see ya.' "

"Sebastian was out of town that weekend?" asked Phoebe, trying to ignore the real satisfaction in this latest revelation.

Emily's eyes went back to the floor. "There was never any guy named Sebastian. I invented him to cheer myself up."

It was so absurd, it was tragic. "You invented a secret friend?" Phoebe asked her, squinting in disbelief at the desperation she had mistaken for smugness.

"I'm not very good at being alone."

"Apparently. So who gave you the rabbit fur?"

"I bought it at a Salvation Army in Oakland for twenty bucks," Emily mumbled.

"Great buy! I mean, if you like fur. I've always found the butchering-of-innocents aspect kind of creepy." Phoebe couldn't pass up the opportunity to get in that dig.

There was silence. Emily couldn't very well complain.

"So who have you been on the phone with all fall?" said Phoebe, almost beginning to enjoy herself. "AT and T?"

"For a while I was having daily phone sessions with my therapist in Oakland," her sister confessed.

"You're in therapy too? Jesus, is there anyone who isn't? And *every day*? God, even at my craziest, I only went twice a week. Not that it helped. Though, to be fair, the person I saw was actually at school *learning* to become a therapist, so she had no clue what she was doing. I'm actually convinced the whole business set me back years. She was always—" Phoebe stopped herself mid-sentence, realizing suddenly that not only was she being way too friendly to Emily, she sort of missed having someone to tell her problems to, if only her problems with therapy. (Maybe she would place a call to Freudian Capitalist Atul in Fort Lee after all.)

"My therapist says I have a lot of work to do on my sibling issues," said Emily, drawing a long yoga-style breath through her nose.

"Sibling issues?" cried Phoebe, further astonished. "Only younger sisters are supposed to have those!"

"Who says?"

"I do."

"Yeah, well, it wasn't easy growing up three years older

than you!" cried Emily with what sounded for the first time to Phoebe's ears like genuine emotion. "You were the baby, so it was okay for you to fuck up. I didn't have that luxury. Mom and Dad started looking up to me the day I entered junior high. As if I knew what I was doing. I mean, look at the guy I married!"

"Jorge's not so bad," said Phoebe, enjoying her new role as her sister's tormentor (and therapy topic). "I mean, if you can get past the brown fixation—literally everything the guy wears is brown! What's up with that? Does he have some kind of unnatural attachment to his you-know-what?"

Emily snorted audibly. "If you only knew."

"He does, he does!" Phoebe squealed, back in thrall to the forces of puerilism.

Emily snorted again. Then so did Phoebe. Then their cracking up turned into belly laughter, which in turn offset a series of stomach convulsions. Before long, they were butting heads and bent over in delicious agony, mouths agape as they tried in vain to draw fresh breath. Whether they would be back at each other in a matter of hours, ready to draw blood, was anyone's guess. In the meantime, they milked the moment for all it had to offer, collapsing onto the floor.

Phoebe found her head burrowed in the very cleavage that had seemed, until recently, poised to swallow her whole—when the doorbell rang.

She rolled over to find Roger/Roget's reddened mug pressed up against the glass. Like most adult American males, the mere suggestion of girl-on-girl action drove him into an orgiastic frenzy; he saw the practice exclusively as a prelude to his own pleasure. As for the addition of two sisters to the equation, and not just any sisters but sisters he had individually felt up, Phoebe could only wonder at the images coursing through his brain. "I got it!" she called to her parents, even though she had no immediate plans to do anything, the better to leave him standing out in the cold for a few more minutes. Then she turned back to Emily and said, "There's someone here who'd like to go to forty-third base with you," thereby unleashing another round of hysterical giggling and drooling. (Though their motives were distinct, both sisters had ample incentive to laugh in the guy's face.)

Five minutes later, Phoebe deigned to open the door and Roger/Roget stormed onto the porch. Ripping his jacket off as he walked, he revealed the same turquoise T-shirt he had worn on their first date. Phoebe had grown to find his fashion faux pas charming, but she saw how that could change. Predictably enough, he was now in a foul humor. "What the hell is going on here?" he demanded to know. "Hey, Emily—bye, Emily," he mumbled at the sight of her sister scrambling from the room.

"So, which of us did you come to see today," Phoebe asked him, after Emily had left, "girlfriend number one or girlfriend number two?"

"What the hell are you talking about?" he asked back.

"Your attempt, some weeks ago, to screw my sister!"

"Give me a break. The chick pursued me like a dog."

"I'm so sure."

"Okay, fine." Roger/Roget scowled at his sneakers. "At some point I may have copped a feel."

"Purely for *her* benefit, I'm sure," Phoebe shot back.

"Look, I admit it wasn't torture or anything. But do I look like I ran off with her?"

"I don't care if you eloped to Vegas," she told him, her temperature again on the rise. "The point is, you two-timed me with my own sister!"

"Yeah, but I mean—"

"You mean what?" she cut him off. "That you didn't think I'd find out?"

Roger/Roget grumbled something unintelligible, his eyes still on the floor. Then he lifted his gaze to Phoebe. "Look, I didn't even know if you were into me back then! To be honest, you were kind of a bitch at dinner that night."

"Blame the victim, why don't you?"

"Yeah, well, first you made it pretty clear that you didn't even *want* me to come to dinner, which was a little hurtful, to be honest. And then, before I'd even had a wine cooler, you had to make this big point of how I wasn't going to be staying over that night—and this to your father! Do you know how embarrassing that was?"

"Yeah. I'd been on exactly *one date* with you. And you hadn't exactly been pleasant during it, either. I seem to remember some line about how shrill you found the violin!"

"I didn't want to come on too strong."

"Is that why you gave Emily your phone number that night while I was sulking on this very porch?"

"Look, I'm sorry! Okay?" Grimacing with regret and frustration, Roger/Roget looked away. "I think I may have gotten a little overly attached to your family. I don't have one of my own."

"Oh, that is such a lame excuse!" Phoebe railed back at him. "I can't believe you're playing the orphan card! Does that mean you're going to be making a pass at my father soon too? How about my mother? You know what they say about redheads."

"Yeah, but it's a wig," he said.

Phoebe made a hissing noise.

At which point Roger/Roget began to refit his arms into the sleeves of his bomber. "Maybe I'm not cut out for relationships," he said, sighing as he started toward the door.

"As a first step, you might try sticking to *one* sister!" Phoebe called after him, missing him already, afraid she'd pushed things too far, wondering if he'd move back to New Rochelle and if she'd live through it. The last room of her "motel" had already been filled. Panicking, she darted ahead, positioning herself between Roger/Roget and the door.

For a few moments, they stood silently facing each other. Then he reached for her, moaning, "Phoebe."

"Go away, you disgust me," she told him, but in so gentle a way that he surely understood it was merely that she wasn't ready yet to forgive him. Her weak slaps at his chest came from that same vengeance-seeking but ultimately warm place in her heart.

How was Jorge to know that this was the case? Swiss Army knife raised in his fist like the Statue of Liberty's lantern, he appeared suddenly behind Roger/Roget, bellowing, "Freeze and identify yourself!" in his left ear. Roger/Roget spun around.

Needless to say, the sight of Jorge's glistening blade sent Phoebe's boyfriend in a mad scramble for the corner, where he stood immobilized with fear, his arms plastered to the plastic tarpaulins that Leonard had dropped over the screens. "It's okay, Jorge—thanks," said Phoebe, now positioned between them. "It's just an old friend of mine who's had too much to drink." (In the background now, she could hear Roger/Roget muttering "Bullshit.") "And this is my brother-in-law, Jorge. Jorge, Roget." Both men grunted. Having fun, she turned back to Jorge. "Roget is actually my father's conductor at the Newark Symphony Orchestra." Making the connection, Jorge ground his teeth together and spat on his knife then wiped it dry on the thigh of his corduroys, having apparently run out of clean places on his sweater. Meanwhile, Roger/Roget made himself even smaller in the corner, his eyeballs popping like marbles. "But listen, Jorge," Phoebe continued. "Do you think you could give us a few minutes alone? I know it doesn't look like it, but Roget and I are actually in the middle of a conversation."

"Gladly," Jorge sniffed, one eye twitching. "I approached the porch merely to address your mother's concerns for your safety."

"You can tell her everything's under control," Phoebe told him.

"Very well." His posture so erect that he appeared to be leaning backward—maybe he'd spent too long in the Back-Saver—Jorge left the room in a modified goose step.

"Jesus!" Roger/Roget cried after he'd gone. "That guy's a fucking psychopath!"

"No, just another slime bucket who can't keep it in his pants," Phoebe felt compelled to clarify. "Though I have to give him credit. When he strays, it's not for the usual bimbo."

Before Phoebe had the chance to elaborate, Roger/Roget had fallen before her on one knee. "Phoebe," he began again, this time in a supplicant tone, "please forgive me. You're the only Fine sister for me."

But Phoebe still had one question. "How do I know now

you aren't saying the same things to Emily when I'm not here?" she asked him. "My great-uncle Moses the Menshevik used to take all six of his grandnieces aside at family holidays and tell each one she was his favorite. I only learned this recently, of course, having always thought I was special to him. But Uncle Moses isn't the point. The point is, once someone lies to you about something, it becomes difficult to believe anything they say ever again."

"But I love—making love to you," he replied, eyes twinkling. "I mean, I love you."

"I thought you'd never admit it," she smiled, her heart threatening to leap out of her chest.

"And your sister is a critical bitch."

"Now you're really talking," murmured Phoebe, closing her eyes in sync with Roger/Roget's wet and wonderful kisses. Her trust, if not fully restored, was at least, like the instruments in Georgiu's shop, now on the repair docket.

It made no more or less sense that Georgiu should be the next visitor at 281 Douglass Street. That said, it was not by any of the accepted methods (doorbell, telephone, pitching pebbles) that he made his presence known, but rather by means of a grotesque and prolonged belch. At the sound of it, Phoebe again jumped free of Roger/Roget's clutches, only to find the craggy tree stump himself leering behind the glass. "Georgiu!" she cried, noting to herself that, apparently, appraisers made house calls, after all.

It also seemed she'd forgotten to close the door tightly after Roger/Roget, as Georgiu let himself in, mumbling, "Ah, young love, how it primes the juices." He had some kind of cheesecloth sack tossed over the shoulder of his one-piece blue mechanic's uniform, and his twenty white hairs were sticking straight up in the air, like a nouvelle-cuisine preparation of endive.

"Great timing, as usual, Geo," said Roger/Roget, shaking his head.

To complicate matters, Roberta had found her way onto the porch, as well. "It seems I've become the impresario of a three-ring circus!" she trilled at the sight of the three of them. "Now, which one are you?" she asked, pointing at Georgiu. Acknowledging Roger/Roget's presence was still beyond her.

"This is Georgiu, the man who's fixing your viola," Phoebe cringingly confessed, knowing that her mother was suspicious of all persons connected with the accident. "And this is my mother, Roberta Fine."

"Delighted," he said, bowing.

"Welcome," said Roberta, with a tight-lipped smile. "I was planning on making an appointment to see you, anyway. So now I won't have to."

"So many fine ladies in one house," Georgiu added, with half-mast lids that appeared to be weighing him down.

"Well, thank you," replied Roberta, her tone warming slightly. Like Phoebe, she never tired of compliments. "Please, come in." She motioned for him to enter the main portion of the house.

Roger/Roget took the liberty of accepting Roberta's invitation as well, so that Phoebe found herself following both men and her mother into the den.

She smelled Leonard's pipe before she saw Leonard, leaning up against the art history bookcase, his legs crossed jauntily before him. He only smoked on special occasions, which made Phoebe fear the worst regarding her sister and Jorge's plans for the future. Before him on the sofa, like a couple of high-school sweethearts seeking permission to spend the Saturday after prom night at someone's beach house at the Jersey shore, the two sat, looking happy if a little apprehensive. (It frightened Phoebe to think that her father might be dispensing marital advice.) Even scarier, Leonard and Jorge—Phoebe noticed suddenly—were wearing practically the same pair of wide-wale corduroys, though Leonard's were less mustard than a golden shade of beige. And unlike Jorge, he had paired them with a blue corduroy blazer whose suede patches were detaching from the elbows.

Addressing her husband, Roberta was the first to speak. "I assume you need no introduction to Mr. Mankuvsky," she began.

"What's up, Len?" said Roger/Roget, who continued to seem unfazed by Phoebe's parents' rejection of him.

"Hello," Leonard said coldly.

"As for our other visitor," Roberta went on, turning to Georgiu, "if you'll forgive me, I didn't catch the full name."

"Ceausescu. Georgiu Ceausescu," he replied.

She turned back to her husband. "Mr. Ceausescu is fixing my viola, it seems." A quizzical yet determined look came into her eyes. "Georgiu Ceausescu. I swear I know that name from somewhere."

"Perhaps one of your esteemed colleagues has had his instrument repaired, appraised, or otherwise glorified under my roof?" he suggested.

Roberta had other ideas. "By any chance did you attend the Peabody Institute for Music in the early nineteen sixties?" she asked.

Shock and embarrassment washed over Georgiu's wrinkled face, and he pursed what remained of his lips. "It is true that I studied the violoncello there many years ago," he said quietly, "before I made the transition to luthier." Then he sneezed, as if wishing to wash away all traces of his admission.

"Well, *that's* where I know you from, then!" cried Roberta, clearly tickled by the connection. "I could swear you were in my Intro to Ethnomusicology class."

"God, what an incredible coincidence!" said Phoebe. She couldn't help but think the connection boded well in terms of fostering trust between her mother and the man assigned to fixing her instrument.

Roger/Roget had his own reasons to be happy. "George, man, you're like a total phony too!" he said, laughing. "What, did you grow up in Westchester or something?"

"Scarsdale," said Georgiu, looking miserable.

"Aw, man!" he crowed. "Well, what the hell. I started life as Roger Mancuso from Whitehead, New Jersey, so I guess we're even."

"You *what*?" said Roberta.

"He only lived here for a few years," Phoebe cut in, wishing he'd chosen some other time to unleash this potentially explosive tidbit of information about himself. For all she knew, her mother still harbored ill feelings toward the guy on account of his callous treatment of her beloved viola one day after school in fifth grade.

"You grew up in New Jersey?" asked Emily, looking disdainful. As if she hadn't been born and bred there too.

"It seems I am the only authentic foreigner in the room," said Jorge, with a self-important smile.

"Oh, shut up." Emily turned to face him. "You're about as authentic as your hair implants." Jorge's mop-top was a weave?

"Here they go again," Phoebe muttered under her breath, pleased to see order restored on that front, at least.

"A very curious revelation," said Leonard, sucking on his pipe. It wasn't clear if he was talking about Jorge's hair or Roger/Roget's hometown.

"Ro-ger Man-cu-so"—Roberta slowly repeated the name—"who came to my house twenty years ago and ate all my granola bars?"

"That's me," he said.

There was silence. Phoebe hid her eyes.

"Well, you've certainly demonstrated perseverance where my daughter is concerned, I'll give you that!" Roberta declared finally with a laugh, before turning to Phoebe in an accusatory manner and asking, "Why did you keep this a secret from us?"

"I told her I'd spank her in public if she told anyone," Roger/Roget answered for her. Again, Phoebe winced in agony.

"I see," Roberta said quickly. "Well!" Her smile turned suddenly yielding. "Unless I'm mistaken, Roger—I mean, Roget—you showed an early interest in the viola?"

Phoebe held her breath, hoping—praying, really—that he wouldn't squander the opportunity to express his deep appreciation of the viola's rich palette (and potentially win back the favor of her mother).

"A very keen interest, in fact," he answered, sounding eerily like Jorge. "And I still remember with profound gratitude how you allowed me to hold your precious instrument that afternoon. To be honest, it was a turning point in my life. I was either going to end up in jail or onstage. After that day, I knew it was going to be the second. Which may help to explain the unfortunate incident that took place in your music room last month. I'm afraid I couldn't resist the opportunity to revisit that early thrill. In fact, my hands were literally trembling with excitement as I lifted the viola from its case. And—well, I'm afraid I lost control of the situation, to put it mildly."

Would Roberta see right through Roger/Roget's performance? Would it matter if she did? Phoebe kept her joy in check—until Roberta burst forth with: "Well, the story certainly makes more sense in that context." After which point Phoebe exhaled with relief.

"I can't say I remember any of Phoebe's little friends with the last name of Mancuso," said Leonard, about five minutes behind, as usual. "Bert, which one was he?"

Roberta waved her hand in front of her face. "Lenny, I absolutely can't stand the smell of that pipe anymore."

Roger/Roget turned to Phoebe. "How come your old man calls your old woman by a guy's name?"

"Don't get me started," she told him, with a clenched jaw. "Dad, did you hear that?"

"My apologies to all and sundry for the many crimes I have committed," Leonard announced, in an unnecessarily projected voice, sounding, frankly, a little drunk. "Puffing on the old pipe is just my way of celebrating good news." He stashed the offending pipe behind his back, but not before taking a final drag.

"What good news?" asked Phoebe, dreading his answer.

"Well, my elder daughter appears to have repaired relations with her husband. Or, at least, they're bickering again like an old married couple. Not that Bert and I ever resorted to physical violence." All eyes turned to Emily, who now had her hands around Jorge's neck, while Jorge pleaded for mercy. (It was difficult to say if they were joking around or not.)

"There is, perhaps, more good news as well," said Georgiu, stepping forward. "It seems that the luscious daughter here"—he made a zigzag motion in the general direction of Phoebe—"and her virile young swordsman"—he tipped his head at Roger/Roget—"had their little accident atop a genuine early-eighteenth-century Giuseppe Antonio Guarneri del Gesù. Some novices in the room may ask, Who was Guarneri del Gesù? I would answer, only the fifth, last, and most illustrious of the Guarneri clan of Cremona, and, along with our other friend Antonio—Stradivari, that is—perhaps the greatest luthier of all time. Why, then, does the instrument bear the imprimatur of our friend Monsieur da Salo? On account of its magnificent tone-producing capacity, our other friend Giuseppe took it upon himself to revive and revamp his Brescian predecessor's model of a hundred years earlier. So it is that I come today to reveal the true, identifying ticket." From his satchel, he slowly withdrew the back of Roberta's instrument, scroll attached, but still no sign of any front.

"My viola!" gasped Roberta.

"Told you it wasn't sixteenth-century," said Roger/Roget. He elbowed Phoebe in the ribs, but she was too caught up in the unfolding drama even to yell *ow*.

Peeling away the da Salo label with his thumb and fore-finger, Georgiu displayed an ancient yellowed rectangle stamped with the dim outline of three black letters. "Among the spectators, surely there is at least one familiar with the initials 'I H S.' No?" he asked.

"Islip High School?" offered Roger/Roget.

"Ah, but there you are wrong." Georgiu smiled. "The letters were Giuseppe's cipher, unsolved to this day. It was on this account, however, that the man was nicknamed 'del Gesù,' as in Jesus, our lord and master—or *he who contains the mystery of being*."

"The Fines are Jewish," Roger/Roget told him.

Georgiu made his sad clown face. "Presumably, they are still aware of the existence of one messianic carpenter?"

"It's fine," Roberta assured them both. "We're not very religious."

"Are you telling us that my mother's viola is worth a lot of money?" asked Phoebe, anxious to get back to the fiduciary angle.

"On account of its compromised position, perhaps not a billion zillion dollars," Georgiu replied, frowning at the butchered instrument. "But, assuming the repair goes as scheduled, certainly half that at least, if not more—one can't always predict these things, as they ultimately depend on the gullibility of the presumably Asiatic customer, who may or may not become confused by the number of zeroes." He threw his head back and laughed wildly.

Roberta coughed to express her discomfort with ethnic stereotyping, but the gesture seemed to go unnoted.

It was Roger/Roget who finally succeeded in shutting the man up. "Could you cut the racist shit already, Geo?" he said. "We're trying to get some numbers here."

Georgiu shrugged. "One million? Perhaps two?"

"I can't believe my family is about to join the ruling class," said Emily, shaking her head with disgust.

"Well, I suppose thanks are due to old Uncle Moishe!" said Roberta, sounding suddenly tickled. "Who knew all those backstreet procedures would reap such fine rewards!"

"Mom!" cried Emily.

Roberta looked confused. "Why, Em—I always thought you were a big supporter of the pro-choice movement."

"I am, that's not the point," she grumbled, clearly irritated at finding her political loyalties (toward the poor and the pro-choice movements, respectively) at odds.

It was Leonard's turn to weigh in. "A million bucks," he considered out loud. "That's a lot of raincoats at the Burlington Coat Factory."

"Assuming you don't gamble it away first," his wife snapped back.

Everyone looked embarrassed except Georgiu, who seemed in a hurry to bring the conversation back to his own profit margin. "Needless to say, I am happy to complete the repair and draw up new papers," he went on, "contingent on receiving the standard cut of the eventual sale."

"Of course," Phoebe eagerly assured him, her heart beating now in twos. She pictured the Greek Revival town house in Greenwich Village in which she would soon be living.

But as Emily pointed out, "It's for *Mom* to decide if she's interested in selling or not!"

The collective eye turned to Roberta, upon whose long face a look of quiet contentment had taken hold. "Obviously, Dad and I will have to discuss the situation in further detail," she told the group after a short pause. "But the way I feel now, I'm inclined to say *good riddance* to the whole damn music business!"

"I'll drink to *that*," said Emily. "The cello was the fucking bane of my existence when I was growing up."

"Your language, Emily!" cried Roberta.

It took Phoebe a few seconds to realize that her mother's notice of resignation came as a huge relief to herself, as well. It removed some of the pressure she felt to make music—any music. And while the violin wasn't the bane of her anything, in truth, she wasn't enjoying playing it much these days. She was enjoying composing even less, which is why she was also considering retiring from work on her—still, after all this time, mostly only hypothetical—solo album, *Bored and Lonely*. She figured there might be other times in her life when she'd be more inspired by the topic. Besides, in recent months, she'd made the exciting if discomforting discovery that what she really wanted to do was run her own business. She dreamt of employees, logos, and tax ID numbers. It seemed that great-grandfather Isaac, of Scranton by way of Bavaria, had left his imprint on the Fine family, after all.

All that was left for Phoebe to do was to change her own name back to Feingold.

It emerged in subsequent weeks that Leonard had had just about enough of the oboe as well. His lungs were no longer expanding the way they once had. With greater and greater frequency, he would emerge from the concert hall feeling as if he'd single-handedly inflated a hot-air balloon. He was tired of the musician banter backstage, onstage, and while car-pooling too. The "Stop, I can't hear another viola joke!" and "His tempi are insane!" and "What's wrong with her reeds? She sounds like the A train," and "Well, they said he left it in the back of a taxi and didn't realize it till the guy drove off," and "How can you forget a Strad?" and "Well, I just faked that one," and "Are you free the fourteenth to do a wed-ding?" and "Let me guess, another *Pachelbel Canon*?" and "I've been playing this fiddle for thirty-five years, and people still ask me if I've got a machine gun in this case—must be all those old movies on AMC," and "I like the bass, but how can you lug that damn thing around all the time? Ever thought of taking up the piccolo?"

And "He played his solo really well, didn't he?" and "You think so?" and "Got anything to eat?" and "You driving across the bridge?" and "He looks like he's conducting Elvis Presley," and "I can't believe he picked on her, of all people; she was no more out of tune than the rest of the section," and "So I had to buy a seat for the cello. Can you believe it?" and "Did it get a meal?" and "What's the difference between alto clef and Greek? Some people can read Greek," and "It's one two three, one two three four five, one two, one two three four, one, one, one two three four five six," and "How long is this maestro's contract?" and "Short, I hope."

And "Are they giving out free tickets for this concert? You can have mine—I wouldn't subject my family to this one if you paid me," and "You locked your keys in the car? Don't worry; in this neighborhood, someone'll break in for you," and "Conservatively estimated, how many times would you say you've played this piece?" and "You driving uptown? Got room for a tuba? . . . a trombone? . . . a timpanist and his wife?" and "That's the third violist's son playing second stand over there; you'd think he would have steered him toward another profession," and "I heard she got a recording deal," and "See the Nets game last night?" and "The timpanist's rim shots could take your ears off; maybe he should go into magic, he already looks like Merlin."

What's more, Leonard and Roberta claimed to have grown weary of the suburbs—found them dull and confining and predictable, and were looking to add a little more spice to their remaining days on this earth, however many those might be. There was reason now to believe that there might be more than a few. Roberta had had some *actual* tests performed at the hospital, the results of which indicated that the c-word had "taken a leave of absence," just as Emily had from Legal Aid. In the meantime, Phoebe's mother had developed a nasty case of bunions that, perhaps because they were identifiable and quantifiable, seemed to bother her far more than the cancer ever had. Or at least she complained endlessly and bitterly about them, referring to them (naturally) as the b-word. Even so, she and Leonard planned to move back into Manhattan with the money they could expect to reap from the sale of her viola. (The sale of their house in Whitehead would be valuable only insofar as it might finally throw the Oritani Savings Bank off their backs.)

At present, they were leaning toward a converted loft space in one of several trendy neighborhoods downtown, but they were trying to keep an open mind.

Needless to say, upon learning of her parents' intentions, Phoebe was devastated. It wasn't just that Leonard and Roberta were effectively debunking the myth she had constructed around her family home as a kind of sacrosanct space, secure from the forces of crassness and modernization; their leaving meant she would have to leave too. But where would she go? And with what funds? With the cost of New York real estate being what it was, it turned out that her parents were going to need all the proceeds from the sale of the viola themselves. Of course, it *was* their money. And nowhere in the law was it written that the parents of a college-educated woman were required to continue supporting her into her thirties. Still, Phoebe couldn't help but think that she was deserving of *some* kind of facilitator's fee. It was she, after all, however unwittingly, who had instigated the events that had led to Georgiu's discovery that Roberta's viola was, in fact, a Guarneri. What's more, both Georgiu and Roger/Roget stood to come away with a healthy cut of the profits.

"Now, here's an ad for a converted synagogue—wouldn't *that* be cool?" Leonard started up one Saturday morning, having bid Ernest "Palisades" Park good-bye for the last time. The *New York Times* Real Estate section lay open on the kitchen table; the back issues of *Allegro* had been put out on Commingled Paper night.

"Yeah, really cool," muttered Phoebe, trying to stave off a hernia.

"It's in a neighborhood they're calling Loho," he went on. "I don't think I've heard that acronym before. Could be a misprint for Soho, of course."

"It's not a misprint, it's a fancy name for the neighborhood Grandma Edith grew up in," she told him. "Otherwise known as the Lower East Side."

"No kidding! Well, listen to this: It comes with granite countertops, a Sub-Zero—whatever *that* is—"

"It's a special kind of stainless-steel refrigerator."

Leonard looked up from the paper. "Why would anyone want a stainless-steel refrigerator?"

"I guess they think it looks good," Phoebe offered through grinding teeth.

"Hm. Interesting." Oblivious to her agony, he went back to the listing. "And what's a w slash d?"

"Washer-dryer."

"I suppose everyone needs one of them."

"I don't think you and Mom would like it down there," she said, trying a new tack. "It's very—young."

"Well, we've always loved kids," said Leonard. "You know, we *did* have two of them." He timed his cluck and wink to coincide.

"But it's sort of druggy too."

"Well, your mother and I have never shied away from danger!" He smiled saucily. "At least, not consciously."

"Well, if you want danger, what about someplace in the outer boroughs, like Brownsville or East New York?" suggested Phoebe, thinking that a move to one of those war zones would propel her parents back to the suburbs pretty quickly.

"Oh, no, we have our hearts set on Manhattan!" insisted Leonard.

Her father's good mood was really getting her down. But what could she do? And what would become of her? Fine Furniture Inc. was bumping along, but it wasn't yet bringing in enough money on which to live. And while she felt better assured now of Roger/Roget's loyalties, he still hadn't asked her to move in. What's more, just contemplating leaving Whitehead made her feel disoriented. It was as if she were leaving for Guatemala City all over again—or maybe just college. Except this time she was already homesick. She felt depressed about America's future, too. After watching the Supreme Court hijack the presidential election, Phoebe had begun to feel as if she had never made it out of Central America after all. She also began to address her sister as "Spoiler"—though, in Emily's defense, the state of California had gone for Gore anyway, so her absentee ballot vote for Ralph Nader hadn't mattered anyway.

But life has a way of falling into place at the precise moment when we give up trying to control it. A week before Phoebe's thirtieth birthday, she and Roger/Roget were waiting in line at Hank's Franks at the Little Ferry traffic circle—in exchange for a lengthy back rub, Phoebe had agreed to try a hot dog—when he elbowed her in the ribs and said, "Hey, Fine. You seem a little down these days. What's going on?"

"I dunno," she lied. "I guess it's just my parents selling the house off and stuff."

"Where are you going to go?"

She shrugged.

Neither of them said anything for a few minutes. Then Roger/Roget let out a long sigh and announced, "All right, you've dropped enough hints. I'll marry you."

"You'll *what*?"

"I said, *I'll marry you.*"

"How do you know I want to marry *you*?" asked Phoebe, as deliriously excited as she was put out by his method of proposal.

"Point made," said Roger/Roget. "Wanna get married?"

"Okay," she answered.

"Cool."

They kissed and advanced in line. But something didn't feel right. "Shouldn't we go celebrate somewhere?" she asked. If not the white wedding type, Phoebe wasn't yet ready to cede the moment to history, either.

But Roger/Roget only shrugged. "We're already here. Might as well get a dog."

"We should at least tell someone! I mean, you're supposed to call your parents when this kind of thing happens."

"I don't have any parents."

"Well, I do." She ripped his cell phone out of his jacket pocket and began to dial home.

"God, this line is taking forever," he mumbled.

"Could you try to act a *little* more excited?" she lit into him, beginning to doubt their long-term compatibility. "I mean, what's the point of getting engaged if you're not even into it?"

"Sorry, I'm just distracted. . . . Finally! Two dogs, please, one plain, the other with relish, mustard, ketchup, mayo, and a pickle."

"That is so disgusting. Are you really going to eat that?"

"Hey, I'm celebrating!"

"You drive me crazy."

"You know you love it." (He was probably right.)

Back in Whitehead, amid packing boxes, Roberta picked up the phone after the sixth ring. "*Bonjour.* Fine family residence."

"Mom? It's Phoebe," she began. . . .

"Oh, Be, we're so thrilled for you two!" Roberta exclaimed at hearing Phoebe's good news. Since her viola had been revealed to be a Guarneri, her mother had undergone a 180-degree reversal in her attitude toward Roger/Roget. She had even taken to calling him by his fifth grade nickname. "Tell Stinky I hope he grows to think of me and Dad as the parents he never had," she continued. "Such a sad childhood! But lucky for us; we always wanted a son. And between you and me, I've never been able to think of Jorge that way. He's always been a bit, well—how do I say this?—too *pompous* for my taste."

Phoebe got through half her hot dog before gagging. Roger/Roget devoured his in sixty seconds flat. Then they went to the ShopRite in Fairlawn and bought each other plastic rings from the twenty-five-cent machines by the automatic doors. Then they drove to an empty parking lot in Moonachie, where they made even more cramped love in the backseat of his Corvette. Then they went to the multiplex on Route 4 in Paramus and caught the latest Bruce Willis action vehicle. Then they went back to Roger/Roget's place and listened to Mahler's 2nd Symphony. (Phoebe fell asleep in the middle.)

"*¿Puedas mirar el* front wheels of the *carro* behind you? *¿Seguro?* Okay, *bueno. Ahora, quiero que* put your *blinkito* on—okay, *bueno.* Now, maintaining your speed, *quiero que* turn the wheel *a la derecho*—okay, *cuidado,* not so herky-jerky, *bueno.* Now, steady her. *¡Buenisimo!*"

"Was that okay?" said Phoebe, breathless, sweating—and now safely ensconced in the outermost lane of Interstate 80. How had she ended up there? One afternoon, she'd been idly leafing through a coupon mailer promoting local commerce that had found its way into the Fines' kitchen—only to discover that the Vaya Con Dios driving school of East New York, New Jersey, was offering private instruction at 50 percent off their normal rates. With the promise of God in attendance, even if it wasn't her God, it was a difficult offer to refuse. There were other motivating factors as well for finally learning to drive. For one thing, she was tired of relying on other people to get her from here to there. For another, if she had any hopes of becoming a suburban soccer mom—albeit one with a thriving junk dealership on the side—it seemed clear that she would eventually need a license.

What Phoebe hadn't prepared for was being lured onto a major thoroughfare on her first outing. Nor did the fact that her instructor, José, had a brake pedal beneath his own seat provide much solace. While eighteen-wheelers throttled by, she gripped the wheel of her student-driver car/mobile leper colony as if dangling from the ledge of a skyscraper. She had never been so terrified in her entire life. It was also pretty exciting. It turned out that the older you got, the more intense life became—so much for America's idolization of youth!

Meanwhile, just as Georgiu had predicted, a Japanese electronics executive and amateur violist by the name of Toshi Somethingorother appeared, seemingly out of nowhere, and, though it was still in two pieces, made a substantial seven-figure offer on Roberta's viola. Roberta and Leonard, in turn, placed a bid on a 2,000-square-foot loft on Leonard Street in Tribeca. If all went well, they were about to go into contract.

Emily returned to the West Coast shortly after Jewish Christmas, at which point, disillusioned with public service, she began interviewing at corporate firms in San Jose. It was still unclear what was happening with her and Jorge, though they seemed to be living in the same house, if not sleeping in the same bed. (There was reason to believe he had yet to be invited back from the sofa.)

And Phoebe went back to referring to her fiancé as Roget,

as opposed to "Roger/Roget," while she decided to keep her last name, Fine, as is. At a certain point, she'd come to realize, we became the sum of our aspirations, not our origins. Besides, it seemed to Phoebe that a lot of happiness came down to what you chose to call things: adversity or challenge, seducer or lover, garbage or gold mine, "nice imitation of nothing" or Giuseppe Guarneri del Gesù.

Why
She Went
Home

A Reader's Guide

Lucinda Rosenfeld

Lucinda Rosenfeld converses with her
mother, Lucy Davidson Rosenfeld, writer
of books on art and architecture.

Lucy Davidson Rosenfeld: Is Phoebe's father, Leonard, patterned
after Dad [a professional cellist], or is Leonard supposed to
typify classical musicians in general?

Lucinda Rosenfeld: Well, there's a little of Dad in Leonard, but
Leonard is much ditzier than Dad, whom I think of as very
competent. Also, I've always—probably unfairly—assumed
that oboists were borderline insane, whereas cellists are
rarely crazy. In fact, they're often the ladies' men of the
classical music world.

LDR: Okay, what about Roberta Fine? As a mother, am I *that* annoying?

LR: Never.

LDR: Speaking of annoying, is Phoebe gloomy and difficult just
to irritate her parents?

LR: No! Where did you get that idea? Phoebe isn't trying to
make *any* impression on her parents. Sometimes, they just

annoy *her*—so she acts difficult in return. She loves them, of course, too.

LDR: Well, if Phoebe has ostensibly fled New York City to get away from the world of the cool and the trendy—and her parents are clearly very uncool—why don't they please her more?

LR: They do please her! She enjoys thrift shopping with her mother. She takes pleasure in attending her father's concerts. At some point in the book I say that Phoebe better enjoys socializing with her parents than with any of her old friends. But she's also a troubled person, easily wounded and easily disappointed by and in the world, and, unfortunately, that world includes her parents. In short, no one's immune.

LDR: So you're saying that Phoebe's negative experience in New York City is mostly the product of her bad attitude rather than bad luck?

LR: Well, maybe a little of both. She tends to seek out negative experiences that reinforce her alienation. It's one of her worst qualities.

LDR: Would you say that, by the end of the novel, Phoebe revises her soured view of the world?

LR: Somewhat. Maybe a little more than somewhat.

LDR: Let's move on to some general questions. What did Dad and I do that helped turn you into a writer?

LR: You kept a lot of books around the house, for one. Though, in all honesty, growing up, I was never a voluminous reader. I generally preferred making things with my hands and playing sports. I guess the most important thing you did was leave me alone to think and daydream and do chemistry experiments with toothpaste and whatever else it was I did to fill the time. I'm deeply opposed to parents who over-schedule their children.

LDR: Would you say that you feel liberated by writing?

LR: As an overly sensitive person who's always feeling slighted by one person or another, I can definitely say that writing helps me process all the emotions I feel during the day. In that sense, yes, it's liberating.

LDR: How does the fiction writer take the people and events she knows in real life and turn them into characters and scenes?

LR: Writing is a process of distillation. It's also a process of transformation. So it doesn't really matter if the origination point is real or lifted out of the sky; wherever you end up will be radically different from where you started, anyway. The important thing is to keep honing in on the kernel at the center. In other words, what is this story really about? Sometimes, the way things "really happened" can get in the way of that question.

LDR: In those instances when you have cannibalized real-life events, is it even possible to think of them now as anything but part of a novel?

LR: That's too personal a question. I'll pass.

LDR: Let's move on to Phoebe's love life. I feared that Phoebe was just settling for Roget. Or does she really love him?

LR: One of the most surprising things about publishing *Why She Went Home* was the reaction I got to Roget. Almost no one I talked to thought he was good enough for Phoebe. I had one reader who urged me to write a third installment of the Phoebe Fine Chronicles, if only so Phoebe and Roget could have a quick divorce and she could find someone better! But yes, I think she does love him.

LDR: I was going to ask you later, but since you raise the question: Are you planning a third Phoebe Fine book?

LR: Right now, I'm renovating. At least, that's my excuse. Ask me in six months.

LDR: Does writing a novel have anything in common with building or renovating a house?

LR: Well, in the same way that, when you're renovating, it's difficult to see what the room will look like until there's paint on the walls, and furniture on the floor, with a book, you simply can't know what you've written until the last "i" has been dotted (to use a convenient cliché). Before then, outline or no outline, it's just an amorphous, undefined blob. That's probably why writers look so demoralized all the time.

LDR: Let's get back to Roget. Is Phoebe attracted to him because he's awful to her and therefore plays into her low self-esteem? Or does she see better things in him than we do?

LR: Wow, I guess you disliked him too! I intended Roget to be direct, talented, and passionate—even if he lacks polish and sophistication. One hopes that he'll improve his manners under Phoebe's influence.

LDR: So, Roget is the "anti–New York" man? Or does he wish for the success on the bigger stage of, say, Lincoln Center or Carnegie Hall?

LR: That's an interesting question, and I'm not sure of the answer. Does anyone ever turn down the opportunity to be famous and wealthy? I'm not sure anyone does—or, maybe, knows how.

LDR: Well, if Roget stays in his second-rate position at the Newark Symphony, will *Phoebe* be satisfied?

LR: Yes, I think so. She's given up on the New York definition of success, in favor of something smaller-scale, but possibly sweeter.

LDR: Let's talk some more about the New York–New Jersey divide. Which elements of Phoebe's story do you consider suburban in nature? Or are they all just rejections of the outside world?

LR: That's another hard question. I think Phoebe genuinely likes New Jersey. At the risk of sounding pretentious, she likes its lionization of the practical and the mundane, over the beautiful and the dramatic. Would she be just as happy in Wyoming? Probably not. The real thing New Jersey has going for it is that she grew up there. Having failed to find a satisfying adult life for herself, she still thinks of Whitehead as home.

LDR: So how does returning to a childhood environment help Phoebe to grow up? Or is she simply regressing?

LR: Well, I think she has to regress to realize that she's regressing—if that makes sense.

LDR: Okay, what about Phoebe's desire to collect her neighbors' trash? Are we supposed to understand it as some kind of grand metaphor for her life? If so, I admit it went slightly over my head.

LR: Well, people generally throw things out that they no longer need or want. In that sense, collecting their garbage is a way of peering into their pasts and, really, the past in general, which is debatably Phoebe's main problem in life. So, yes, I guess it's a metaphor.

LDR: Another topic: How much do the clothes each character wears suggest his or her personality?

LR: Looking back, I realize that I used clothes as shorthand for how invested each character is in the world of appearances, as represented by New York. As the reader can clearly see, Phoebe is positively schizophrenic on the subject. She hates to care how things look, but she does care. Immensely.

LDR: Who is your favorite character in the book—aside from Phoebe?

LR: My favorite characters are always the ones who do and say the most embarrassing things. I guess I relate to them! In *Why She Went Home*, the award would have to go to Leonard.

About the Type

This book was set in Sabon, a typeface designed by the well-known German typographer Jan Tschichold (1902–74). Sabon's design is based upon the original letter forms of Claude Garamond and was created specifically to be used for three sources: foundry type for hand composition, Linotype, and Monotype. Tschichold named his typeface for the famous Frankfurt typefounder Jacques Sabon, who died in 1580.

About the Author

LUCINDA ROSENFELD was born in New York City on the last day of the 1960s. She is the author of *What She Saw* . . . , the first installment of the Phoebe Fine Chronicles. Rosenfeld's fiction and essays have also appeared in *The New Yorker, Creative Nonfiction, The New York Times Magazine*, the *Sunday Telegraph*, and many women's magazines. She lives in Brooklyn and has no pets.

14. According to the old adage, one person's trash is another person's treasure. Why is "Dumpster diving" so exhilarating for Phoebe? There's the suggestion that this could be Phoebe's new vocation. How might it suit Phoebe better than her office/media job in Manhattan? Is it more likely to make her happy?

15. In Chapter 15, Phoebe lists "Ten Reasons Why Sex Is Overrated." Do you agree that sex is overrated? If you agree, can you expand on Phoebe's list? If you don't agree, could you make a counter-list of your own?

16. In Chapter 7, Phoebe wonders, "When had money become the object of her frustrated ambition . . . ? Once upon a time, not that long ago, sex had been her obsession." How can money replace sex? Are Phoebe's money issues resolved by the end of the book? What is the relationship between money and happiness, in general?

17. Do you think Phoebe and Roget have a good shot at "happily ever after"? Why or why not?

18. Can you imagine a third book in the Phoebe Fine Chronicles?

9. At the end of Chapter 15, Phoebe realizes that "she had come back to Whitehead not so much to care for her mother as to have her mother care for her. So she could imagine that she was still someone's daughter, still young and sweet and un-tarnished and in need of protection." Do we ever really stop thinking of ourselves as young? As someone's daughter or son?

10. Also at the end of Chapter 15, Phoebe decides that "wher-ever you were in life, the baggage simply followed you there—if not on your own flight, then on the next one in." Do you think this is true or false? More generally, how much about your life can you really alter by moving locations and/or making other external changes to your situation?

11. The classical music world of New Jersey is the book's un-likely backdrop. What role does classical music play for Phoebe? How do our parents' professional lives inform our own? How do they exert pressure over us?

12. Author Bliss Broyard comments, "*Why She Went Home*'s candid take on family values couldn't come at a better time." What does she mean? How do the unique qualities of the Fine family parlay into a particular set of Fine family values? On the other hand, do you think there are universal values that should apply to every family?

13. The tone of *Why She Went Home* is decidedly comic. How does humor serve to enhance or take away from the serious-ness of the subjects that Rosenfeld takes on, from illness to aging to loneliness? Can a book be tragic and comic at the same time? In what ways is life tragic and comic at the same time?

or Emily's fault for being so hostile? What is it about sisters in particular that make them so competitive? How does Phoebe come to understand Emily differently by the end of the book?

4. In Chapter 6, Phoebe returns to New York City for a night out with her girlfriends. Why does she suddenly long to be "trapped in her junior-sized trundle bed" in New Jersey? By retreating to the suburbs, do you think Phoebe is escaping life or trying to build a better one?

5. What does Phoebe mean by questioning Manhattan's "dogged insistence on existing in the present tense, above and beyond history"? To what extent can a place be said to live in any tense?

6. Phoebe slowly becomes attracted to her father's orchestral conductor, Roget, who is nothing if not rude. What is Roget's appeal to her? Is her choice of Roget an example of Phoebe's taste in men maturing or continuing to fail her?

7. In Chapter 1, Phoebe wonders if she'll "ever love another man as much as she did Leonard Fine." How is Phoebe's choice in romantic partners connected to her love for her father?

8. Considering Rosenfeld's earlier novel, *What She Saw . . .*—in which every chapter recounts Phoebe's experiences with a different boy or man—how has Phoebe changed as a character? In what ways has she stayed the same? To what extent is she still dependent on men and male attention for her sense of self? How have her views on sex changed? How has her definition of "home" changed?

Reading Group Questions and Topics for Discussion

1. Almost thirty, with her work and love lives stalled, Phoebe Fine moves back to her parents' suburban home with precisely no plans for the future. She's a creative, intelligent woman from a loving—albeit eccentric—family. Why can't she seem to settle into adulthood? Does she expect too much from life? Not enough? More generally, by Phoebe's age, do most people know who they are and what they want—or do we spend our whole lives trying to figure that out?

2. Phoebe wants to be supportive of her mother, who has cancer and is receiving chemotherapy treatments, but there are times when she shrinks from the very sight of Roberta's "awful auburn wig with the short bangs." In what way is Phoebe's reaction to a family member's illness true to life? In what way is Phoebe especially selfish? How does Phoebe's mother invite a lack of sympathy? How does that dynamic change by the end of the book?

3. Phoebe and her sister's rivalry and antagonism date back to early childhood. Why can't Phoebe seem to let go of her envy of and anger at Emily? Is it Phoebe's fault for caring so much,

LDR: What does Halloween have to do with Phoebe's many disguises?

LR: Hmm. The connection never occurred to me until just now, proving that critics (and mothers) are smarter than writers (and daughters). But yes, disguise is central to Phoebe's sense of uncertainty and frequent changes of persona.

LDR: And finally, are you Phoebe?

LR: No! At the same time, yes. But ultimately, no. I'm much more ambitious than Phoebe. She's my defeatist side. Also, for the record, I left northern New Jersey at seventeen, for college, and have never moved back. Instead, I've lived in Brooklyn, New York, since 1993.